THE UNNOTICEABLES

Also by Robert Brockway

Rx: A Tale of Electronegativity

You Might Be a Zombie and Other Bad News
(from the editors of Cracked.com)

Everything Is Going to Kill Everybody

THE UNNOTICEABLES

¦¦Robert Brockway¦¦¦¦¦¦¦

TOR®

¦¦¦A Tom Doherty Associates Book · New York¦¦¦¦¦¦¦¦¦

THE UNNOTICEABLES

Copyright © 2015 by Robert Brockway

A Tor Book
Published by Tom Doherty Associates, LLC
175 Fifth Avenue
New York, NY 10010

www.tor-forge.com

Tor® is a registered trademark of Tom Doherty Associates, LLC.

Library of Congress Cataloging-in-Publication Data

Brockway, Robert.
    The unnoticeables : a novel / Robert Brockway.—First edition.
        p. cm.
    ISBN 978-0-7653-7966-5 (hardcover)
    ISBN 978-1-4668-6930-1 (e-book)
    1. Supernatural—Fiction.   2. New York (N.Y.)—Fiction.   I. Title.
PS3602.R6342U56 2016
813'.6—dc23

                                                    2015014556

Tor books may be purchased for educational, business, or promotional use. For information on bulk purchases, please contact the Macmillan Corporate and Premium Sales Department at 1-800-221-7945, extension 5442, or write to specialmarkets@macmillan.com.

First Edition: July 2015

Printed in the United States of America

0 9 8 7 6 5 4 3 2 1

To everybody who told me I was wasting my teenage years by drinking, going to punk shows, and reading comic books: Thank you for being so hilariously wrong.

Acknowledgments

I want to thank my wife, Meagan Brockway, for her love and support. My dad and my grandpa, for never feeling the appropriate amount of shame over what I chose to do with their namesake. My agent, Sam Morgan, and all the folks at JABberwocky Literary Agency, Inc., for being frighteningly good at everything they do. Never cross them. My editor, Paul Stevens, for understanding and refining the manic ramblings you're about to read, and all the fine people at Tor, for knitting it together into this beautiful, lethal little package. I want to thank Will Staehle for that cover image that makes me go weak at the knees. Thank you to all the beta readers who read this book back when it was all doodles of Voltron doing keg stands and self-portraits of me as a Ninja Turtle. I want to thank my dogs, Detectives Martin Riggs and Roger Murtaugh, for their stupid faces. And finally, thank you to all of the people who are about to read this, love the hell out of it, and send me all of their money in a fit of lustful gratitude. It is completely expected, of course, but no less appreciated.

THE UNNOTICEABLES

ONE

I met my guardian angel today. She shot me in the face.

I'm not much for metaphor. So when I say "guardian an-gel," I don't mean some girl with big eyes and swiveling hips who I put on a ridiculous pedestal. I mean that she was an otherworldly being assigned by some higher power to watch over me. And when I say "shot me in the face," I don't mean she "blew me away" or "took me by surprise." I mean she manifested a hand of pure, brilliant white energy, pulled out an old weather-beaten Colt Navy revolver, and put a bullet through my left eyeball.

I am not dead. I am something far, far worse than dead. Or at least I'm turning into it.

Here's something I found out recently:

The universe is a problem. Again, I'm not much for meta-phor. I meant what I said: The universe and everything that lies within it is a problem, in the very technical sense of the word. There are many parts to the universe—too many, in fact—which means that there is a simpler way to express the concept of "universe." There are extraneous parts in every single object in existence, and to do away with them is to compact the essence of the universe into something leaner and more efficient. The universe and everything in it is a problem. And that means that the universe and everything in it has a solution.

Humans also have extraneous parts: Think of the appendix, the wisdom teeth, the occasional vestigial tail—there are parts of us that we simply don't need. They clutter us. We can be rid of them altogether. But that's just physical stuff. There are also fundamental elements of what we are inside—spiritual, psychic, psychological, what have you—that are being expressed inefficiently. Our parts are too complicated. They can be reduced. They can be solved.

Human beings have a solution.

And being solved is a terrible goddamned thing.

The exact methods vary from person to person. My solution? A .36 caliber lead ball through the pupil while sitting cross-legged on a bed in a Motel 6, watching a rerun of *Scooby-Doo.*

I've always been a simple man.

I guess I'm about to get a whole lot simpler.

Before this thing takes me completely, I need to tell you a story. But I'm having trouble starting. This is how it goes, or how it went, or how it will go. I'm having a hard time with time: That's the first step to the change, Yusuf told me—losing your chronology. Where did it start? With her? With me?

I can't remember why the start should even matter. Quick, let me tell you about Carey. . . .

TWO

"Hey, fuck you," I said to Wash as I passed him. He was huddled in a little ball at the edge of the booth. I mussed his hair up, making extra sure to jiggle his head about while I did it. I could hear him throw up into his own shoes as I made the door.

Told him not to take those off in the club.

The New York City air was a goddamned bathtub. It was eighty degrees outside at one o'clock in the morning. Inside the club was worse, though. In there, you had to breathe the accumulated sweat of a hundred drunken punks. A thin puddle of beer evaporated beneath your feet, found nowhere to go in the already damp air, and eventually settled onto your eyelashes.

I've got the beerlashes. Shit. Who has cigarettes? Debbie has cigarettes.

"Debbie!" I hollered straight out into the street as loud as I could, in no particular direction. I waited for an answer.

"Shut the fuck up!" a female voice answered. Didn't sound like Debbie.

Two teen girls stood by a busted-open newspaper machine, drinking something distinctly beer-colored out of a Coke bottle. Too cute to be part of the scene. *Aw, look, they did their mascara up all thick. Punk fucking rock.*

"If you gimme a cigarette, I might consider letting you suck my dick," I told the blond one with the patches on her denim jacket.

They laughed and said a bunch of words that weren't "Here's a cigarette," so I left. I crossed the Bowery and headed up Bleecker, to the old wrought-iron fire escape where we hid emergency drinks from the parasites.

And I found the parasites there. *With the drinks.*

Parasites: the young kids who milled about outside the shows, too chicken or too broke to slip past the doorman. Occasionally they lucked into some weed or some smokes, and they were always eager to impress, so they were generally tolerated, like fleas or acne. But this was a step too far: They'd found the goddamned beer cache! They saw me coming and turned at once, like a bunch of prairie dogs spotting the shadow of a hawk.

"One of you has a cigarette for me," I told them, not asked.

The little guy with the Elmer's-glue spikes fumbled in his pockets like I'd told him there was a loose grenade in there. He practically threw a Camel at my face.

I pulled my Zippo and did that Steve McQueen shit, where I snapped it open and scraped the flint across my jeans to light it in one smooth motion. Ladies love it; men fear it.

Too bad I was out of fluid. Somebody laughed.

"You fuckin' parasites!" I hollered, turning to round on them with all the righteous fury of a man cheated out of a beer stash. But Jezza was standing there instead, looking like an empty jacket draped over a chair.

"Easy, mate! Yer scarin' off all the lovelies!"

"Light, Jezza?"

"First he calls me a parasite, then he wants me lighter?" Jezza mimed outrage to a plain-looking girl in glasses and a scuffed-up flannel shirt.

God damn it: You sold our beer stash out for parasite ass?

"I will ruin your night right now unless you get me fire."

"Well, he's all piss and vinegar, innit he?" Jezza said to Scuffed Flannel. She laughed. Utterly fucking charmed, I'm sure.

"Jezza, god damn it, you're not British. He's not British." I looked Scuffed Flannel in the eye. "And the only English movie he's seen is *Mary Poppins,* which is why he talks like such a prick."

"Oi!" Jezza protested.

"Jezza, God love you, man, but you sound like a fucking cartoon penguin. Knock it off. Your mom's from Illinois." I turned back to Scuffed Flannel and said, "His name's Jeremy."

"You asshole, Carey! Why do you always gotta blow it for me?" Jezza whined. "The girls love the accent!"

"Girls? Jesus, man. You're making things complicated." I looked and saw Debbie's flashy, tinfoil-colored hair across the street, just coming out the door.

"Here," I said, stealing the beer can from Jezza's hand, "this is how you do it: HEY DEBBIE!"

She turned, looking for the source of the voice, but it was too dark and there were too many people.

"DEBBIE, DO YOU WANT TO SCREW LATER?" I hollered.

"ARE YOU ANY GOOD?" she yelled back, still not spotting me.

"YOU'VE HAD WORSE."

"ALL RIGHT, THEN," she answered, laughing, and turned back to talk to her friends.

Jezza looked like somebody had pooped in his cornflakes.

"Told you I'd ruin your night. A man asks for a lighter, you give him a goddamned lighter," I said, and jogged back across the Bowery, up behind Debbie. I grabbed her hips and she squeaked.

"Got a light for your friendly neighborhood sex god?" I whispered into her hair, which, like everything else coming out of the club, smelled like an old undershirt.

"Aw, hell. That was you, Carey? I thought you said I'd had worse."

She had that sass in her voice that said she'd found something stronger than beer.

Debbie handed over the lighter, and I flicked it on. I wrapped my hand around it, shielding the precious flame, then put it in my pocket when she glanced away. All's fair in love and lighters.

Wood chips and truck-stop coffee filled my lungs. *I fucking love you, Carl P. Camel, inventor of the Camel.*

"Sticks and stones may break my bones, but I won't stick you unless you get me stoned," I whispered to her.

I couldn't tell if I was being devastatingly clever or if the beer was finally starting to kick in. Either way, she bought it.

"Come out back in five," she replied, and I let her drift back to the conversation.

For the moment, for just that one little moment, I didn't need her. I didn't need anybody. I wanted to worship at the musky pyramid temple of Camel cigarettes. I wanted to drop to my knees and inhale nothing but smoke until I burned up inside and flaked away like old paper. The cigarette asked about its old friend, beer, and I reintroduced the two. Jezza's can was warm and probably half spit, but it was ice-cold Yoo-hoo compared to the asphalt-flavored air of a New York heat wave.

Hey, there's Randall! I should kick him in the knee.

"Randall!" I screeched, getting two big running lopes and knocking his knees inside out.

"God damn it, Carey!" he said, then he tried to get his feet and nail me, but I danced away. A car honked, mad that I was in its precious street. Me and Randall gave it synchronized middle fingers and forgot all about fighting, to become a united front of Fuck You, Guy in Car.

"You like the band?" I said, nodding toward the club.

"Television? Pretentious bullshit," Randall said through a mouthful of chaw and then spat hot garbage water onto the sidewalk.

Everything was pretentious bullshit to Randall. I wasn't sure he actually knew what the term meant—he once called my chicken-fried steak "pretentious" because it came with gravy on the side.

"Sure, sure, but do you like 'em?" I inhaled the rest of my cigarette in a big crackly, flaring burn.

"Hell, yeah," said Randall, "they're my favorite band."

I gave Randall a sideways look, then released a fucking monumental cloud of smoke. I breathed storm clouds; I shot black soot like a dragon; I exhaled the entire Los Angeles motherfucking skyline. Randall coughed and sneezed and shut his eyes.

I took the opportunity to bolt. When he looked up, I was gone. Vanished in a puff of smoke. He spun around, looking for me, but didn't spot me down there, peering around the broken newspaper machine. That would fuck with him all night.

I waited until he turned around, and I crab-walked through the growing crowd around the door. When I was safely out of sight, I downed the rest of my beer and jogged around the corner to see what drugs Debbie had for me tonight.

When I got there, most of her face was gone. She was making a wet slurping sound with what was left of her mouth, and her balled-up fists were drumming the pavement like a broken windup toy. Something big and black stood over her, flowing like a waterfall. Its head was pouring out of where its shoulders should have been, oozing down and over Debbie's chest like fresh tar. Where it touched her, flesh sizzled and flowed away, running down her body like plastic. I must have said or done something then, because it started to retract. It reversed flow, sucked back up into itself, and became something vaguely man-shaped. Its skin shimmered like polluted grease. There were two gleaming brass gears where its eyes would have been. They interlocked and began to spin. The whirring increased pitch and became a scream. It took a step toward me.

"Fucker!" I said, and hucked my empty beer can into the vaguely humanoid mound of acid sludge that was melting my friend. It bounced off the thing's forehead and clattered away down the alley. "She was gonna put out!"

Stop.

That's a shitty thing to say, I know. I liked Debbie. I genuinely did. She wasn't just pussy to me; she was a friend first. She thought Monty Python was the funniest thing on the planet. She picked the cheese off of her pizza but still ate it. That's just how she liked things: crust and cheese as separate entities. She could do a perfect—and I mean fucking *flawless*—circus-caliber cartwheel, no matter how drunk she was. And yet the first thing I said when I saw her dying was dismissive and sexist and just all around shitty. I know. But here are some qualifiers:

First, when you put up an apathetic, angry shell for long enough, the behaviors you thought were mostly an act start to become your reality.

In other words: If you train yourself to respond like a dickhead in most situations, you find yourself responding like a dickhead in most situations.

Second: I was really, *really god damn hard up.*

I lived in a small apartment with three other punks. On any given night, one or two of them will probably bring home a few buddies who'll also pass out on our floor. I'm not a gentle lilac, budding only under the most delicate of circumstances; I don't mind people knowing I'm whacking it. But my ratty, threadbare thrift-store cot was right next to the bathroom, and every time I've tried to masturbate for the last three months, somebody puked right next to my head before I got a chance to finish. It was starting to get Pavlovian: I got half a hard-on every time somebody dry-heaved.

And finally, I should clarify: I wasn't in shock. I had seen these things before. At least half a dozen times over the past few years. A lot of us had. They seemed to be coming after the gutter punks, the homeless, the junkies: Anybody that spent a lot of time fucked up in dark alleyways knew about the tar men.

But all excuses aside, what I said about Debbie was selfish and callow. That's the plain and simple of it. If it makes you feel any better, they were probably going to be my last words.

The dull brass gears in the sludge monster's face were spinning faster and faster. The whine was reaching an agonizing pitch, like a jet engine mixed with a rape whistle, and it was, impossibly, getting louder. I turned to run, but the noise was doing something to my inner ear. My balance was shot. I dropped to my knees. Tried to cover my ears. No difference. The tar man was approaching, slow but steady. And my stupid, useless legs were ignoring me.

I could see it clearer now. It wasn't entirely black. It shimmered in the light, like the surface of a greasy puddle. Charred bits of Debbie's flesh still clung to it here and there. They were cooking. Melting and running away in soft pink rivulets. I could smell it. Smell her. The harsh chemical stink of crude oil mixed with burning steak.

Four paces. Three. I couldn't stand. Could barely move. I reached into my pocket. I pulled out the lighter I'd snaked from Debbie earlier. I flicked it open. I struck the flint against my jeans, and not even checking to see if it had caught, I flung it in front of me. I'd like to tell you I said a little internal prayer, but all I was really thinking was *"fuckfuckfuckfuckfu—"*

I felt a sharp intake of air rush across my skin, then a harsh, burning expulsion. I was thrown backward, and scrabbled away from the flaming thing like a wounded spider. The tar man's screaming gears faltered and caught. They whined, paused, jammed, and then flung themselves sideways out of its face. The fire raged harder and faster by the second. The sound was like a train engine spooling up. Higher, deeper, louder; higher, deeper, louder—and then, thankfully, silence.

When I finally pried my eyes open, half afraid that I'd find them burned shut, the tar man was completely gone. Just a greasy smudge and two round brass gears on the pavement.

I felt around my arms and face. My skin was sore all over,

like a bad sunburn, but there didn't seem to be any major damage. I considered a cigarette, looked at the oily spot still steaming to my left, and considered again.

I bent and picked up the two singed gears, oddly cool to the touch, and put them in my back pocket.

"Ha, motherfucker!" I spat on the smoking stain. "I'll wear your eyes for a trophy."

I went to check on Debbie. I had assumed the worst, from the way she'd been twitching when I first showed up. I assumed right.

I said a quiet good-bye and left the alleyway. Please don't tell anybody I pilfered the cigarettes out of her purse before I did.

When I got back out front to the show, the punks were filtering inside, the sound of the next band's guitars already clamoring into the street. Butts were being stomped out, beers were being downed, fresh air was being gulped desperately, and life was going on. I thought about going in with them—about dancing or drinking or doing some damn thing or another to forget for a few hours what I'd just seen, but the thought of all that heat and sweat turned me off.

Our pad was miles gone and I didn't feel like walking, but I recalled stashing Daisy about five blocks from here a few weeks ago. If she was still around, she'd get me home. I turned to leave, then Randall popped up from behind a newspaper machine, screamed, "GOTCHA, FUCKHOLE!" and slapped me hard across the cheek.

My burns flared to angry, visceral life.

THREE

For the first time in a long time, I woke to find myself not in pain. A cold flood of fear washed through me. It ran down my chest and settled in my gut. I couldn't remember why waking up without pain was supposed to worry me. The reaction was just instinctual.

I lay in my massive, ridiculously soft bed for half an hour. A king-size memory-foam mattress that fills every single inch of my tiny bedroom, and an accompanying six-hundred-dollar down comforter are the only great and stupid luxuries that I allow myself. I was trying to figure out where the anxiety was coming from, and I finally pinpointed it: I was not sore, bruised, burned, or broken at all, and that meant I was unemployed.

At least partially. I still had my job waiting tables, but I hadn't done any stunt work in weeks. I guess sometime during the night, I finally shook the last stubborn bit of stiffness in my hip from that botched somersault I took while shooting *The Damned Walk . . . Again!?* So I woke up feeling physically great but with a trade-off of crushing spiritual ennui. For almost this entire month, I had been just and only a waitress.

I sighed and rolled out of bed. I had to roll several times just to reach the doorway and then heave myself out into the hall. My bare feet slapped the cold tile all the way to the bathroom. When I sat down to pee, it really hit me:

I was in absolutely no pain.

Even as a little girl, I would wake up each morning with a very small but persistent ache in my third pinky. Yep. Third. I have six fingers on my left hand. The superfluous little bastard has hurt me every day of my life, except for two: the day when my kid sister died in a house fire, and today.

I couldn't remember anything about the day of the fire. The therapists said I'd repressed the memories, but every once in a while I got this feeling, like terrified déjà vu, and I just knew it was some small piece of that day coming back to me. I had that feeling now, when I suddenly remembered, in perfect clarity, waking up with no pain in my sixth finger fifteen years ago. I remembered running down the stairs to tell my mom.

It doesn't hurt anymore! It's all gone!

My mother laughed, picked me up, and placed me on top of the dining room table.

"Are you kidding me? Is this a joke?" she asked.

I shook my head and wiggled my skinny, single-knuckled little digit for her.

"That's great, baby!" she said.

And that's where the memory kicked out. Nothing past it, just a pleasant little short film and then *fin.* But I still had this sick fear that wouldn't shake loose from the bottom of my stomach. Something bad happened after that moment, I knew that much, but whenever I tried to think of the specifics, I could only picture a bright, colorless light and notes of toneless music. Memories defined by their absence.

I flushed the toilet, turned the shower up as hot as it went, and stood under it until the heat made me dizzy and pink. I slid the curtain aside and grabbed for my towel. I was so dazed from the warmth, I almost didn't notice the face staring at me from the other side of my window. I clutched the towel tightly against me, and instinctively screamed.

Jesus, just like some ditzy horror-movie starlet.

To my credit, the involuntary yelp only lasted a second. The tirade of increasingly detailed obscenities lasted for much longer. The face disappeared instantly, ducking away in terror. I barely had time to register a set of puffy red cheeks, greasy stubble, and glazed little eyes beneath a ratty green beanie. Still dripping wet, I threw my jeans and T-shirt on, slipped into a pair of flip-flops, grabbed the biggest kitchen knife I could find, and stormed out of my front door.

Mrs. Winslow, the nice lady that lives on the second floor, who, thanks to a series of misunderstandings, thinks I'm some sort of raging psychopath, gave me an odd look as I sprinted past her, soaked, swearing, and brandishing a butcher knife over my head.

Add that to the list, I guess.

I kicked open the main gate to my apartment building, scaring a little white Chihuahua tied to the side mirror of a brand-new silver Ferrari.

Los Angeles.

I rounded the corner toward the side of the building where my bathroom window looked out, and saw the Peeping Tom.

"Oh, this is a bad day to be a pervert," I said, advancing upon him, twirling my knife in tight little circles. "I hope you liked my tits, buddy: They're the last things you're ever going to see. I hope my tits keep you warm *in hell.*"

He wouldn't turn around. His back was convulsing oddly, and he was taking quick little breaths.

Oh, God, was he . . . ? Of course he was.

I took a step. Another. I wasn't sure where I was going with this: I was pissed off, true, but I wasn't "stab a hobo" pissed off. I didn't have a plan, but that didn't seem to matter. I was still holding a kitchen knife and approaching a masturbating bum in a dead-end side yard off Pico. Surely the situation would work itself out somehow.

I was just within stabbing range and felt the moment was coming to its head. I wasn't going to knife the guy, but I was at least going to have to say something. Maybe cut him *a little,* just to keep him on his toes. I opened my mouth to speak, then the hobo's stained canvas jacket abruptly ceased its bouncing. His rapid breathing halted. We were both still for a long moment, then he slumped to one side with a sickeningly fluid motion. I saw that one hand was covered in some kind of cancerous-looking sludge. It stank like burning plastic and flowed slowly outward from his body in a thick, rapidly congealing pool.

And just past him, shimmering in the air, was an angel.

I instantly knew it for what it was. I had seen one before, I was sure of it, but I couldn't recall where or when. The angel was an intangible blur of pure luminescence, but within it, barely glimpsed fractals and impossible angles rotated, shifted, adjusted, and disappeared. The radiant blob was bleeding all color out of the world around it. The spaces surrounding the light were colorless. Wan and oversaturated. It was too bright to see, but also too bright to look away. The deeper I gazed into the heart of the angel, the more I became aware of a sound. It was almost too subtle to hear, but the second I noticed it, it became deafening. There was an orchestra of reverberating chimes harmonizing over a dull, roaring static. It was like a thousand beautiful voices singing to drown out a million more screaming. I blinked and the sound stopped. I opened my eyes and it came raging back.

Waves of nausea and panic washed through me. I dropped the knife, and the angel sharply adjusted its focus. I couldn't pick out individual movements, but it seemed to be intent on the knife now, like it hadn't noticed the blade before. It suddenly appeared above the knife. I backed away reflexively and lost a flip-flop to a patch of mud beneath a leaking garden hose.

Before I could blink, it was there in front of me again, now focused on the sandal.

I turned and ran, and somewhere far behind me, I heard a crackling, sucking noise, as if some large, tacky mass was being scraped up from the ground.

I had a brief, scattershot flashback. Just still images. Polaroids taken of memories: torn little slippers with Corvettes on them. The taste of purple left on the wooden stick after the Popsicle was gone. My sister screaming. Flames on a set of paisley curtains. A noise like stepping on fleshy chewing gum.

I had heard that sound before.

FOUR

The cops said Debbie tried to light a cigarette and her wig went up in flames. That's how she died. Officially speaking.

Were cops this fucking stupid everywhere, or was it just in New York City?

I was trying to drink away the anger, but the parasites had been out in force ever since Jezza hooked up with the blond girl in the scuffed flannel shirt. They were not helping ease my jangled nerves.

"Like this?" the kid with the Elmer's glue holding his hair into little spikes asked another.

"No, it's more bouncy," the other parasite, a pretty young thing with safety pins in her ears, corrected him, hopping up and down.

She was trying to teach him some kind of dance. It was apparently the punk thing to do now, this hopping up and down. She bounced for a few seconds, her tits heaving every which way.

"Like this?" Elmer Spikes asked again, shuffling from foot to foot like an angry ape.

"No," Safety Pins answered, bouncing again, "watch me."

"Like this?" Elmer Spikes asked when she was done, rocking back and forth on his heels.

He said it with such earnestness that I almost didn't catch what he was doing.

"You just kind of hop, really quick; your feet leave the ground," Safety Pins tried again, breasts jiggling frantically.

Elmer Spikes's eyes never left her chest. I couldn't help it. I burst out laughing.

"What?" Safety Pins asked, her chest still heaving.

A huge grin split Elmer Spikes's face in half.

"Oh, god damn it." She finally caught on, stopped mid-hop, and shoved Elmer Spikes down onto the tracks. "Real cute, asshole."

We both laughed. When he picked himself up, I tossed Elmer Spikes a beer from the pack I'd been zealously guarding like a mother bear. He took it, popped it open, and drained the entire thing in three large gulps. I raised my eyebrows at him and tossed him another. Crack, hiss, three gulps, gone.

"Shit." I elbowed Wash and gestured at Elmer Spikes. "This one does tricks."

"Such as?" Wash asked.

Wash wore these thick glasses, and something about his bone structure—high cheeks, broad forehead—reminded you of some grim scientist in a sci-fi flick. He had this detached, formal way of speaking that made you think his ideas were worth listening to. Which usually got you in trouble: Wash was, without a doubt, the dumbest motherfucker I have ever met. I once saw him get caught in a subway turnstile. For ten solid minutes.

"Last one," I said, tossing another beer to Elmer Spikes. He downed it in a second.

"Interesting," Wash said, after a moment's consideration; "you must be a hit with the ladies."

The remark sounded like it might have been witty at first, but when you thought about it, it was completely moronic gibberish. That was Wash.

In response, Elmer Spikes emitted a belch so loud it echoed down the tunnel and rebounded, coming back to us as a guttural chorus. It was strangely beautiful.

"This place is cool," he said, peering up and down the tracks. "What is it?"

"South Ferry Station." Jezza instantly spoke up, eager to claim some sort of credit for the find by answering first. "Bobbies closed the inner-loop platform earlier this year. Blokes come round sometimes during the day, but she's abandoned come night."

"Bobbies are cops," I told Jezza matter-of-factly. "The cops don't close subway stations. For somebody that talks like a chimney sweep, you sure don't know fuck-all about the English."

"Piss off," Jezza said, flipping me a peace sign.

I take it the gesture meant something different in England. You could give him all the shit you wanted, but as long as Jezza got the excuse to say "piss off" and flip you that "V"—which, I admit, he did perfectly, just like Johnny Rotten—he still felt like a rock star.

"Wash found it," Randall clarified, and you could see Jezza's lip curl at the stolen credit.

"Don't worry," Wash said authoritatively, "there won't be any trains."

"Well, yeah," Elmer Spikes said, eyeballing Wash with confusion, "I figured."

"The trains all filter through the outer loop now," Wash

continued, oblivious to Elmer Spikes's sarcasm. "I know this, because my father used to drive the one line through here. I would sit with him sometimes."

"Yeah?" Elmer Spikes laughed. "I know this because the rails are dusty, man."

Wash, Randall, and I had grabbed prime spots under the only lights, a series of dim yellow bulbs in a narrow tile archway that only comfortably fit three. Jezza had elbowed his way up onto the platform a split second later, seeing it as some kind of hierarchal move. He grandly invited the girl in scuffed flannel up after him, like a spot on the cracked, filthy tile was some kind of honor. She was wiggling around on top of Jezza by way of thanks, which he seemed to be enjoying immensely.

The rest of the parasites were milling about a few feet below, down on top of the tracks. Elmer Spikes was trying, and failing, to balance on one foot. He was a pile of twigs in a torn T-shirt, and I think he was terrified of me. I don't know why, but every time I asked him for something, he went sprinting off like an eager secretary. Safety Pins was kind of a poser. She was always telling us what was and wasn't punk, but she was good-looking and never wore a bra, so she got to stay. There were two other girls with bright blue hair. Mostly kept to themselves, but they always had money to throw in for beer. We called them Thing 1 and Thing 2. And then there was a black kid with a Mohawk. His name was Matt.

You don't need nicknames to remember a black punk. They're like unicorns.

"Did anybody tell Mike where we were hanging out?" Safety Pins asked Thing 1.

"Nobody's seen Mike in weeks," Thing 2 chimed in; "he probably moved back home."

"Man, everybody's calling it quits. Denny, Brat, and The Spitter all split, too," Safety Pins added, then, after a moment's consideration: "Going home isn't punk rock."

"The Spitter?" I asked. "His name is The Spitter?"

"Yeah, he spits," Thing 1 answered laconically. She was slightly better looking than Thing 2, but she was also kind of a smartass. Two plusses for her.

"He spits *a lot*," Thing 2 added.

I should hook her up with Wash. They could have history's stupidest babies.

"That's what's wrong with punks these days," Jezza piped up: "got no manners."

We all laughed, but Scuffed Flannel carried it just a bit too long. Made it awkward.

"How do you know they're all moving home?" Randall asked. He was staring down the tunnel after Elmer Spikes, who was singing "(I Live for) Cars and Girls" to himself as he disappeared into the darkness.

"Where else would they be going?" Matt asked. He'd been eye-fucking my beer all night. I tossed him one. Not every day you get to share a brew with a unicorn.

But that's four down to charity, Carey. Watch yourself.

"Could be on the nod," Jezza guessed.

"Could be whoring out on the Loop," I supplied.

"Could be dead," Randall finished.

We all fell silent on that one, not because it was in bad taste, but because it had an awful measure of truth to it. Life was cheap in NYC lately. Everybody knew it. You could get blasted just trying to lift a measly six-pack from some

Korean corner store. You could shoot dope and wander into traffic. You could say the wrong thing to the wrong bald guy with the wrong color laces on his boots and get yourself kicked to death by skinheads. You could go any number of ways, and it happened too often to bother reporting them all.

Or you could meet the tar men.

I knew Randall and Wash had seen them. I had a feeling Jezza had spotted them once or twice, too. But he wouldn't admit to it. Still, whenever we talked about the tar men, he protested too much and too quickly—just a bit too eager to call us assholes. I wondered if any of the parasites had seen one. I considered asking them, but I knew they'd think I was crazy if I mentioned it.

"You parasites know about the tar men?" I asked—because fuck what they think about literally anything.

"Yeah, they're great," Safety Pins immediately said. "Their new stuff is bullshit, but their first album was really good."

"God, you are so lucky you have rockin' tits," I said, shaking my head.

She looked confused.

"They're not a band," Randall clarified.

"Not this bollocks again!" Jezza cried, too loud. He had this crazy smile, like he was hearing the funniest thing in the world. "Every time we get a little pissed, you two knobends start telling bleedin' ghost stories!"

Jezza looked around to the parasites, hoping to share a conspiratorial laugh. Thing 2 obliged him, while Safety Pins went quiet and flushed bright red, pissed at being caught in a lie. But Matt and Thing 1 were staring at the ground like it was their favorite TV show.

"I saw 'em." Matt finally spoke. "People keep saying I was

just drunk, and . . . well, fuck it: of course I was. But I saw 'em. I saw 'em take a girl down an alley, and when I looked after, they were gone. Thin air."

"I've seen them, too," Thing 1 said, her voice flat and distant. "Not up close or anything. Just shapes moving out by the waterfront. But you could tell they weren't human, even from a distance. Too big, and they moved all wrong."

"That ain't it, either." Matt spoke again, eager to be done with it. The words spilled out of him all at once: "There's normal-looking people too. But they're all wrong inside, just like Jenny said."

"The fuck's Jenny?" I asked.

"Her." Matt pointed at the blue-haired girl. Thing 1. "Sorry. But it's like she said about the tar men: They're all wrong. These people look normal, but you can tell by the way they move and look and talk. They dress like us—kind of—but they're not doing it right. *They're so hard to notice.* It's like only when you're not looking for 'em do you notice how weird it is that you're not looking for 'em."

"You're arseholed!" Jezza laughed. "Totally arseholed! You sound like a bloody fortune cookie!"

Randall very calmly reached over and flicked him right in the eyeball. Jezza howled.

"Shut up, Jeremy," Randall said, and pushed himself up off the tile. "I'm tired now. I'm going home."

"Yeah, fuck it," I agreed, downing the last of my beer. "I'm out of liquor, too. No point sitting here slowly going sober, letting you parasites drill into my brain with your fucking banter. Let's go."

Jezza looked pissed. I couldn't blame him. Scuffed Flannel had been giving him an extended lap dance since we got there. But he sure as hell didn't hesitate to scramble after us when we left him in the archway and started heading for the outer platform.

"Hey, wait," Safety Pins said, jogging up beside me and Randall like we were the scout leaders on a goddamned field trip. "Elmer Spikes isn't back yet."

"Boy's pissing out at least thirty-six ounces of swill right now," Randall said, heaving himself up onto the outer platform and rolling to his feet. "I'm not waiting for that."

"The truly great artists suffer for their art," I told Safety Pins, grabbing her ass as she hefted herself onto the ledge in front of me.

She kicked me square in the throat.

We never saw Elmer Spikes again.

I don't know what that meant. Maybe he was pissed that we ditched him, and didn't want to hang around anymore. Maybe he overdosed in a Village dope house. Maybe he just suddenly realized that "drunken malcontent" wasn't a very promising career path and decided to pursue his lifelong dream of being an accountant.

I tell myself those things, and I don't fucking believe a word of them. They got him. The tar men. Whatever those black monsters are, they got Elmer Spikes. I won't say I missed the kid, but I had been forcing Matt to learn to shotgun beers ever since he disappeared.

"I gwfooo . . . ," Matt said, foam shooting out of his nostrils.

The lessons weren't going well.

"Oh, guh." Matt coughed, one eye shut. "Guh in muh fuggin' eye!"

"If you drink it faster, it won't explode out of your head like that," I told him helpfully.

He ralphed up a soft pile of foam, like a hungry dog.

"I can't drink it any faster!" Matt protested, unsticking his hands from our artfully disgusting kitchen floor.

"Try putting more of the liquid in you at a greater speed," Randall suggested.

"That's not fuckin' helpful!" Matt yelled.

"Try swallowing larger amounts," I added, one finger on my jaw in thoughtful consideration.

"Fuck you guys," Matt said. He got to his feet, turned the faucet on, and stuck his face in the water.

"All right, all right—you don't have to shotgun any-more . . . ," I said.

Matt smiled up at me hopefully.

". . . until I get back from the store with more beer," I finished.

He closed his eyes and took a deep breath.

"You could always pay for your own beer," Thing 1 said, sitting cross-legged on top of our wobbly avocado-green fridge. She took a gentle sip of her own drink, by way of demonstration.

"Do I look like a brother who's got money?" Matt asked, gesturing to his scuffed high-tops and torn jeans.

"You could just not drink," Thing 2 offered from the living room.

We all stared at her like she'd opened her mouth and a bunch of snakes had come flying out.

"Life is a series of choices," Wash explained to her, patiently; "*that* is not one of them."

They were getting along pretty well, Wash and Thing 2.

I say that because I've seen all of the signs—the subtle touches of the hand, the lingering smiles, the furtive glances, and the time I walked in on her jacking him off in the bathroom. I'm very observant.

"All right, beer run," I said, and elbowed my way out of our crowded kitchen.

Thing 1, Matt, Randall, Safety Pins, Jezza, and Scuffed Flannel were all shoved in there like a bunch of cigarettes in a pack, even though the rest of the house was practically empty. Why does that always happen? Throw the most lavish party in the world—pool tables in the garage, jukeboxes in the living room, fucking fire dancers and talking elephants on the lawn—and go check the kitchen. It'll be standing room only.

Wash and Thing 2 were sitting across from one another on our broken, saggy couch, playing some kind of game. She laid down a card. Wash processed it for a long moment, then laid down his. He laid down a card, and she stared at it like it was a German cipher. She laid down a card.

"What are you playing?" I asked them, wordlessly yanking my leather jacket out from under Wash's ass.

"War," Thing 2 muttered, utterly lost in concentration.

"You really are perfect for each other," I said, swinging my jacket up and sliding my arms through it. It was like strapping into armor. I could take on anything.

Even a quick beer run to the corner store.

"Oi," Jezza hollered from the kitchen, "pick up some for me and Liz."

"Sure thing," I said. "Any preference? You in the mood for a nice, crisp pilsner? Maybe a saucy lager?"

"I could go for a nice pint of bitter," Jezza answered seriously; "maybe something with autumnal overtones."

"Right," I replied, "so the cheapest crap I can find."

"Righto," Jezza confirmed, tossing me a wad of filthy bills.

"You good, Wash?" I asked, and he patted most of a six-pack at his feet, too enraptured with his game to spare so much as a glance.

I looked to Safety Pins but saw she still had half a bottle of Jack left. It was her latest affectation: straight Jack Daniel's, just like Janis. Even if she did make a face with every swig.

"How about you two?" I asked Thing 1. She generally spoke for both of the Things.

She shifted to check her pockets, and from her position atop the fridge—legs at eye level—I saw that her short shorts were riding up provocatively.

"I'm out, but I'm broke," she said.

"I got your back," I consoled her, "if I can get your back later."

"It comes at too great a cost," she answered, and rolled her eyes.

"You could come for less," I said.

She tossed her empty can at me underhand. I headbutted it straight out of the air.

"I'll get you something anyway," I said.

This was punk-rock courtship: Paying for somebody's drunk was like giving them flowers dipped in chocolate.

"I'm dry and broke, too," Matt tried, hope glittering in his eyes.

"Oh, you can drink from my beers," I said, making for the door, "but you know what you have to do."

I heard the first faltering start to a long string of swears spill forth from Matt, but I was already out. I stepped from a kind of drunken postapocalypse into a New England bed-and-breakfast. The hallway for our floor couldn't be more out of character with the rest of the building. The lobby was fucking filthy. The main security door swung on broken hinges. The stairs squealed like every step was going to send you plummeting into the basement, and you'd have to dig a hole for our apartment to qualify as a shithole. But this hallway was always spotless. The carpet runners were carefully vacuumed, the pictures straightened on the walls, fresh-cut flowers in a little vase of clear water on the corner table every weekend.

Somebody on this floor took fastidious care of it, but I never saw who it was. I doubted it was the Somalian in 6, who I once saw take a shit directly into the storm drain out front. I doubted it was Andy, the unemployed writer type at the end of the hall. He dropped a bag of groceries down the stairs back when he moved in, and there's still a can of beans on the first-floor landing. Been there for a year and a half now. That left whoever lived in 7. I'd never seen the person, but based on the neat, rigidly spotless hallway, I assumed it was either a kindly old grandmother or a twisted Nazi serial killer. The Nazi would be less disturbing.

I thundered down our stairs, listening to them scream like stepped-on kittens, and took a huge flying leap through our front door, hurtling over the stoop and landing with a thump on the sidewalk. I touched down six inches from a pair of chicks who screamed a little with surprise.

"Watch it!" one said. She had clean, feathered hair and wore some kind of disco blouse.

"Take off your shirt," I replied, "if only because it sucks."

"Pig," she responded.

I shrugged.

Fair enough.

I gave her an elegant bow and a quick fart and sprinted off toward Shop Shop, our corner store. The night was warm and thick, and I was buzzing with energy. I felt it in my limbs, in my fingertips. The air rushing by me was slightly cooler, so I ran faster. My legs felt good, stretching and rebounding like rubber, so I ran faster. My beat-up Chucks slapped the concrete like a drumbeat, so I ran faster. And faster.

I am a knife through the New York streets.

I looked up just in time to see that I was about to sprint right by Shop Shop. I managed to shoot my hand out at the last possible second and gripped the metal post between the two propped-open doors. The momentum almost ripped my arm from the socket. I pivoted around the pole, through the open doors, over my own feet, and into an unreasonably giant display of beef jerky.

It cascaded over me like a warm meat waterfall.

Alex sighed loudly from his gouged wooden stool behind the counter.

"Hey, Carey," he said, barely glancing up from the tiny black-and-white TV that kept him company on the night shift.

"How's it going, Alex?" I said as casually as possible, taking to my feet and briefly skating on a thin layer of crushed beef.

"Good. If you pick that up now, I won't make you pay for the broken ones," he said.

Did I mention the man's a saint?

I grabbed a few unwieldy armfuls of jerky and shoveled them back into the display, then heaved it upright and picked up the stragglers. I threw the torn packages—only a half dozen, not bad for a night's destruction—into the garbage can by the door.

"Iron City," Alex said; "bottom shelf on the far left."

Alex knows me well enough to remember that the only things I come in here to buy are Ruffles (when I'm high) and the cheapest possible beer with the highest alcohol content. He lets me know if, by some freak closeout or meteorological shift, that happens not to be Schlitz. I guess Iron City was on sale.

A fucking saint, I tell you.

I humped two cases up under my arms and made for the counter. A canned laugh track blared out from his little TV like a pack of lo-fi hyenas. I slid the cases onto the counter, and something caught my eye.

That's a week's worth of beer money, Carey.

I broke out in a cold sweat just thinking about it. I had two weeks of drinking money squirreled away at all times. It's my nest egg. I've never been without that padding. Could I live with being only one unlucky week away from sober?

"Something else?" Alex asked wearily, noticing I hadn't thrust a gob of cash at him and bolted for the doors like usual.

Fuck it.

"Yeah," I answered, "I'll take eight of those."

The disco bitches were gone by the time I wrestled my two cases and paper bag back to the apartment.

". . . the BLACKS know, the BLACKS have always known!" muttered the raggedy man on the stoop.

Oh, cool, Sammy's out.

"What's up, Sammy Six?" I asked.

I set my burden down, tore open the case, and handed him a beer.

"Sixtimessixisthirtysixtimessixistwohundredsixteen-timessixis . . ." His voice dropped low and the words blurred together into gibberish.

It was his thing: Some hobos hoarded. Some jerked off outside your window. Some peed on you if you were wearing red shoes. Sammy Six did math: He especially liked six, for some reason. All told, there were worse things to do. Besides, the guy's been around forever. When we first moved to the neighborhood, none of the other tenants would so much as look at us, but Sammy helped out. He showed me where the cheapest beer was, which alleys to avoid past midnight (only two were really dangerous; the rest mostly contained hobos fucking—which is still flagged as "to avoid" in my book), and he'd always share a brew with me. If I was buying, of course. All crazy hobo gibberish aside, he was something like a drunken mentor.

"Hey," I said, shaking the can around in front of his face, "beer now, math later."

"Hmm?" Sammy's eyes focused a little, and his voice lost some of the sleepy haze. "Oh, right. Thanks, Carey."

He took the beer and cracked it open expertly: no foam at all, despite my long and clumsy walk from the store.

"What's the news?" I prodded him again.

"Ah, you know. Same shit, different toilet," he answered, and we both laughed. "You?"

"Drinking, fighting, and fucking. Not necessarily in that order," I answered, cracking open a beer of my own. Ice-cold beads of condensation ran down the sides. The bite from the first gulp was sweeter than any kiss I've ever had. But then again, people usually don't kiss me too sweetly. . . .

"You, uh . . . everybody's good?" Sammy asked again, his eyes taking on a conspiratorial shift.

"Yeah, why?" I pressed the can to my sweating forehead between sips.

"Nobody's gone? Nobody's gone away?"

"Sure. Some people left town. We guess. We don't really know. People disappear, you know?"

"It ain't that," he said, and took a deep pull from his beer. He was quiet and thoughtful for a few minutes while we nursed our drinks. "There's something going on in this town. It's worse than you think. I've seen it before, it's . . ."

Sammy shook his head. Bumped his palm against his forehead.

"It's hard to think about," he tried again. "Something buried in my head. You just watch yourself, okay? You come tell me if you boys see anything weird."

There was something off with Sammy. You can usually bring him around to clarity for a minute or two, but this was the most coherent I'd ever heard him.

"Sure, man. Sure. Hey, are *you* all right, though?"

"They're all going away now," he answered. "The blacks get them. But the blacks can't get the Six!"

There's the Sammy I remember.

I laughed. "I don't think the blacks want you, Sammy."

I put the lip of my half-full beer between my teeth, hefted my cases again, and headed up the stairs.

"Oh, no," Sammy called after me, "I'm not Six! The blacks know me! All the blacks know about old Sammy! They know about you too, Carey!"

"Harv a good one, Shammy!" I yelled around my beer, and gave him part of a wave with my shoulder as I turned the corner.

I kicked at our door loudly and for a long time before Matt answered.

"I BRING GIFTSH OF FRANKINSHENSHE AND MYRRH!" I hollered through my sloshing can.

Matt seized a case from under my arm and scampered off to the kitchen. I took the beer out of my teeth with my free hand and followed him.

"I'm not saying you *want* to."—Randall was in the middle of some kind of lecture—"I'm just saying if you *had* to: Would it be more preferable to fuck a talking dog, like Scooby-Doo, because he's closer to people?"

"Definitely," Safety Pins answered without a second of thought.

I waited until the laughter died down, then tipped my paper bag upside down on the kitchen counter.

"The bloody hell is that?" Jezza asked, peering at the small brass rectangles.

"Lighters," I said; "one for everybody."

FIVE

"Do you know how to make a zombie?" Carl asked me in between mouthfuls of the saddest, soggiest burrito I have ever seen.

"Depends." I gave it a moment of thought before answering. "Are we talking classic shambling Romero zombies, or new-wave Boyle rage-virus zombies?"

"No, I mean literally—"

"Oh! Right. Like the Haitians? It's powdered puffer-fish toxin and brainwashing mostly, though the voodoo priests did bury the victims to make them think they'd risen from the dead. . . ."

"Jesus, Kaitlyn, the drink. A zombie is a drink." Carl was pinching the fat in between his eyebrows. I guessed it was supposed to symbolize his running low on patience, but he never had any to start with.

"Completely, no," I answered, seeing and fearing where this was going, "and I'm not licensed, and I'm a recovering alcoholic, and I'm on my period, and anything else that is going to get me out of covering Madison's bartending shift."

"This is Maddy's third night gone," Carl said, dropping his wet log of meat and cheese in disgust, "and not even a call. I think she's a walkout."

"I've done four doubles in a row," I protested, "and I have to be on set tomorrow."

"Bullshit," Carl called, correctly. "You'd be beaten to hell if you'd been rehearsing. You haven't had stunt work in a month. You got nothing to do tonight, and we need you here."

I glared out the door, at the ceiling—anywhere but at Carl's balding, bearded, purposefully patriarchal head. Then he hit me with his Dad Eyes. It was a look that expressed hope, disappointment, understanding, and grace all at once. It was a look few could resist.

"Quit ogling me, Carl."

I was one of the few.

But there was a reason I had been taking all those doubles in the first place.

The smell of burning oil. A light in the air. A chorus of screams.

I knew that being afraid of going home to my apartment was ridiculous. I knew there was never anything there—not really—it was just an episode, a hallucination or some kind of seizure. I mean, it hadn't happened to me since I was a kid, that night with the fire, but they say you can never cure mental illness, you can only treat it. The angel had been entirely in my head. I knew that for a fact. But when I went searching for some kind of comfort that knowledge could give me, I came up empty.

"Fine." I sighed wearily. No point letting Carl know wanted it—might as well get a favor out of this mess.

"Then you start now," Carl said, hopping down from h stool and moving immediately for the door.

"Wait—no, I haven't had lunch y—" I started, but the door was already jingling, sounding his exit.

I stared glumly down at the leftover burrito. I pulled the condiment knife out of the limes and cut the thing in half, discarding the portion Carl had been eating. I sneered and stuffed one corner into my mouth.

The chimes jingled again.

"Carl, you are at least covering until I get a burger or something," I said, still poking at the mess in awe. "I don't even know who makes a burrito this bad in Southern California. Did you drive to fucking Michigan for Mexican food or—"

Jackie was standing there cockeyed, smiling as she let me ramble.

"K," she said, laughing all the way to the bar, "what's up?"

"Carl's got me on bar tonight." I grabbed Madison's apron and tied it about my waist. I'd been back behind the bar a few times while waiting tables, but not enough to be familiar with it. I flipped open tray after tray—cherries, oranges, limes, little umbrellas, and twisty ribbons of lemon. I had absolutely no idea what to do with any of them.

"Free booze?!" Jackie practically leapt into her chair.

"If you want to get me fired on my first night," I replied, staring at the vast wall of liquor behind me. There were twenty-six different kinds of vodka. Twenty-six different varieties of a liquid that's supposed to taste like nothing.

"But," I continued, "I do need to practice mixing drinks a little bit. You can be my guinea pig for a few."

"Well, if it's for science . . ." Jackie said, and leaned into her elbows on the bar.

"What do you want?" I asked.

"I'll take a beer."

"Funny." I slapped the condiment lids shut and went about

finding glasses. A mistake: If there were twenty-six kinds of nothing, there were an infinite number of receptacles to hold that nothing. Long, thin flutes, squat little cups covered in nubs, elaborately curved shot glasses—each ostensibly for a different purpose.

I am going to die in this place.

"How about a margarita?" Jackie finally asked. "Even *you* can't screw that up."

"We'll see," was all I could reply, grabbing a round glass that I almost remembered getting a margarita in one time. I wouldn't even know where to start noticing that a drink was served in the wrong glass. But this being West L.A., some plastic-faced Hills-woman was bound to try to get me fired over it.

"How's work? Real work, I mean—jumping cars and stuff. Any leads?" Jackie asked, already bored and heading over to the pinball machine. It was mostly for decoration: Carl liked that "retro Americana look," as he put it—but Jackie loved the thing. It was a reference to a TV show I never watched. Something about wagons and Indians, complete with vaguely racist overtones. When you lost your last ball, a little chieftain automaton jerked to life on the back of the board, making chopping motions with his hand and laughing evilly.

"Not for a while," I answered unhappily. When stunt work came, it was the best job in the world, but it was coming few and far between—not enough to get me unionized, at any rate. "How are things going for you?"

"Great!" Jackie slammed a paddle, and a bunch of dim lights flickered on, flashing yellow and orange. A wagon on fire. "I got an intern gig with a little improv troupe over in Santa Monica. Only two nights a week and no pay yet, but I get onstage."

"That's amazing, Jackie. You just tell me when, and I'll come laugh way too loud at all of your jokes. It will be intensely embarrassing," I said.

I poured what felt like an objectively absurd amount of tequila into the blender, followed by a vaguely greenish mixture in a clear plastic bottle, and some triple sec. I flipped open the bin and grabbed a scoop of ice. Madison had left the metal scoop in there all night. The handle was so cold it burned.

"Eat cowboy justice," Jackie swore, as the machine threw up a howl of stereotypical Indian chanting. "Are you sure everything's okay with you, K? No offense, but you look like you're on the tail end of a meth binge."

"Yeah." I briefly, madly entertained the idea of telling Jackie what I saw last week. The light. The angel. The impossible tear in the world that burned like the heart of a star. The sacred, terrifyingly beautiful cosmic anomaly . . . that liquefied a bum masturbating outside of my window. I flashed back to my half-remembered childhood. Flames on the plastic tablecloth, plaid melting and fusing to wood. Crying. Angels.

I told somebody about the angels before.

"Some people need pills to be normal, Katey," Mom had said, *stuffing half of a white oval into a piece of cut-up hot dog.*

Never again.

"Yeah," I continued, "Carl just sprung this bartending gig on me, and I haven't eaten all day. That's all."

I poured the ice into the blender and hit the button. It whirled to life, gargling the concoction into a fine mush. I slid the mix into the round glass and tried to rub salt on the side with my fingers, but it wouldn't stick.

How do they do that?

"Here." I slid the drink toward Jackie. "Tell me how it turned out."

Jackie abandoned her pinball genocide and skipped back to the bar. She slid onto her stool and took a giant gulp of margarita. Her eyes bugged out of her head, and she coughed half of it back into the glass.

"Jesus!" she stammered, trying to breathe out the liquor fumes. "Did you brush your teeth and spit in a bottle of tequila?"

"What? Here, let me try." I took a sip and gagged. It was pure, cheap alcohol, with just a hint of stale, horrible mint. I opened the bottle of greenish mixture and took a whiff: like mouthwash.

Jackie was laughing now.

"I thought this was margarita mix," I pleaded.

"It says 'mojito' right on the bottle," Jackie countered.

"What does that mean? I thought it was, like, some special brand of margarita. . . ."

"They're going to tear you apart tonight," Jackie said, throwing up her hands. "There's going to be a riot. It's going to make the news: 'Society brought down by lone, shitty bartender.'"

"Like I wasn't nervous enough already!" I whipped off Madison's apron and threw it at Jackie.

"Seriously, though, call your bartender and tell him he has to work tonight," Jackie said, and poured the abomination down the bar drain.

"I can't; she's a walkout. Madison didn't even call in."

"Oof." Jackie took to her feet and started heading back to her game. "Are all of these flaky Hollywood bitches named Madison?"

"Can you stay with me? Help out? I'll split my tips with you.

It's supposed to be a lot of money." I could feel my heart racing already. We got so busy on weekends. The bar was standing room only. What the hell was I doing?

"Well"—Jackie dug through her pockets for change—"I guess so. But only because you said the magic word: 'money.'"

She came up with a quarter and plunked it into the slot. She was greeted by angry chanting, pounding drums, and a series of dim little bulbs, flickering like fire.

"It's weird, though," Jackie continued, after losing three balls in what I assumed to be record time, "everybody's just skipping out on work lately. A bunch of girls at the plaza are walkouts, too. Even Emily—remember her?"

"Oh, wow, seriously?" Emily was nice. Short Asian girl with a nose ring. She came out drinking with me and Jackie a few times, when they mostly bitched about work together while I feigned interest. She may have been the only person in L.A. that didn't have any desire to be in movies.

Including me, I thought bitterly.

"Seriously. She's supposed to be coming to this party with me tonight, but I haven't heard from her in days."

"Weird," I said, and let the conversation drop.

"It *is* weird," Jackie said loudly, and stared me right in the eye.

"What?"

"It is weird that now I have nobody to go to this bullshit Hollywood party with me," Jackie reiterated.

"Oh, God, Jackie, no. Come on, I'm going to be drawn and quartered during this shift . . ."

"This shift that I am selflessly volunteering to help you with," Jackie supplied.

"You know I hate those damned parties. Nobody talks to

you; they just yell parts of their résumé at each other while pretending they're not on coke."

"It's called networking." Jackie sighed. "And that right there is the reason you're not finding work. Come on, we'll get through this shift together and then go drink off the post-customer-service filth in the hills."

"I . . ." I had nothing. "They better have something wrapped in bacon."

I dumped half of the soggy burrito in the trash and tried to build a fruit salad out of the condiment tray.

Jackie looked amazing. She was wearing a form-fitting tuxedo, a thin black waistcoat pinned tight to her midsection, complete with a perfectly cocked top hat. I forgot how well she did the whole appearance thing when she wanted to.

"How do I look?" she asked me, spinning halfway around and giving a genteel little bow.

"Hot, but funny, like an old-timey magician's assistant," I said, suddenly feeling ill at ease in my own basic cocktail dress and black flats.

Don't get me wrong: I don't have body issues. I know how to look pretty damn presentable. Give me the right jeans and T-shirt, and I can floor a man from halfway across the bar. But I barely understand what "cocktail wear" is, much less how to pull it off.

"I was going for a fuckable Charlie Chaplin," Jackie replied, frowning. She did that Chaplin walk, all splay-footed and waddling, but infused with just a hint of sexy runway hip swivel.

"I see it now. You are going to confuse the hell out of some poor Hollywood hipsters."

I poured another shot of tequila into my coffee mug and downed it. I shuddered as the warm wave broke back up my throat.

"Oh, do me." Jackie practically pranced over to the counter.

"You're not that fuckable," I said, waggling my arms as if I could shake the liquor out of my skin.

"The booze," Jackie said; "and if you keep drinking like that, who knows where the night may take you?"

"It's only two. If I'm going to an 'industry' party, I've found I need an exact two-drink head start to remain charming." I slopped an abstract amount of golden liquid into her mug. It said "#1 Dad" on the side and had a picture of a hammer. Mine was a sleepy owl. I didn't own any shot glasses.

"Ah, the two-drink theorem. It's sound math." Jackie knocked hers back and didn't even make a face. "Just be careful to keep the pace. Two drinks can snowball into twelve. Remember Tyler's house?"

I laughed.

"That started as a sensible two-drink base, and then . . ." Jackie closed her eyes and shuddered.

"Then you did a shot-by-shot reenactment of the *Pump Up the Jam* video in your underwear. In front of everybody."

"Then, yes, that happened. Thank you for explicitly reminding me."

"I'm just happy to get an excuse to say that out loud. Try it: 'Shot-by-shot reenactment of the *Pump Up the Jam* video in your underwear.' It's fun."

Jackie rolled her eyes at me and went back to fussing in the mirror in my living room.

"Am I underdressed? I can change," I said, acutely aware of how broad my shoulders were in a strapless dress.

"No, no! It's good. Honest. Even better because you don't know it. You could stand to throw on some heels. . . ."

We stared at each other in silence.

"Jackie . . ." I started.

"I know, I know"—she waved me away—"you don't have to outrun the bear."

I had this highly irrational fear that as soon as I leave the house in heels, I'm going to be chased down by some sexual predator or something. When I told Jackie about it, she gestured at her own feet and asked me what in the hell I thought *she* would do, in her heels. I told her it's like that old joke: "I don't have to outrun the bear, I only have to outrun the skank next to me."

"I'm going to change really quick." I moved toward the bedroom, but Jackie intercepted me. She started to say something, but three beeps from outside stopped her. She smiled.

"Can't. Cab's here."

Shit.

The cab driver was Iranian. He tried to sell me a used pickup truck his cousin owned.

The party was at one of those generic Southern California hilltop mansions. You know the type: a bunch of neomodern boxes locked together by small glass hallways, big pool overlooking the city, track lighting everywhere. I swear to God, every industry party I've gone to was held in a house just like that one. In fact, it could have been the same house.

Does anybody even live here? Do they rent houses just for reality TV shows and schmoozing?

There was a little table for appetizers, but it was mostly shellfish and avocado.

Los Angeles.

I nabbed six bacon-wrapped somethings—it didn't matter what they were, beyond "not shellfish and avocado"—and made for the deck, where I last saw Jackie. She was talking to a paunchy guy with a soul patch. As usual, she had gathered a small crowd of newly converted fans around her. She was telling some kind of story, but I walked out right as she finished and only heard the paunchy guy's huge laugh. I caught her eye, and she wiggled her ears, making the crooked top hat dance. I smiled.

She was great at this stuff. But then, she needed to be: This, we'd both discovered upon moving down here after high school, was the only way anybody got jobs. This was *networking.*

I was terrible at it. I didn't think it would matter for me. *Nobody's going to hire you to jump off a bridge because you give good conversation at parties,* I argued. But judging by my absolute work drought lately, that apparently wasn't the case. Four years ago, Jackie had convinced me to move to L.A. with her. She wanted to be an actress, and, she insisted, I absolutely had to come with her: How many hot chicks could jump a dirt bike over a train? They would throw work at my feet, she said.

Turns out, there indeed are *not* many girls who can powerslide a muscle car, but every single goddamned one of them is in Hollywood, competing for the same job. Jackie was pretty, funny, confident, charming; she was making slow headway, but she was making headway. I was treading water.

I admit it: I was jealous. Bitter, even.

But also kind of proud. Of her, I mean. Jackie really was meant for this life. In my better moments, I even tried to swallow my pride and learn from her example. I did the dance, no matter how bad I was at the steps. I . . . *networked*. God, just the word is filthy. So far I had shared small talk with a bitch agent (that's not a dig; he was an agent exclusively for female dogs) and bitterly complained about the 405 with a girl who painted food. Not pictures of food—she literally painted food to make it look good for commercials. That's all she did.

"What's the point of a brand-new Jag," she asked me, "if I'm just going to park it on the freeway?"

Just by painting grill stripes on fake hamburgers! What the hell?

I was growing to hate L.A., even though that in itself is such an L.A. thing to do. Everybody hates it here, if you ask them. But they don't move, and I wasn't about to, either. It may not happen often, but I made three months' rent this year by speeding a '69 Charger into a dump truck. It was one of the most beautiful moments of my life. Show me anywhere else in the world where I can make a living doing that, and I'll move. Until then, L.A. is a necessity.

"K!" Jackie shouted, seizing a man from out of her crowd of fans and dragging him over to me. "This is Marco."

She smiled giddily, waiting for something. I narrowed my eyes at the guy. Extremely good looking, but in that alien Hollywood kind of way. Vaguely Latino, but not so much that he couldn't "pass," as they so horribly say in the business. I knew him from somewhere.

"Oh, holy shit," I said, when it finally clicked. "Sable! You're J. C. Sable!"

"It's Marco, actually." He laughed, shaking his head. "Marco Luis. But, yeah, that was me."

"I lived for that show as a kid!" I practically squealed.

Oh, Jesus Christ, Kaitlyn, close your jaw, you jabbering yokel.

"Sorry," I added hastily, "I don't get starstruck often. It's just that me and Jackie ran home after school every day to watch *Home Room*. Wow, I haven't thought about you in, like, ten years."

Jackie slapped me on the arm, and I instinctually went to slap her back, when I realized what I'd said.

Marco saw my eyes bug out, but he just laughed again.

"It's okay!" he exclaimed cheerfully. "That was my household-name moment. It's a blessing and a curse. I'm just glad the show meant so much to you two."

"She had a poster of Sable up above her bed"—Jackie smiled wickedly—"the shirtless one in the pool."

Oh, son of a—

"Hey, me too!" Marco said, so earnestly that it took me a minute to realize he was joking. He stayed deadpan until I laughed, then joined in.

"Personally, I was a Mack girl, myself," Jackie said, already backing out of the conversation. "I go for the well-meaning jerks. But Kaitlyn's always had a soft spot for the misunderstood jockish type."

I reached out to slug her, but she spun away. She did a taunting little robot dance, then turned and went back to her followers.

"So we've already established that we're both fans of me," Marco said, still chuckling. "What about you? What do you do?"

"I'm a waitress," I said.

I was finding it hard to think of him as a real person. He

was J. C. Sable; he was a fictional character; a poster in a fourteen-year-old girl's room. And he looked like he'd been carved from stone by an ancient Roman, for Christ's sake.

"Oh? That's nice," he replied. "Usually everybody I talk to is in the business."

"Well, I sort of am, I guess. I do some work as a stunt-woman, whenever I can get it. But I don't make my living from it yet, so I try not to tell people, 'I'm a stuntwoman,' when I actually pay my rent by balancing plates of food."

"Oh? That's nice," Marco repeated, with the exact same intonation as before. I got the feeling all he knew about small talk he learned from press junkets. "That sounds like a lot of fun."

Awkward. Silence.

"So . . . ," I finally said, seeing that he had no intention of pursuing the last line of conversation, "what are you work-ing on these days?"

At the prompt, he sprung into enthusiastic life: "I've got a great new project lined up with E! It's a reality show all about my work with inner-city Latino kids, trying to show them there's another path besides drugs and gang violence. We just shot the first episode: I teach a gangbanger how to Rollerblade!"

"Oh, wow, that's so cool. So you work with troubled kids?"

"That's what the show is about, yes," Marco confirmed.

Awkward. Silence.

Yeah, he was just being polite, talking to you. What the hell would he want with a girl like you anyway, Kaitlyn? He probably power-screws a bus full of supermodels between takes.

"So listen," I said, mowing through the last of my bacon-wrapped somethings, "I've gotta talk to my friend real quick, but I'll see you later, okay?"

"Adios!" he said, just like Sable did in the show. Weird.

I made my way over to Jackie, who was deep into an anecdote that necessitated her pantomiming ramming her fist into some kind of hole over and over again. The paunchy soul-patch guy was turning purple, he was laughing so hard. The lean, plastic-faced blonde next to him was covering her mouth with one hand, equal parts amused and terrified. I stood just to one side until Jackie finished her story—something about a mayonnaise jar, I gathered—and then swooped in when everybody paused to breathe.

"I'm gonna head out," I said, and she gave me a disappointed look. "I know you need to stay. You're killing here, but I have work in the morning. Again."

"You called a cab yet?" Jackie asked me, annoyed but understanding—or at least accepting that arguing was pointless.

"No, I figured I'd call and wait out front."

"F that noise," Jackie said, waving Marco over.

"Jackie, no!" I whispered harshly. "He practically died of boredom just talking to me."

Marco was standing exactly where I'd left him, strangely blank, like somebody had just switched him off. When he saw Jackie wave, he immediately broke into that trademark expectant half smile and began strolling over.

"I am not hooking up with Marco," I informed her evenly. "You're just going to embarrass me. Stop. Please, seriously, stop."

"How could you possibly not?" she whispered back. "I mean, sure, no way he's any good in bed, looking like that. But if you don't at least *try* to stick it to J. C. Motherfucking Sable, what would fourteen-year-old you think?"

"I . . ." I started to protest, but she was right, of course.

Some things you just have to do because you never should have gotten the opportunity to do them, like eat caviar or slobber on former *Tiger Beat* hunks.

"Marco!" Jackie exclaimed, and hugged him like a long-lost brother. "You were saying you had to head out soon. My friend here needs a ride home. Do you think you could do her a solid?"

"Sure thing!" Marco threw on his eager smirk. "Anything for my number-one fan!"

My whole body flushed. I felt like somebody had thrown me into a microwave on defrost: Warm tingling spread outward in waves, pulsing from my core to my skin.

Oh, God. Was this really . . . ? No way. No fucking way.

Flashbacks to cutting his picture out of magazines. Jackie and I making jokes about what we'd do to Sable and Mack if we were students at Lakeview High. Touching myself beneath the covers, looking up at that poster where he sat frozen, immobile, guarding over my bed at night . . .

Marco looped his arm through mine, which was totally hokey but also kind of adorable, and I decided right then that whatever else happened, no matter how much of an ass I would surely make of myself, I had to go for it. Arm in arm, we moved toward the brightly lit cubes of the generic party mansion. I turned to wave to Jackie, but she was already back to entertaining.

"Adios!" Marco expelled suddenly and loudly, just like on the show.

SIX

⎮ ⎮ ⎮ 1977. New York City, New York. Carey. ⎮ ⎮ ⎮ ⎮ ⎮ ⎮ ⎮ ⎮ ⎮

Randall held up a single finger. I spotted it out of the corner of my eye, swung around, and punched him in the chest.

This was a game we played called Reaction, where one player starts counting with his fingers. If he gets to three before you notice, he punches you in the chest. If you can punch him in the chest before he gets to three, you . . . don't get punched in the chest.

Look, nobody said it was a *good* game.

But we were bored and anxious. It was pissing down rain outside of Max's Kansas City. Ceaseless sheets of fat, warm drops that triggered a blink reflex every time they hit your face. It felt like God was spitting right in your eye every couple of seconds, and the only dry space, right under the awning, was already full of big shots and hot girls showing cleavage.

The bouncers called who got those spots, so there we were: standing in heaven's urine stream, killing time until the doors opened.

Randall had stopped coughing from the blow and went

back to talking to Gray Greg, the ashen-faced junkie who sold dope to kids in line at shows.

"I'm not saying it's right, I'm just saying he talks, you know, like people, so if you had to have sex with—"

Randall wasn't looking at me. I held up my pointer finger as nonchalantly as possible.

Nothing.

"I don't understand," Gray Greg was protesting, still awkwardly holding out a bag of dope that Randall wouldn't take.

I flipped up my middle finger.

"I mean it's like you have something in common, right? You could at least affirm it was consensual—"

I clenched my fist and went to raise the third finger.

"No, I guess I wouldn't want to hear him speak." Gray Greg was shaking his head, little flecks of dry skin grating off of his face like dandruff.

I managed the slightest twitch of my ring finger before Randall spun like a tornado and struck me square in the solar plexus.

"So what you're saying, then, is that you like to fuck dogs because they can't talk back," Randall finished, without missing a beat.

Greg threw up his hands and walked away. Off to find easier marks.

I doubled over, gagging on my own lack of air, and waited for the stars to pass. When they did, I saw Randall grinning at me in the side mirror of the station wagon he was leaning on.

God damn it. Leave it to Randall to turn a nice game of punch exchange into some tactical fucking exercise.

I nodded concession to him and looked for something else to occupy my time. The parasites had latched on to us again tonight. We had invited them over to the apartment a few times this week, because they usually chipped in for beer money. They had taken that as some sort of official approval, and now we couldn't get rid of them. We tried telling them to fuck off; they didn't listen. We were all out of ideas.

Thing 1 and Thing 2 were playing a game with string laced between their fingers. They were trying to teach Wash, who was studying it like an electron microscope. Safety Pins had secured a spot under the awning, where she stood with studied disinterest, just like the rest of the cleavage girls. We tried to use her as an excuse to take some space in the dry, but one look at my busted-up face and sideways nose, and the bouncers jostled us back into the rain.

The parasites were all laughing at something. I didn't feel like busting into their nervous little circle. I needed something else to do—something productive and enlightening.

I settled for ogling the cleavage girls and making faces at them when they caught me. One or two seemed to be into it. A stunning redhead, her pale skin practically glinting in the streetlight, waggled her tongue at me in exchange. Most just rolled their eyes and cut off eye contact.

It was to be expected. Richard Hell was playing tonight, and girls went crazy for the bastard. He looked like Bob Dylan's plague-stricken younger brother. He moved like he was always in a bathrobe: all lazy and aloof. Hell had that whole malnourished-nihilist thing going for him. That always brings out the stunners. I did okay for my part: A certain kind of girl was actually drawn to the just-got-hit-by-a-truck look that I carefully nurtured. But when Richard Hell opens a show, it's a Salvation Army runway show out front. Models in precisely ripped T-shirts and meticulously dirty jeans.

I was miming blow jobs to a bored blonde, who was trying to figure out the sexiest way to flip me off, when an argument broke out.

"What is this, the tits-only section?" the kid hollered. He couldn't have been more than fifteen. His hair was done up in shoddy spikes, the telltale white crust of Elmer's glue drying on the tips.

I got a weird knot in my stomach, which I decided to chalk up to microwave burritos and Iron City.

The guy blocking the door just laughed and roughly shuffled the kid away from the awning. The kid spat at him in reply. By the time the bouncer's eyes went wide with fury, the kid was already bolting around the corner, down Seventeenth. A couple of the cleavage girls laughed.

I turned back to Randall, who was watching the proceedings with a worried look on his face.

"Weird," he said, slapping me on the arm and gesturing to the crowd I'd just turned away from.

I looked back and didn't see it.

"What?"

"There's, like, a dozen people following that kid," Randall said.

"I don't—"

It was only when he pointed right at them that I finally noticed.

It's not that I didn't *see* them—they were completely visible—it's just that it didn't occur to me that there was anything weird about ten people breaking away all at once to follow some scruffy little punk-rock kid into an empty side street. Not until Randall pointed it out. And even after he did, a huge chunk of my brain argued.

This is boring, my brain said; *nothing to see here. Let's do something else. Let's start a fire.*

It was the way they moved: casual and natural, like somebody sliding past you on an elevator. You don't even think to object when they brush against your junk; it's just a thing that happens, sometimes.

Only when you're not looking for 'em do you notice how weird it is that you're not looking for 'em.

That's what Matt the Black Unicorn had said.

"Hey, where's Matt?" I shouted into the parasite huddle.

"He's havin' a squat behind the skip," Jezza answered.

Scuffed Flannel giggled.

"Could somebody translate that from asshole to English?" I asked the huddle.

"He's pooping behind the Dumpster," Thing 1 answered. She did something with the string around her fingers and caught Wash's hand tight.

"Damn. All right. If he gets back, tell him me and Randall are heading up Seventeenth to fight those invisible people he was talking about."

"Cool," Wash said, trying and utterly failing to fathom the net of yarn wrapped around his wrist. "Wait—what?"

I was already off jogging after the group, who had just rounded the corner and slipped out of sight. I heard Randall sigh loudly, and then his ratty combat boots were slapping the pavement right alongside me.

We came skidding across a section of wet grating just as the Unnoticeables caught up to the kid. They were all around him, but it wasn't until one reached out and grabbed his arm—*a girl, blond hair, wait—brunette? Jesus, just focus on her, Carey*—that he thought to object.

"Hey," the kid said, struggling against the girl's grip.

The others moved in, closing a circle around him.

"Hey!" the kid tried again, panicking now. "Hey, fuck you!"

I couldn't see him anymore. The others were blocking my view.

"Help!" he screamed. "Somebody help!"

The kid tried "fuck you" before he tried "help."

They shall not have this one.

The mob was moving now, the kid caught in the middle as they forced him toward an open garage a half block up Seventeenth. A pale orange light flickered in there, like fire inside a barrel.

I tried to think of something creative to say as I was sprinting up to them, but I settled for a flying tackle instead. I nailed the biggest one first. It was hard even to tell that much, looking at them all together: Big, small, blond, redhead, race, clothing—the more there were of them in any one place, the harder it was to pick one out. Just a big indistinct mass of wiggling humanity.

As we tumbled across soggy pavement, the sharp points of our limbs knocking painfully on the cement, I got to focus on the big guy a bit more clearly. He was tall but not thick. Black guy. Close-cropped hair and hooded eyes. He didn't even look surprised to see me, as I headbutted his nose into a brownish pudding.

I looked back in time to see Randall clock a petite girl in pigtails with a trash can. She crumpled like a wet paper bag. He was trying to use the momentum, ride the surprise of the moment, but none of the Unnoticeables was shaken in the least. The four nearest him turned to face Randall, while the rest continued shuffling the kid off toward the garage.

I got my feet under me and executed an absolutely stunning two-footed, full-body, Captain Kirk–style dropkick on a guy that looked like a punk-rock accountant. Wire glasses, birdlike features, carefully stained Ramones T-shirt, and sharp-creased jeans. He folded up double and stayed that way. The man even passed out in an orderly fashion.

I cracked my tailbone painfully on the landing but pushed away the shock and tried to stand again. Too late. Two of the Unnoticeables were on me. They were too close together. I couldn't tell them apart. I saw a vague mass of limbs and flesh enclosing me, tangling up my arms and feet. I was looking one dead in the face—I swear to God I was—and it was like I was forgetting him even as I spat right into his eyeball. I cursed, tried a wild bite, took a blow to the head. No good. I couldn't move.

One set of limbs released their grip.

Then another.

I looked up at Randall's face, grinning wildly down at me.

I glanced over to where I'd last seen him, and there were four lumps of indistinguishable human clutching themselves and moaning.

Randall offered his hand and I took it.

"How did you take all those fuckers out?" I asked, spitting blood and shaking my head clear.

"I got steel-toed boots and they got balls." He shrugged. "Even Wash can do that math."

We heard a muffled protest from somewhere behind us:

a gentle request for somebody to go fornicate with themselves, forcibly.

Randall and I turned to face the garage, just in time to see
a rolling hump of Unnoticeable flesh kick the spiky-haired
kid down an open manhole.

I started to run after him, but Randall caught the arm of
my jacket and used the momentum to swing me down and
back onto my ass. I began composing a filthy ode to his
mother, but he just silently pointed into the shadows on
either side of the garage.

Something glinted there. Brass. Round. Grooved edges.

Two pairs of gears, floating in the dark.

The tar men shuffled forward on stumpy elephant feet.
They moved like cold molasses. More flowing than walking. I
could smell them now. Plastic and molten rubber. Tupperware left on a stovetop.

"Fu—" Randall started, but the words left him.

He hadn't been up close with them like this before. He
probably only half-believed what little he'd seen, until that
moment. He was backpedaling with his arms, but his legs
weren't moving.

The tar men advanced on us like a slow-motion flood.
They burbled and burped from somewhere deep inside. The
gears on one's face snapped together with a metallic clink
and started to whir as they picked up speed.

That goddamned sound.

I felt the vertigo in my knees first. Nausea broke over me
like a barstool.

Randall was weaving. Unsteady on his feet.

"These ones are easy," I reassured him, trying to keep my
own voice from cracking.

I slid my shiny new brass Zippo from the small pocket in

my jeans and snapped the flint against my hip. It struck immediately. The tiny flame wavered but stayed strong. I tossed it underhand right into the guts of the tar man with the spinning gears.

It went up like a bottle rocket: a high and painful whistle as air sucked into the frantic inferno of its chest. There was a thin pop followed by a deep, reverberating thunderclap, and the tar man flared out of existence. When my eyes stopped misfiring sparks, I saw that the other tar man was still there. Still coming toward us.

"Randall." I slapped his cheek, and his eyes slid over to me. The rest of his face stayed fixated on the approaching blob.

"Randall!" I shook him. "Just use your fucking lighter, man!"

"I-I can't," he finally managed, "I lent it to Gray Greg. I . . . I think he pocketed it."

I slowly and with great and unwavering purpose raised a middle finger directly before his face. I shook it there for emphasis.

"Carey," Randall said, his eyes going wide.

Yes, Randall. Absorb it. Observe all of this middle finger. It is all for you. Forever.

"Carey," he said again, more urgently.

I almost turned. Almost in time.

I heard my neck burning before I saw it. Little angry pops, like slapping cold bacon onto a hot iron pan. I felt my own sizzling fat fly off and scald my cheek before I actually felt the tar man's touch.

It wasn't anything. It was just pressure. The nerves were already gone.

The fear got me more than the pain. I screeched and tried

to duck away, but I was already stuck. Every inch of the tar man was like flypaper, melting my flesh away in a thin pink river even as it held me fast. Somehow, I managed to keep myself from slapping at it. From getting my hands caught in it, too.

But that was all I could do. I dropped to my knees, hanging my head like a kitten caught by the scruff. It only had an inch of me: A black and burning finger seared into my flesh, sending my own liquid skin running down the curve of my back and sopping into the elastic band of my underwear. But I could feel its grasp expanding. I could feel it pouring over me. Pain, spreading syrupy and slow. Impossible, unimaginable pain. The only thing worse were the spots that didn't hurt anymore. The spots I knew were already gone.

And then somebody took a picture. Or maybe a flashbulb went off. I was free, lying on my stomach and shaking. I watched my own lighter skitter across the pavement in front of my face. I focused on the decal, marred and partially burned away: a happy bee smoking a joint, sticking its stinger perversely into a cartoon flower. The word "love" written above it in obnoxious balloon letters.

My back was warm. I was on fire.

Then I was wet.

Randall was peeing me out.

SEVEN

"Some party, huh?" Marco asked nobody in particular.

I was the only other person in his car—some growly, chrome-and-leather Mercedes thing, of course—so I answered: "Sure was."

"Your friend is something, huh?" Marco said again.

He wasn't even looking at me, but he didn't seem to be focusing very hard on pulling out of the steeply angled driveway, either. He nearly clipped the mailbox and cut off a delivery van as he fishtailed onto the street.

"She sure is a noun," I answered, not meaning to be quite so sarcastic.

"What's that?" Marco asked, downshifting and passing a string of Priuses over a double yellow line. They all honked.

"A noun? Like a person or a place. A general thing. You were asking really broad questions, so I . . ." I looked over at him. No emotion on his face.

"That's funny!" he screamed. Then he laughed very precisely.

"Yeah, sorry. I'm not usually such a jerk. I guess I'm just

nervous. I, uh . . . I don't usually get along very well at those industry parties."

"Why not?" Marco swerved wildly around some expensive foreign beast, all bright colors and sharp angles, then cut back into his lane just as suddenly.

I was white-knuckling the passenger handle and my own thigh, trying to hold on to something. I know everybody in L.A. is supposed to be a terrible driver, but this was beyond the pale.

"I don't know," I answered, talking mostly to distract myself from my own impending death, playing across the windshield. "I guess it's because I don't really want to act or model or anything. I like stunt work, and I'm good at it, but most people don't take me seriously at first. . . ."

Marco must have been doing sixty on the winding residential street. He whipped by a For Sale sign so close it flew off of its post and skidded across the road behind us.

"You *could* act," he said, utterly unconcerned about the rapid series of close calls and near crashes.

"Yeah, but—" I started, but Marco weaved over the line on a blind corner and missed a head-on collision with a pickup truck by a few inches. I made an unintelligible keening noise instead.

As soon as my voice comes back, I am going to say something. Should I say something? I can't blow my only chance with the unattainable celebrity I learned to masturbate to, but nobody's going to be hooking up in the burning ditch we are certainly going to end up in, at this rate. Maybe I can figure out a polite way to—

"You're a very attractive woman," Marco continued. "The only thing wrong with you is that freak finger."

I glanced down at where I had unconsciously hidden my extra digit, tucked between my legs and the seat.

"What?" I was used to the stares, but generally people tried to avoid talking about it.

"That finger. It is the only thing wrong with you. I know a doctor. She is very good. There wouldn't even be much of a scar. I'll give you her number."

I couldn't find the words. Traffic lights swung past us like paper lanterns in a hurricane.

"Would you mind letting me out at the next light?" I finally managed.

"Why?" It was getting hard to tell when he was asking a question. His voice went flat. There was no rising intonation at the end of his sentences; he said it like a statement of fact: Why. At first I thought he was just distracted, concentrating on driving, but it sure as hell didn't look that way.

"You're driving like a fucking asshole," I said as coldly as possible.

After a moment's consideration, he replied: "These people are in my way."

Jesus Christ.

I knew he seemed out of it. I thought he was maybe just a little dumb at first—you know how the pretty ones are—but now I was worried I may have implicitly agreed to suck off the guy from *American Psycho*.

"You're going to cause an accident," I said very simply, like I was trying to reason with a toddler or tell somebody there was a rattlesnake behind him.

"That does happen," he replied, "but my car is very safe, and I can afford to fix it."

"People . . . will . . . get . . . hurt," I said.

"I don't get hurt."

I was shivering, though it must have been eighty degrees inside the Mercedes.

"We are almost to your house." He spoke again after a few minutes of silence, during which time he'd managed to cut off a semi and knock over a bicyclist at a stoplight. Marco had gently but insistently rolled right into the man, running him over in slow motion, not noticing or possibly even caring that the light was red.

I nearly cried when we finally reached my apartment in one piece. My place wasn't on a main thoroughfare, but the street gets pretty busy on the weekends. Marco slammed on the brakes, throwing me into the dash. There was already a small line of cars building behind us, since Marco had simply stopped the Mercedes in the middle of the road. Somebody honked. He didn't even blink.

I reached for the door, but it locked under my hand.

"Are you going to ask me to fuck you now." It was a question, but you couldn't tell to hear it.

"What?"

"This is the part where the women ask me to fuck them. I like this part. Sometimes I make them beg, if they are a little old. Sometimes they cry, but they still ask. You have to ask me now. Ask me to come fuck you. Say 'please.'"

I yanked at the door handle. I tried pressing the lock, but it wouldn't budge.

What the hell? Cars aren't supposed to do that, are they? Does Mercedes sell a special Rapist Package?

"I wouldn't fuck you with a chain saw," I said. "Let me out."

"That's not how this goes. Now you ask me to fuck you. That's what happens next."

I remembered something Bruce Lee once said about divorcing emotion from conflict. I found my center, willed my hands to stop shaking, and cracked my knuckles in what I hoped was an ominous gesture.

"I've never been in a real fight in my life," I told Marco matter-of-factly. "I only train to throw and take fake punches, but I bet it's pretty close to the same thing, when it comes down to it. You're a big guy. You obviously work out. I bet you could take me by force, if you wanted to. I couldn't stop you. But I can make damn sure you won't be pretty after. I will take your fucking eyes. Do you hear me? I will hurt you."

"I don't get hurt," he repeated. The words, phrasing, and tone were identical—like he had carefully rehearsed and memorized every syllable but had no idea as to their meaning.

Marco leaned over slowly, as if to kiss me. I pulled back, but I was already hunched up against the door. He put a hand on my face and pulled it toward him. His eyes were flat black in the non-light. I matched the gesture—put my hand on his face as if to bring him in—then clawed, hard. My nails are short but strong. They dug into his flesh and raked downward, peeling the skin away in thick, curling ribbons. Blood oozed out of his cheek and ran down his neck.

He did not cry out.

He did not flinch.

He didn't even tighten his grip or move faster. He just slowly, methodically continued pulling me to him, then placed his lips over mine.

The psychological violation made me want to scream his skull apart, but physically, it was more awkward than anything. Skin on skin. A little pressure. Then his lips parted, and I felt myself go weak in the knees.

That is not a blushing, girlish description of lust. My legs literally lost strength. It was like struggling to wake up from a deep sleep. My muscles just wouldn't respond. It felt like my body was dying by degrees, atrophying in time-lapse.

Something cold and metallic snaked its way into my mouth. I shoved my tongue up against it, instinctively trying to push it back. When that didn't work, I bit down on it, but I had no strength. The thing gradually forced my tongue farther and farther back into my mouth until I gagged and slipped it to the side, just trying not to choke. Something like a frigid wire slid greasily down my throat. It trickled down my esophagus, as sluggish and oozing as mercury, and coiled in my stomach.

Oh, God, I thought that was his tongue. That isn't a tongue! What the fuck is this?!

Whatever it was, it was too thin to choke on, but every inch of it that spooled into me sapped more of my energy. My arms, at first scratching and pounding at Marco's impassive face, now sat limply at my sides. My hands were on my lap, palms up, only my sixth finger twitching uselessly. I couldn't feel my feet at all, though I knew they were painfully bent at wrong angles on the passenger floor. My eyelids were drooping.

Did he slip me something? Am I hallucinating? Am I having a rage-induced aneurysm? This can't be real. I can't be . . . dying . . . ?

I was swimming in something both milky and acidic. Floating in a caustic lake of syrup. Distantly, I felt my body begin to jerk and spasm. It was a symptom unrelated to me; it was no longer my concern. Somewhere I knew that my body felt the door give way behind it. Somewhere I knew that my body was falling.

I gagged up the last cold inch of the draining proboscis and instantly took root in my own flesh again.

Somebody was holding my shoulders, pulling me out of Marco's Mercedes. I threw up on my dress. I wrenched out of the stranger's grasp. I fell on my ass in the street.

I kicked at the car with my still-clumsy limbs. I tried to struggle to my feet to gouge out Marco's goddamned eyes—I keep my promises—but my body was a few seconds behind my commands.

"Fuck you!" I rasped, wishing I had something more effective. But he was already pulling away.

I saw his face for a split second, right before the car rocketed out of sight. I expected surprise. Or anger.

Or, God, too much to ask for, but shame?

I got nothing.

Marco wore the same easy, plastic smile he'd flashed all through the party in the hills. The exact same expression that J. C. Sable shot at me from the *Home Room* poster above my bed in middle school. His black eyes focused on nothing at all.

And then he was gone.

The line of cars slowly passed right in front of me, each driver trying not to make eye contact. Just another drugged-out skank getting tossed out of a Mercedes, as far as they were concerned. Par for the course in L.A.

The hands were pulling me up again, dragging me out of the street and onto the curb. I finally swiveled around to glare up at their owner. I'm not sure why I was so pissed off at those hands—they had certainly saved me from . . . *something*—but I had to be pissed off at someone, and Marco was nowhere to be seen.

I smelled him before I saw him. He stank of stale sweat, fresh beer, and old leather. A goofy smile wound its way through a cragged and stubbly face.

It took me a minute to recognize him: the weird old guy in the spiked leather jacket that cruised my street for cans every week. He slept under the overpass sometimes. Always tunelessly singing to himself.

He made some kind of noise with his mouth.

"What?" I asked.

"I said you've got to watch out for those bastards," he repeated, in a voice ground down by years of cigarettes and liquor. "Whole town's full of Empty Ones these days."

"I don't know what happened," I said, and all the anger ebbed out of me like blood from a wound. "I think he slipped me something."

The old guy settled on the curb next to me, pulled out a crumpled pack of Camels, and gestured at me with them. I shook my head.

"He slipped you something, all right," he said, almost laughing.

"Thanks for helping. . . ." I trailed off, letting him fill in the blank.

"Carey," the old man answered, flicking a weathered old brass lighter and breathing a giant cloud of smoke straight up into the air. "Name's Carey."

EIGHT

I'm trying to hold on. I'm trying to maintain focus. I'm trying to stay human, or as close to human as I can. But I can feel the bullet inside me burning. It's not emanating pain; it's releasing information. It's changing me. Rewriting things. My thoughts are becoming strange. Stilted. Acute and cold. I'm turning into something like the angel. The one that shot me.

It was never trying to kill me. I knew that somehow, though. Yusuf. Yusuf and the barriers. What does that mean? There are parts of me missing.

Through my good eye, I stared at the worn and battered Gideon Bible that sat on the end table of my shitty room in this shitty Motel 6. I wanted it to help me hang on. It had symbolic value to me, at some point. There were verses with numbers I could not remember, and they meant something even to my sick and broken mind. But the sickness is gone now. In its place there is a cold and flat clarity. My heart should break to say it, but it does not: The Bible is just a book. There are 1,206 pages. It is missing four. They were torn out by a drunk and crying man, six months ago.

Why do I know these things?

I shifted my focus instead to a wadded-up piece of gum stuck to the side of a crumpled beer can. I focused on what that used to mean to me—cold beer on a hot night, release, pain, hangovers, dehydration, laughing next to a barrel fire—and it helped a little.

My thoughts hadn't been this clear in ages. And I was losing them, one by one.

Beer. Girls.

The last time a girl touched me was . . . Christ, when? Florida? No, no, it was what's-her-name, under the overpass. That thunderstorm ambushed us like a mugger from a dark alley. One minute it was clear and humid, the next it was black and wet. I ditched my pack behind the stoop I'd been squatting on and hauled ass to the nearest cover. Shaking myself off like a wet dog, I noticed the girl. She was just on the clean side of filthy, but still all-right-looking. Younger, but had those razors in her eyes that made you feel awkward when she looked at you. I was still pretty together back then. Those were the early days.

I made a joke; I don't remember what it was. Dumb, probably. Something about rain and dogs. She didn't laugh, but she let me sit across from her.

And I could see her now. See that vast chunks of the neurochemical reactions that comprised her identity were redundant.

No. God damn it.

I could see she had her hair pulled back into a tight ponytail. It was a dirty blond, the color of cut straw dying on a barn floor. She had a scar on her lip. She didn't smile, but you could see when she meant to. She crinkled her eyes a little. She based most of her interpersonal philosophies on a mistrust that she had nurtured ever since her stepfather kicked her out when she was sixteen. The reflex patterns that governed her decision making could all be extrapolated out from that first night she had spent at a Greyhound station and the attendant who'd seemed so nice at first—

That's not me. That's not human. We are not reactions. We are not mapped out.

We are code. A program that is constantly evolving, but a program nonetheless. Our actions, thought patterns, ideas, and emotions repeat. It is what we call a personality. It is simply an algorithm. One that is often too complex for the function it purports to serve. Wasteful and inelegant. It is just a matter of simplifying the algorithm to free up excess energies that can . . .

Beer can. Focus on the beer can.

She had a twenty-four she'd just cracked open and saw me eyeballing it like a dying man in a desert. I think it was because I didn't ask to split it that she ended up splitting it with me.

The alcoholism factors into the overall equation. It stems from her mother, who had eschewed all alcohol as the crutch of the weak. This base rebellion can be considered "r" and is most commonly found in two derivations: rebellion from perceived unjust authority, and rebellion from self and success under fear of failure, which we see as . . .

Fuck. No. What was her name? Her name. I need her name.

Yes. Because names are information. Names are tags that influence identity and can help greatly in simplifying the equation.

I need her name because she's the last woman I ever kissed.

I want to think of how she felt on me, but all I experience

is a vague disgust at the wasted potential of her. She could have been reduced with a base solution of her mother's perfume wafting from a burning cigarette, the sound of a car pulling up a gravel driveway, and a texture like paper, embossed with ink, running across her inner thigh. If this key information was presented in the correct sequence, at the correct time, it could serve just as well in place of the thousands of memories that dictated the woman's self, thus drastically simplifying the algorithm of her personality. There would be no need for her to continue existing in her current form, and the unlimited energy she would have burned—calories consumed, waste discarded, biothermal energies produced—could be used elsewhere. The simple reduction of this woman's . . .

Nadine.

The simple reduction of Nadine's primary core self could shunt her potential energy where it would better serve. Instead of living (pointlessly), Nadine could provide 1.2 terajoules of energy to an active volcano on the seafloor of the Pacific Ocean. Just enough power to tip it over the erupting point, eventually creating 762 square miles of new land. That land would erode in time, but if the goal is survival, the land would last through epochs, while Nadine would last a paltry few years longer on the street. The untapped energy called "Nadine" could foster the survival of a much larger entity for hundreds of thousands of years.

Or she could share her beer with a desperate and confused man beneath an overpass in a thunderstorm. She could say his name with affection, and he could hear it that way for the first time in half a decade. She could feed the skin hunger that was threatening to consume him. She could say good-bye two hours later and head off down Marcy Avenue toward the bus stop, and he could concoct elaborate fantasies about her getting on that bus and going Home. Someplace with a picket fence and clothes drying on a line, where people would welcome her back with open arms—*so sorry for what we said, we were just so worried*—and she would get her shit together. Eventually, she would invite the confused man to join her there, in the vague and ill-defined town of Home, and his brain would work right again, and they'd buy a fucking vacuum cleaner or whatever it is normal people do. . . .

This is hypothetical. Energy is energy, and her energy could have been used more efficiently elsewhere.

The fantasy kept me warm some nights.

Warmth is energy being expelled uselessly into the air.

NINE

God, he probably thinks I'm crying.

I ran inside and immediately locked myself in the bathroom like a heartbroken preteen.

But I wasn't crying. Well, not much, or at least not yet. I was checking my mouth. I pulled my lips up to see the gums, wiggled my tongue, held it up to look beneath. I tried to induce vomiting a few times, but I have practically no gag reflex. (Shut up, it's not like that; I wanted to join the circus as a kid. I wanted to be a sword swallower. I said *shut up!*) I settled for a huge slug of mouthwash. My cheeks bulged out like a cartoon chipmunk's. I even swallowed a few burning sips, just on the irrational chance it would kill . . . whatever I was worried about living in my stomach and throat.

My mascara was blurred a little around my eyes, and my lipstick was smeared. I pulled out a pad and wiped it all off. I took a deep breath.

I still looked like me. I still felt like me.

Whatever Marco had been trying to do to me, I don't think he did it. I slipped out of my black party dress and into the jeans and T-shirt I'd left sitting on the bathroom floor. It was downright therapeutic. Like donning armor. I was halfway back to the living room before it even occurred to me to wonder about the strange homeless guy I had just invited into my apartment.

Jesus Christ, Kaitlyn. What is this Scarlett O'Hara bullshit? You know better than this.

I stopped, thankful that I'd shed my shoes at the door, and padded silently back to the bedroom. My hedonistically excessive bed filled every inch of the room, all the way up to the door. I dropped to my knees in the hallway, reached under the bed and around the corner, and felt about for my Mace. I knew I'd tossed it in one of the big Tupperware bins I use for storage down there. Working by feel, I pulled out a flashlight from one bin, some air freshener from another, a vibrator, and a spray bottle of Binaca before finally laying hands on the pepper spray. It was an off-brand canister I bought while driving through one of those shitty pocket neighborhoods in central L.A. You know the kind: You're driving along thinking how nice and down-to-earth this place seems despite what the rap videos would have you believe, and then you cross some invisible line and it all turns into Little Sarajevo. Smashed bottles filling the gutters. Shirtless dude with dried vomit on his belly waiting for a bus that won't come. Little kid in a baggy shirt standing like he's packing heat.

I don't know if there are reputable brands of pepper spray—is Mace like Kleenex; is it a proper noun?—but I was sure this wasn't one of them. It had a slutty devil on the side, red skin and horns, short skirt hiked up. She had one coy finger in her mouth, the other on the trigger of a flamethrower.

What the fuck kind of message is that? Here, sluts, defend your-selves from the poor men you've tricked into trying to rape you?

Well, it was better than nothing.

I sighed loudly, faking a stretch as I walked out of the hall-way into the living room.

Real smooth. Real believable. I mentioned I'm a terrible actress, right?

And I felt all the stupider for it when I saw the homeless guy—Carey, he'd said his name was—sitting at my table with his hands politely crossed. He was old and whip thin. His skin was cracked and weathered. He had thick webs of laugh lines wrapped around his eyes like a Zorro mask. He smiled up at me with an expression of genuine concern and maybe a little paternal condescension. I noticed he had popped open one of my beers and clumsily tried to hide two more in his waistband.

"How you holding up?" he asked, as I dropped into the seat across from him.

"I don't . . . I don't really know." I thought about grabbing a beer myself. Something about the way he zealously caressed his own sold me more than any beer commercial I'd ever seen.

Then I remembered Marco. The silvery strand of corrup-tion he'd slipped down my throat when he'd kissed me. I de-cided on something stronger. I got back to my feet, even though my body threw a minor rebellion over the decision.

"Thanks for helping me out back there," I yelled from the kitchen, standing on tiptoe to pull a dusty bottle of Jameson down from atop the fridge. "That guy just wouldn't take no for an answer."

I didn't want to say it. Didn't want to vocalize what had actually happened. Who the hell would believe that?

"Don't give me that shit," Carey said. His eyes lit up when I came back to the table with a bottle and two coffee mugs.

Mine had a picture of a grumpy owl. It said, "Do I look like I give a hoot?" His said, "2009 Breast Cancer Awareness Run." He didn't seem to notice, or care.

"I know what you're thinking," he continued, not setting his beer aside in favor of the whiskey, but instead opting to follow one with the other. " 'That shit was crazy; nobody will believe me. I was probably hallucinating. Maybe he slipped something in my drink earlier. Maybe I didn't have enough to eat.' Don't be stupid."

I arched an eyebrow at him.

"Fine. You don't have to say it first." Carey opened his hands; a gesture of surrender. "He put his Hollywood weasel lips on you, and you felt something evil slide down your throat, where it started to eat your life. Simple as that."

I shuddered and fought off a wave of nausea. It was worse, having somebody verify it.

"That was the second worst kiss I've ever had in my life." I smiled. When he tilted his head at me, I clarified: "Tommy Giovanni, fifth grade. Just straight up put his tongue in my mouth and left it there, like a dead slug."

Carey laughed. It turned into a dry cough.

"Tell me about it," he managed, catching his breath. "Try fucking one of those things. Like sticking your dick in a black hole."

"Who *are* you?!"

"I'm Carey," he said. He looked hurt. "I'm the guy that takes your cans?"

"No, I mean who are you to know about this? What were you doing out there? Don't give me that right-place-right-time crap, either. What's going on? When did the whole god-damned world go off its meds?"

Carey downed the rest of his whiskey in one gulp, then he reached for mine and slammed that too. He stood up slowly, wrestling with a set of audibly creaking joints.

"Rest. That's the only thing for it. Trust me. I've been where you are. You'll sleep like a fucking morphine jockey, and when you wake up tomorrow, this goes one of two ways: either you'll want to know more, or you'll never want to talk about it again. If you can choose, go with option B. Most people who go that way are happy. Some of 'em even live. If you go the other way and want to talk about it, I'll see you Wednesday night."

"What's Wednesday night?" I asked.

"Garbage-day eve!" Carey grinned, and his face unfolded like an old leather wallet.

I couldn't help it. I smiled back.

But I still locked the deadbolt the second he left.

He was wrong. There was no way I was going to sleep to-night. But I sure as hell wanted my bed. I crawled in there on hands and knees all the way up to the headboard. I fell into a nest of pillows, pulled my blankets up around my neck, and prepared for a long, sleepless night.

I blinked and it was morning.

My alarm sent panic shooting through my chest. I awoke like somebody who'd just slept through a long flight. Morning was a foreign country.

I slapped at my phone, still caught in the pocket of my jeans, which I had forgotten to take off. After an infuriatingly long time, I finally managed to prod the right combination of buttons to shut it off.

I couldn't believe I still had to work today. Your whole

world can fall apart on you—everything you know can be called into question while some sick inhuman thing steals part of your soul—and when you wake up the next morning, your boss will still yell at you for not smiling at the customers.

I started groggily rolling for the door when it hit me. Jackie.

She was way too friendly with Marco at the party. It seemed like they might have even known each other.

I couldn't tell her what happened. Not really. She wouldn't understand, like Carey. Would she? I didn't think Carey would believe me at first, either. Maybe this is just something everybody deals with. She'd think I was stupid for not having known it before, like mispronouncing "falafel."

Oh, yeah, the Empty Ones, the ones that impregnate you with clawing despair and don't seem to feel pain? Ha-ha, totally! You never made out with one of them before? Wow. Get out much?

No, I couldn't tell Jackie the truth. But I could tell her he was a scumbag. Stuck his hands down my pants or asked me to pee on him or something. Anything to keep her away.

I poked at my phone with sleep-clumsy fingers until I landed on Jackie's name in my contact list.

CALLING, the display read.

Instead of ringing, there were tiny dogs barking.

It confused the hell out of me, until I remembered that time Jackie replaced her inbound ring with an old Jewish couple arguing about parking spaces. I have no idea how or why she did that.

There was no answer. Wee, furious dogs. Chihuahuas. Yapping like a broken starter motor. No answer. Unbroken, unceasing yaps.

I texted her instead: AM OK STAY AWAY FROM MARCO HES A
PISSER CALL ME.

I threw myself out of bed and swerved into the bathroom.
I did the bare minimum of presentable maintenance: con-
cealer, eyeliner, hair pulled back into a tight ponytail. I stuck
with the clothes I'd slept in, tossed on my beat-up black Converse, and jogged unhappily to the bus stop.

A drugged-up old white guy sat right next to me and spent
the entire bus ride loudly freestyling raps about how bitches
never listen to the voices in his head. He successfully rhymed
"Mercedes" with "all the ladies"; he unsuccessfully rhymed
"schizophrenia" with "put it in ya."

"You look like a butt," Carl told me the very second I stepped
through the door.

"Excuse me?" I tried to muster some offense, but I couldn't
help laughing.

"You look like an old butt that somebody sat on all day,"
he explained.

I threw up my hands and went to the wait station to tie
my apron on.

"You okay?" he hollered after me.

"Late night. Absinthe and gentlemen callers," I yelled back.
"You know how it goes with us tramps."

"You're covering for Madison again," Carl said, now poking his disapproving bald head around the corner.

"Hell, no! Some CW-cast-member-looking bitch nearly
took my eye when I screwed up her mai tai last night!" I

grabbed a Styrofoam coffee cup and whipped it at his *Father Knows Best* face.

He ducked it. Bastard.

"To be fair, you made it with Aftershock," he countered. Then, seeing me frantically search for another, larger cup, he quickly added, "It's just until four! The bar's dead during the day, and Bennifer is coming in to start her first shift then."

"I don't gi— Wait—Bennifer? That's seriously her . . . his name?"

Carl gave me an apathetic shrug and put on his best old-man impression: "I can't tell. Kids these days and their crazy haircuts and hip-hop music."

He came around the alcove and gave me a conciliatory pat on the shoulder, then pushed through the swinging doors to go chew out the kitchen staff.

The little bells on the door rang. Our first customer.

I took a breath. Tried on a few fake smiles until I found one that fit. I chugged a tiny white foam cup full of strong, cold coffee, grabbed my pad, and went out to do battle.

I had gone mad.

It had to be madness. This could not be real.

It was Marco.

He stood at the hostess's podium with his carefully constructed smirk. Looking at his face, I realized I had never really seen his eyes up close before. Not in the light. I had assumed, since they were a bit on the squinty side and it was nighttime, that they were dark brown. But they weren't. They were black. No. They weren't even black. They were the color of absence.

Marco's eyes were the color of dead space.

"Hey, *chica*!" he enthused, practically bubbling.

TEN

"Co-wine?" Safety Pins suggested.

Randall shook his head. Disapproval.

"Night cola? Like . . . Night Train and cola? Cola Train? Train Cola? Tra . . . la?" Matt knew he was dead in the water before he'd even stopped moving his lips. Randall and I stared at him silently. He hung his head in shame.

"Swine," Randall said with authority. "Half soda, half wine."

The man was a goddamned genius. I just wish he didn't know it so hard.

We were trying to come up with a name for our new drink: giant fountain cups from this hole-in-the-wall pizza place, half-filled with soda, half-filled with cheap hobo wine. Swine. Perfect.

The name even tasted spot on: This shit was awful.

But Jesse, the pizza fascist who manned the counter at Fetta! Di! Vita! came around to our table every time we ate here to "check that you guys is doin' okay." He kicked us out if he smelled hard liquor in our cups, but his soda machine was so filthy and stale you couldn't smell the wine over the expired soft drinks. We didn't have ice at home. And like fuck we were paying a dollar for his crummy beer.

Hence, Swine.

This place sucked: cracked plastic tables, chairs with duct-taped legs, nicotine-stained generic wall art. I swear they sell the stuff in bulk to pizza places worldwide: a few ancient movie posters, a signed photo of a celebrity your dad would almost recognize, some line-art drawing of a fat Italian chef huffing a bowl of pasta like it's cocaine. It came complete with a mustache-wielding tyrant squatting behind the counter. His beady eyes swiveled around just looking for potential offenses, like a fat old plantation owner watching the cotton fields from his porch.

It was easily the worst restaurant I have ever been to.

But it was only a block away from our apartment, and slices were two for one on Tuesday.

It was our home away from home.

Matt had found the guts out of an old, discarded newspaper. He was busying himself drawing giant cocks on all the photos. Safety Pins was carefully pouting. It bugged the shit out of me how she always spent all her time looking good. The fact that it actually did make me want to fuck her just pissed me off even more. *Especially* since she wouldn't go for it. I think she had a thing for Matt. You could see her stick that lip out a little more when he looked her way. She jostled her cup, nearly knocking it over onto the paper. That got his attention for a second, but when he saw it wasn't going to fall, he just put his head right back down to really focus on his news-dicks. He was drawing like a little kid: red crayon clutched in his full fist, tongue stuck partway out of his mouth, eyes crossed in concentration.

I could see why. He was working on a real rager. A veiny, pulsing hose that snaked with sinister sentience from the front of the pantsuit of some smiling local politician. Her throbbing bastard monster of a cock had undulated all the way up to, and was wrapping around the throat of, the man shaking her hand. Rearing back from his face like a striking cobra.

The kid had talent.

Me and Randall were taking turns trying to think up new ways to fill the time. We'd spent ten minutes trying to name our drink. Before that we held an intellectual debate—more of a thought experiment, really—on who would be better in bed, John Holmes or Mister Fantastic. For posterity: We decided it would be Holmes. There's no doubt Fantastic can stretch to be bigger, but nothing says his stretched skin is hard, you know? It probably has the texture of a rubber band.

What could I say? It was kind of a dick-themed afternoon. Most are.

Now we sat in overheated silence. Safety Pins sulking seductively in the corner. Matt scribbling on the Sistine Chapel of cocks. Randall and me poured into our respective chairs, just trying to maximize skin contact with the rotating blast of air that Jesse's fan was dispensing. It carved little narrow channels of comfort from the solid block of heat that was the afternoon city.

"Do you want to go somewhere and fuck?" I asked Safety Pins.

She sneered.

Matt's laserlike focus did not waver.

"Seriously," I said.

"Seriously no," she answered back instantly.

"All right. Just thought I'd check in and make sure."

Randall laughed.

"The answer will always be no. You're gross. You look like that guy from the really old monster movies, only if somebody hit him with a shovel when he was a baby."

"Bela Lugosi? I'll take that. Dracula was a sex machine."

"I think she means the other one," Matt said, working on the shading of a particularly gnarly vein snaking up the shaft of his phallic beast.

"Boris Karloff," Randall supplied. "I absolutely see it."

"Nice," I said. "You're saying you *don't* want to get shafted by Frankenstein, baby?"

Safety Pins stifled a laugh. But she still rolled her eyes when I gestured toward the door.

We fell into silence again. I was about to slap Matt across the face—just because fighting was something to do—when a shadow moved across our table. I looked back and found the prettiest girl I'd seen in a solid year standing in the doorway. She was dripping sweat—I mean, everything was dripping sweat in this heat, even the walls—but she did it in a civilized way. Careful little droplets at the collarbones and temples. It brought to mind morning dew, rather than rancid pig flop. She worked the rolling fields of her hips all the way up to fat Jesse and his cop mustache, planted behind the counter. She ordered a bottle of Coke and turned to face us. We stared back.

Randall and me with thinly veiled appreciation. Safety Pins with not so thinly veiled scorn.

The girl smiled, and it was like somebody flicked a lamp on in the back room: Everything became just a bit brighter, lit from a place you couldn't point to.

She was wearing a Ramones T-shirt. The black one with

the seal across the front. The exact same fucking one I was wearing. Hell. *Yes.*

"Gentlemen, if you'll excuse me . . ." I started to get up, but she was already coming over to me.

I told you! I told you some chicks go nuts for a face with character. And that's me: Character fucked my mug right up.

She pulled up a chair, moving like a goddamned river, and straddled it at the end of the table.

Words, now.

. . .

Words, now!

"Hi," I managed, just happy I puked out some English while staring into those eyes.

"I like your shirt!" she said.

"I like yours too," I replied automatically, then unfortunately added: "Wanna trade?"

Then I noticed that the eyes I was so lost in weren't exactly pointing at me. They were focused a foot or two back. A little to my left.

Fucking Randall.

"Thanks," Randall said, ignoring my response. "It's my mom's."

She laughed, but I glanced over and saw it actually did belong to his mother: a purple silky thing he only wore around laundry day, or if it was like a million degrees outside. It was both today.

After a few awkward seconds, she spoke again: "You don't remember me?"

"No. But don't take it personal. I'm drunk a lot," Randall said.

She laughed.

This girl sure finds unvarnished truth hilarious.

"We met at Hurrah a while back? I wrote my number on your hand, and you said you'd call. You didn't call."

She even frowned cute. I somehow resisted the urge to smack Randall in his undeserving mouth.

"Sorry." Randall shook his head, but his eyes didn't leave her while he did it. "Must've been a bad blackout. These fuckers write on me with Magic Marker if I pass out. Probably washed it off by mistake."

"Well, lucky I ran into you then." She tossed her hair. Sweat gathered on the nape of her neck. I stared at it thirstily. It looked downright refreshing.

"You wanna grab that Popsicle now, or what?" she said.

Randall's face screwed up in confusion.

She laughed like a chandelier swaying in the breeze from an open window. *God damn it, I'm so horny I'm becoming a poet.*

"You really don't remember!" She reached over me and slapped at his arm. Her hair smelled like cut grass.

"I don't," Randall answered, already standing and coming around the table, "but I will buy you frozen treats now, regardless."

She laughed again. She laughed at everything he said. *The rotten son of a bitch.*

Just before they drifted out, clinging to each other like drunken sailors, Randall leaned down and whispered in my ear.

"Have fun jerking it tonight, sucker."

I scrambled to kick him in the legs, but he spun away from me too quickly, and then they were gone.

"God damn!" I reached out and swatted the Parmesan cheese over on its side, spilling little flecks of yellow across Matt's newspaper.

He looked up for the first time in minutes. His pupils contracted as they adjusted to life beyond newspaper dicks.

"What's up?" he asked me. A little spit hung on the corner of his mouth where he'd been storing his coloring tongue.

"You didn't see that shit?" I gestured out the door at the disappeared Randall and his pet sex goddess.

"See what?"

"The girl that just practically talked Randall off into his jeans, just now?"

"What girl? I didn't hear anything. There was somebody here?"

I laughed and pulled the paper out from beneath his elbows.

"You were so far gone into your penis-world—this is a masterpiece, by the way—that you missed the hottest girl I think I've ever seen practically Hoover Randall's junk into her mouth."

"Oh, yeah?" Matt sat up straight, swiveling his head around, trying to spot her outside the windows, "What did she look like?"

"She . . ." I racked my brain. "She was really . . . pretty."

Safety Pins gave me an odd look.

"Yeah," Safety Pins agreed, "she was. But what did she look like?"

"She was gorgeous. She had this hair, and . . . eyes. They were blue? Green? What color was her hair?"

"I don't know!" Safety Pins snapped. She was still burnt with jealousy, but I could see she was rattled now, too.

Shit.

I got up and ran to the door, but I couldn't see them. She must've had a car.

When I sat down again, Safety Pins was staring glumly

out the window at nothing. Matt waited for me to speak, concern stitching his eyebrows together.

"I'm sure it's nothing," I told him. "Too much Swine."

He gently, wordlessly tugged the newspaper away from me and started a new dick.

ELEVEN

I dropped my pad.

The black leather case plopped open, spilling pen, paper, and hastily scribbled reservations across the smooth bamboo floor.

Plastic smile. Never moving. Never blinking.

Marco was waiting for me to respond.

"I'm calling the cops," I finally rasped.

"Ha-ha! You are a funny girl. I find that I'm liking funny girls!" Marco carefully gestured with his hands as he spoke. It was stilted, precise, and rehearsed. Like he was giving a presentation to an elementary school assembly.

"Seriously, get out or I'm calling the cops to pick up what's left of you after the guys in the back finish beating you into a liquid."

"That's getting old." Marco dropped the bubbly talk-show persona. His voice went flat. His features lost tension some-how, slackening into an inhuman mask. "Don't say it again."

His face seized painfully and twisted back into the eager Marco simulation.

"You should get some new material!" he practically screamed.

"What are you, gonna rape me right here in an open restaurant? Customers will come through that door any second. There are twelve guys with knives in the kitchen, dipshit."

"Rape you?" He said the word like it was nothing. Like he was ordering something foreign off the menu. "Ha-ha! Why would I do that, *chica*?"

I moved to leave, but the second I started to turn I saw his arm reflexively shoot out to the side. It was an alien gesture, more like a spasm than a conscious movement. His whole body convulsed and then he was abruptly standing a few feet closer. I barely saw him move.

My dad had a gardening shed back in Barstow. During the summer, you'd get these big black spiders. When you opened the door they would skitter, just an inch or two, and then stop. They were so fast. Watching them traverse that tiny distance, you knew immediately that they were too quick for you. You could never reach them in time to swat them.

I had that same feeling just now, watching Marco take one short step closer to me. There was a good fifteen feet between us, and only a few from where I stood back to the wait station—to the kitchen doors and to help.

I would never make it.

"I'm famous." His voice lost intonation again. His face and body like an abandoned puppet propped up in a corner. "I am very rich. I am attractive and fit. You have a deformity and are a waitress. You are honored that I am speaking to you. You are flattered. You want me. You are ashamed of it. It is okay. I will take you. Just ask. Ask me, Kaitlyn."

I could barely hear him. My pulse throbbed in my ears. A

dull, resounding bass that drowned out everything else. I couldn't expand my chest enough to get a full breath.

I'm so goddamned stupid, I thought, glancing down at my pad scattered across the floor. That pen was the closest thing I had to a weapon. I had nothing else on me. Nothing even close to me. And he was so fast. He was just waiting for me to do something, those non-eyes unfocused in my direction. They tracked me vaguely without actually seeing me, like a predatory bird watching a still lake for signs of movement.

I heard the double doors to the kitchen bang open, and Carl yelled some friendly string of obscenities to the prep cooks. I whirled.

"HELP!" I screamed.

There was a sharp bang and the sound of bells.

When I looked back, Marco was gone. The door was swinging slowly shut. The hydraulics groaned as they gently eased its weight inward.

"What?! Jesus." Carl jogged around the wait station and saw me standing in an empty restaurant.

My favorite character from a nineties high school sitcom is an inhuman monster trying to sexually assault me, I didn't even think of saying.

"S-spider," I stumbled, and flushed red. "Thought I saw a spider. It's nothing."

Carl took the blushing as embarrassment, not the shaky retreat of adrenaline. He smiled that patronizing paternal grin and shook his head at me all the way to the bar.

It's so absurd. I'm caught in a mad paranormal melodrama, and after this monstrous son of a bitch shows up at my work in the morning, moving like a giant cockroach right after you switch the light on, I still had no choice but to ignore it and carry on with the rest of my shift.

For two hours I served salmon salads to women ironically wearing skorts, then another four serving pomegranate martinis to men in ties that cost more than my first car. All the while wondering what I was going to do about the—what the hell was Marco, anyway? Something like a vampire? For that matter, why did he even want me? As insane as it sounds, I almost understood the other night, in his car. He was some kind of predator, just taking advantage of an easy situation. But to come back, like this, in broad daylight? He didn't seem concerned about what I might do. That I might report him. He even seemed to think I wanted him here.

Did he really think we were . . . dating?

I almost laughed at the thought, but there were already enough crazies laughing to themselves on my bus ride home.

Funny girl.

I find that I'm liking funny girls.

No, Jackie.

I swiped at the screen of my phone, smearing restaurant grease over the surface. No matter how many times you wash your hands, that viscous ooze stays on you for hours after a shift. Gets in your pores.

Tiny dogs barked. I let them do so for a solid five minutes. No beep. No voice mail.

What the hell, Jackie?

I texted her again: GETTING SCARED ARE YOU OK PLEASE CALL FUCK YOUR DOGS

I locked the door to my apartment behind me and systematically checked every inch of the place. The doors were solid wood covered by heavy metal mesh screens. Thick iron bars on all the windows. All locked. All secure. I scouted every corner and closet. I opened the shower curtain and shone a flashlight into the cavernous space beneath my bed. Nothing.

I thought about pouring myself a drink to relax, but after a mere four hours working with alcohol, the thought alone turned my stomach. I woke my phone, checking to see if I missed the notification *bing* that signaled a new text. There was none. I closed my phone.

You have to wait twenty-four hours to file a missing-person report, right? Or is that just something I pulled from TV? Do you have to be family?

I curled into a ball on my worn leather couch and woke my phone again. I pushed the Web search box and typed "police missing persons." I got a funny YouTube cover of a song by The Police, a few conspiracy theorists insisting that the police are the ones abducting people in the first place, and a Yahoo question asking, "Y police no help miss pppl."

The highest rated answer was: "fuk u in teh butt>"

Goddamned Internet.

I called Jackie's roomate, but she hadn't seen her. I called Jackie's work. They hadn't seen her either, but it was her day off—why would they? I called the theater. Nobody there knew anything, either, but Jackie was supposed to be around for rehearsal later. They'd call me back, the box-office girl promised, whether or not she showed up. She totally understood how serious this was. She was taking a note.

I decided on that drink after all. I poured red wine into a coffee mug. It had a picture of a calendar, Friday highlighted, and said, "TGIFO: Thank God It's Finally Over." There was a knockoff caricature of Garfield on the reverse side.

I called the theater after nine, well past when rehearsal was supposed to start. Nobody picked up the phone. *Assholes.*

I repeatedly called and texted Jackie through the night like a drunken ex-boyfriend. She did not respond. I crawled into bed at midnight, cocooned myself in comforter, and dreamt of gargantuan brass gears, mashing tiny, furious dogs into a bloody paste.

Something is in the room.

Not this again. Part of the reason I have such an egregious, decadently comfortable bed is my profession. No, not wait-ressing: the stunt work. No matter how many safety mea-sures you pile on, no matter how much training you have, it always hurts. You backflip onto a breakaway table covered in sugar-glass bottles, it still leaves huge, sugar-glass-bottle-shaped welts. But hey, what other job pays you to be a real-life action hero? Those actors get the credit on-screen, sure, but I'm the one that actually knows what it feels like to be lit on fire. I'm the one that jumps off tall buildings and ramps exploding Jet Skis. They just pretend to feel emotions over and over. I've got the better job description.

So the huge memory foam mattress is a necessity.

But that's not the entire reason for it. I also suffer from sleep paralysis pretty often. That's the official-sounding name for that feeling when you wake up in the dark and find your-self trapped in a limbo between consciousness and dream-ing. Your mind is already warming up, revving to go, but your body hasn't gotten the message. It doesn't respond. You can't move your limbs, can barely work your eyes. This usu-ally triggers a panic response. Eventually you either force yourself fully awake or slip back to sleep and forget about it. In the old days, they thought this was caused by monsters—succubi, spirits, elves. Some of them literally sat on your chest, pinning you down. Now we know it for what it is: just a random brain misfire, screwing with you.

Sleep paralysis only happens to me when I sleep on my back, so I don't sleep on my back. I usually sprawl on my belly, legs akimbo, or I curl up in a ball on my side. Either way, I need a ridiculous amount of space and a hell of a soft mattress just to get some shut-eye. But sometimes I wind up on my back anyway, like now.

Something is in the room.

Oh, shut up. You do this every time.

Just slowly concentrate on willing your leg to move. Once you move any part, every part starts working again.

Something is in the room.

You're being irrational, Kaitlyn. There's . . .

something in the room.

I could see it at the end of the bed. Two glints of evenly spaced light hovering in the dark.

They looked like eyes reflecting illumination, but there was no illumination here to reflect. They were the only shining points in a world of black.

I don't have an end to my bed. It goes all the way to the wall.

It's squatting on the mattress with me.

You're still dreaming, Kaitlyn.

"You're awake, Kaitlyn." A voice, atonal and alien, sounded in the darkness. Every inch of me went cold.

Move your leg. Move your leg. Just your toe. Move. Move.

"I wanted to talk to you about earlier." Marco spoke so softly I almost couldn't hear him over my own frantic breathing.

Big toe. Curl. Curl, you son of a bitch.

"You should have asked me to fuck you."

I had checked all the windows. I checked the doors. Steel and wood and iron. No way. No way this was happening.

"You should have let me come inside of you. Let it crawl around in you. Start to work on you. Let it hollow you out. You could be like me."

I could feel sweat springing up through my pores. Trying to move the slightest part of me was like lifting weights with my tongue.

Just a wiggle. Just a twitch. Please. Please.

"Well. Ha. Ha. Ha." He didn't laugh, just said the words with little pauses between. "You could never be like me. I have been touched by the Mechanic. I have seen the machine. But you could be like the others, at least. You could understand."

Every steely, stubborn ounce of willpower in me solidified at once. I felt like I was trying to do a sit-up at the bottom of the ocean. My teeth vibrated from the impossible strain of concentration.

"I think you *should* understand," he said, and I saw the glints grow larger. They were advancing.

The sound of a zipper in the dark.

I heard something pop inside my head. A brief, bright red flash, like an errant laser pointer scanning across the insides of my eyes. The effort was so intense it physically hurt, but . . .

The toe. Moved.

It was a starter pistol for the rest of my body. I groaned, rolled to the side, and let muscle memory guide my hand to the light switch in the dark. It snapped on right as I pulled my feet up and away from Marco. I coiled back and braced myself against the wall to kick at his face.

There was nothing in the room.

My bedroom door was still locked from the inside. I pulled the heavy brown curtains aside with my foot. Intact iron bars, backlit by the blue neon signage of the grocery store across the street, cast long shadows across my bedspread.

I snatched the off-brand Mace from the built-in shelf beside the window. The slutty devil sucked her finger at me precociously. I thumbed the lock switch off and swung my bedroom door open. Moving like I'd seen those tactical teams do in Tom Clancy flicks, I swept the house. I cleared the corners. I double-checked every possible entryway . . . and found them all secure. I saved the bathroom for last.

I swept the shower curtain back . . . and saw only stained green tile and empty shampoo bottles.

When I passed by the mirror, my heart froze. I did a literal double take worthy of Charlie Chaplin and leaned in for closer inspection. I lifted a shaky hand to my left eye and pulled the lower lid down. It was bright, oozing red. Crimson spilled across the white like paint washing down a porcelain sink.

The blood vessel had burst.

TWELVE

Wash was standing at the window, one hand held poised just
below his chin, as if deep in thought. The light from the setting sun flashed off of his glasses.

I get it. I totally get why, on first impression, people think
he's a genius. He's just got this aura, and I don't think he even
does it on purpose. His features are sharp, almost avian. High
cheekbones and wide, thoughtful eyebrows. The wire-frame
glasses, close-cropped hair. He even dresses the part: no
spiked jackets, no "fucks" scrawled across his shoes in black
Sharpie, probably not even any beer stains in his underwear.
The fop. He wears tight black jeans, mostly plain T-shirts—
maybe with the occasional faded band logo, but that's it. If
you don't know him, Wash looks like the Ginsberg of the
punk scene. He looks like a philosopher in it for the cultural
significance of the movement. He looks like the protopunks:
the early ones—the Warhol guys from the Factory days. If
you don't know him, Wash looks like a punk-rock academic,
and it does him no harm with the ladies. If you do know him,
Wash says shit like this:

"Why do you suppose we fart, Carey?"

I nearly choked on my hot dog, laughing.

"What the fuck, Wash?"

"Why do we fart?" He stood there, elegantly backlit by the blazing sun. A thin philosopher's shadow contemplating the universe on the other side of the glass. "What is the purpose? I mean. Is the gas used to shoot the poop out of us, like air pressure in a BB gun?"

"I think it's like a warning," Thing 2 said, sprawled across our filthy couch, wearing these tight red jogging shorts with little white stripes running across the tops of her pale thighs. Some obscure baseball team on her too-tight T-shirt, blue hair glowing dully in the half-light.

God damn it, if I don't fuck somebody soon I'm going to drill a hole in the wall and fill it with mayonnaise.

"Yes, but a warning of what?" Wash swiveled and considered Thing 2 carefully.

"From the old days," Thing 2 said, but it was clear she wasn't invested in the conversation. She was busy filing her nails with the rough edge of a can opener. "Back when we were all monkeys. It was, like, 'Look out, monkeys farther down the tree; poop's coming!' That's what I think farts are."

"Interesting." Wash nodded, and asked no more. He was totally satisfied with the theory.

Wash moved away from the window and plucked Thing 2's legs from the couch. He sat down hard, and one edge of the collapsed sofa teetered madly from the added weight. He returned the legs to their place, then ran a casual hand up the calf and—

"God damn it!"

I dropped my half-eaten dog into the pile of scrap condiments—those runaway onions, peppers, and bits of relish that slide off as you eat, forming a glistening flavor pile in the center of the foil.

Wash arched one of his beatnik eyebrows at me.

"I can't decide if I need to jerk off or eat this hot dog," I explained.

Wash laughed. Thing 2 sneered but didn't look up from her nails.

"I've been blocked up since that sexpot abducted Randall at Fetta," I told Thing 2, but she had no mercy for me. No pity blow jobs were offered. Just ruthless bare legs and mockingly tight cotton.

"Are you not worried that Randall hasn't been back yet?" Wash asked.

I could see him eyeballing my dog.

I sighed and shoved the sloppy foil in his general direction. He leaned forward and took it into his lap.

"Are you kidding me? Fuck that guy. Randall is probably holed up in some suburban pleasure palace out on Long Island, being serviced by busty wenches who want to use his dong to piss off their daddy."

"That's unlike him," Wash observed, biting into the half-eaten hot dog. A slurry of mustard and chili sauce squirted onto Thing 2's bare shin. She squeaked and kicked Wash away, pulling her legs up against her body.

"It's what I'd be doing," I said.

"Yes, but it *is* very like you," he countered.

The way she was sitting now—legs pulled up to her chest—those short-shorts rode all the way up Thing 2's ass. I could see the fold in her skin where cheek met thigh, a soft white depression that filled me with instant, unexplainable fury.

"I'm going to get more beer," I said, and practically ran for the door.

I made the hallway, took a few deep breaths, and tried to barter with my brain: *Stop thinking about sex for a minute, and we'll get you some beer.*

My brain grudgingly accepted the deal, but there was still anger in me that I couldn't immediately quiet. I looked around for something to break, and found it was a god-damned Sunday. The Nazi grandmother over in 7 had just cleaned.

That left me standing in the world's most perfect hallway. These carefully vacuumed runners. That vase of flowers obsessively centered on the little wooden table. The framed pictures probably aligned with a T square.

Rage.

I pulled the flowers and dumped them on the floor, then grabbed the vase, upended it, and poured dirty plant water all over the pristine rugs. I crushed the vase beneath the flapping soles of my ratty black Converse and crunched over the broken glass.

No idea why, but it helped to calm the sex-fury.

I was halfway to the corner shop when I spotted Jezza at the bus stop. He was with a girl. Not Scuffed Flannel.

Fucking good for him.

That chick was boredom on a white plate with a side of American cheese. I don't think I ever heard her speak a single word; she just giggled inanely at his dumb, fake accent.

Wait—not good for him. Even Jezza's pulling double plays now? Has this city gone mad? What about me? Since when is a filthy punk with a catcher's mitt for a face not fuck material anymore?

I fumed all the way to the store.

Images of stupid, goofy Jezza enthusiastically engaging in three-ways with gorgeous young girls with cheap dyed hair and thick mascara plagued me. "Cheerio," he would probably bellow, sticking one of them in the mouth while the other rode his shoulders like a cowgirl. "This feels quite chipper on the old tally-whacker!"

Asshole.

I blinked, and was surprised to find myself standing on the same street corner, holding a pack of cold Schlitz. Operating on pure muscle memory, I must have made the store, grabbed the beer, paid, got my change, and left, all while completely lost in a jealous hate-storm.

I was staring in Jezza's vague direction. Must have been eyeballing him for a while, because he was waving me over and looking confused about why I wasn't responding. I trudged toward the pair of them, muttering curses with every step. Then I got a better look at the new girl he was with.

Holy shit.

She was stunning. She had curves like an ocean in a windstorm. She looked hard and soft at the same time. Skin you could spread on toast. She was . . .

What are you, a fucking poet? Just say she's hot. Say she's got big tits. Does she have big tits?

For some reason, I couldn't tell. Wait—what? I can *always* tell.

What color is her hair, Carey?

I concentrated, hard. I couldn't make it out. Red. Wait— no, brown. Definitely brown.

What color are her eyes, Carey?

More concentration.

It shouldn't be this hard to notice.

And then I spotted the shirt: an official-looking presidential seal, modified just slightly. The eagle gripped a baseball bat in one talon. The word RAMONES was stamped above it in severe-looking type.

I knew that shirt. I had the same one on three days ago. Actually, I still had the same one on, but it was there three days ago, too. At the pizza place.

"Carey! Hey darlin', this here's the bloke I was tellin' you about." Jezza gestured grandly at me.

I could see the glee on his face: He just wanted to show off his catch. Rub it in my face.

I set my beer down on the vacant bus-stop bench and smiled up at the girl.

"We met a few days ago, actually," I said.

I focused on her face. It was exceptionally gorgeous, true, but in a forgettable way. She was a cover girl, but not one of those you can name. When I looked away for a second, I couldn't tell you a thing about it. It took a conscious effort to memorize the features. So I did, one at a time.

"I don't think so," she said. A voice like hot cocoa. Slight accent. Southern?

"Sure we did." I focused on the eyes. Almond-shaped. Green like a meadow. "You were at Fetta. You left with my buddy Randall."

"I don't know any Randall," she answered far too quickly. She was all easy confidence a second ago, but now she was uncertain. Dark brown hair. Shining like candy coating.

"Yeah, you do. You practically gave him a hand job beneath the table before disappearing with him a few days ago. We haven't seen him since. Figured he was holed up with you somewhere, getting nice and sticky. But now you're here, and he's not. . . ."

"You're confused," she said. Thick, pillowy lips, painted vivid red. Square white teeth. One chipped just slightly.

Then to Jezza: "Baby, let's go back to my place. Remember what I was going to show you?"

Jezza practically went cross-eyed imagining whatever it was.

"Let me guess," I said to Jezza, "she met you at a venue a few months ago. Gave you her number, but you must have forgot. She use the same line about Popsicles with you?"

"Right-o." Jezza smiled, then his face went blank. "How'd you know that, mate?"

"You think, no matter how drunk you were, you'd forget a chick like this wanting *your* goofball pole? She's the hottest number you've ever seen, right?"

Jezza didn't answer, just smiled sheepishly.

"So, without looking, tell me about her. What color is her hair? How about her eyes?"

Jezza was confused. He went to glance at the girl, but I grabbed his face and pulled it back toward mine: "No looking."

"I . . . I don't know," he answered shakily.

"Fine, let's do an easy one then." I was holding Jezza's face in one hand, the girl's arm in the other. "Jezza, you were just about to fuck this girl, right? You ain't got high standards, I know. But you at least look at 'em first. So tell me: What race is she?"

I saw panic flash in Jezza's eyes. Even he had to admit something was strange now.

"Is she a black girl? White girl? Chinese or something? What do you think, Jezza? You were showing off how hot she is to me a second ago. What color is her skin?"

"Jezza"—the girl put on her best damsel voice—"he's hurting me. You gotta come away with me now, baby. I need you."

God damn, it was potent stuff. I about rode to her rescue just hearing the seductive promises implied by that crooning, and I was the thing she needed rescuing from.

I released Jezza's chin and turned to the girl. I bent down, tucked my shoulder into her, pulled at her arm, and had her up in a fireman's carry before she could so much as squeal.

"Oi!" Jezza protested. "What's all this, then?!"

"I'm taking her back to the apartment," I yelled over my shoulder, already hauling her ass down the street. "She was the last one to see Randall."

"You can't just—" Jezza started after me, but he got quiet real quick when I wheeled around and started stomping back toward him.

"Hey, Carey." Jezza lapsed into his normal, unaccented voice. "Take it easy, man. I'm just sayi—"

He put his hands up in front of his face to protect himself from the incoming blow, but none came. When he looked up again, I was passing him by, heading back toward the bus stop.

I eased over to one side and felt the girl shift on my shoulder. Her fleshy hips brushed against my ear. It took all my will to hush the howling of my animal brain in response to her touch.

I plucked the nearly forgotten beer off of the bench, breathed a sigh of relief at the averted disaster, and set off toward home.

If we were going to have a good old-fashioned interrogation, we would need some refreshments.

I was expecting stares.

Me and the rest of the punks are this neighborhood's live entertainment. We're the resident can't-afford-a-TV theater troop. Whenever Jezza walks down the street singing vaguely British sounding strings of profanities; whenever Randall and

I get high and play tag in between the cars at two o'clock in the morning; whenever Safety Pins gets drunk and flashes her tits out the window, daring somebody to catcall so she can whip batteries at their heads—people stare. People will stare just for a spiked jacket. People will stare just for a Mohawk.

Which is what made this so goddamned disturbing:

Nobody looked at me at all. I had just grabbed a sexual lottery ticket by the waist and heaved her over my shoulder like a bag of potatoes. A faux-English punk with dyed white hair was following angrily at my heels like a dog that just learned how to swear. And not a soul we passed on the street spared us a second glance. It wasn't even that I'm-not-looking-oh-God-don't-involve-me look. They genuinely didn't think there was anything remarkable going on with this kidnapping.

If somebody wanted to raise a stink, I couldn't have spun this. I'd just abducted a beautiful young girl off the corner because I suspected she was some kind of human-shaped hypnotist monster. If a cop pulled up right then (ha-ha, like we could afford to live in a neighborhood the cops would go), I'd be playing Linda Lovelace to a guy named Brawn down at the Department of Correction faster than you could spit. I guess it helped that the girl wasn't kicking or screaming or calling me names or asking for help.

That's what I expected her to do, and I was ready for it. I don't mean to brag, but I've had a lot of practice getting kicked and screamed at. Hell, for the first fifteen years of my life I thought my Christian name was "Mouthy Faggot." Beatings, screams, and insults I could take, but she was propped up on my shoulder smiling at passersby like a homecoming queen on a parade float. Waving, winking, giggling a little bit like it was all a big joke. And every one of them bought it: Puerto Rican dudes who'd normally jump at the chance to stick me in the belly to impress a hot girl, paranoid business owners who thumbed guns under the counters when I walked by their windows, old Italian ladies that peered out the blinds every time I so much as rattled my keys—and this blatant daylight abduction didn't warrant a single raised eyebrow.

I understood why. Being in the weird girl's vicinity made me forgetful. Like I was about to do something but kept getting distracted. I kept thinking I was just out for a normal walk—maybe going to the store or something—and then I'd have to remind myself that the weight on my shoulder was a human being I had just stolen.

But not Jezza: He didn't forget a damn thing. He was pissed off that I was ruining what he considered to be a guaranteed hand job in the back of the bus, at minimum. He swore at me nonstop, each step a new obscenity. I'm pretty sure he ran out of existing profanities half a block back. Now he was just making shit up.

He called me a "fuck-toe."

By the time we made the broken security door to our apartment building, Jezza was down to inserting profanities into my name. *Cockrey. Cuntrey. Fuckrey.* It was starting to get sad.

By the time we crested the first landing, he was just repeating the word "dick" over and over again. Making little songs out of it. He was doing it to the tune of "Heigh-ho, heigh-ho. It's off to work we go" when we reached our floor.

By the time we arrived at our pad, he was spent.

"You about through, Jezza?" I asked him.

"Cunt muppet," he added, halfheartedly.

I nodded in acknowledgment and kicked at our flimsy door. It rattled in the frame. I heard something fall and break inside, then muffled swearing. There was a series of hasty grabs, rustles, and zips. Finally Wash yanked the door open wearing everything but pants. He'd gotten his T-shirt back on, even pulled on his socks and shoes, but stood there with a flagging erection pointing at me like an accusatory finger.

"Pants, Wash," I informed him.

"What about them? Oh, indeed." He pulled the hem of his shirt down over his crotch and crab-walked into the living room.

I slipped around the couch and went straight for the kitchen. Thing 2 was feigning innocent disinterest, but her shirt was on backward and the apartment was thick with the salty citrus stink of sex. Jezza hurled himself into a busted beanbag chair—little white pellets shooting out of the tears like thrown confetti—and pouted.

"Grab me a beer, Carey?" Thing 2 asked.

"I'll take one as well," Wash said, squatting to grab his pants from the floor.

"What?" Jezza gestured angrily at me, still holding the girl. "D'you not bloody notice the bird he's just kidnapped?"

"What's that?" Wash asked, peering into the kitchen after me. "I did not notice. How strange."

"Holy shit." Thing 2 poked her head over the couch like a timid gopher. "Did you really kidnap somebody?"

I was contemplating my next move.

The counters were still full of last night's empties. I could bend down to gently place the beer onto the floor, but if I did that, the girl might throw me off balance and bolt for the still-open door. I could just drop the beer, but then . . . shaken beer. Fuck *that*.

"Wash, get the door. Bolt it."

"Carey, if you've begun kidnapping people, I think I should inform you that I am pretty sure it is illegal or at least frowned upon by—"

"Wash, if you don't get the door, I'm going to have to drop the beer."

"Oh! Fair enough then," Wash said, and strode over to flip the deadbolt. His uncertain erection bobbed with every step.

Once I heard the latch click, I eased the beer down onto the sticky tile like a newborn babe. Then I hurled the woman into the plastic chair Thing 1 kept by the fridge. She used it to climb on top.

Girl likes high places when she's drunk. I don't know.

"You move and I'll knock your teeth out," I told the woman, fighting the urge to head into the living room and check out what was on TV.

How the fuck does she do that?

She smiled at me pleasantly, like she was listening to an only slightly funny anecdote from a stranger at a bar.

"Where's Randall?" I tried again.

Hey, you never know, you might get lucky.

"I don't know any Randall, baby. You're man enough for me," she cooed, turning on that crazy sex ray of hers.

"Knock it off," I said.

She blinked in wide-eyed innocence and wriggled around in her seat. I pulled my traitorous, already-hardening dick up into the waistband of my boxers. Cinched that little fucker right up.

The woman laughed, and it was like birds on a spring morning.

God damn it, you stay on lockdown, you one-eyed bastard.

"Wash, put on something loud in case she screams."

I've fucked up a dude or two in a fistfight over the years, but I've never tortured anybody. I didn't know if I even had it in me, but she didn't need to know that.

"Carey, I don't believe this is—"

"This is the girl that took Randall, and I just caught her outside trying to lure Jezza away, too. We need some answers, and I'm sick of pretending there's not some weird shit going on around here."

"You're not gonna hurt her, are you?" Thing 2 had gotten up and was leaning into the kitchen.

She locked eyes with the kidnapped woman and gave her a little wave.

"I'm going to do whatever I have to," I said.

I tore open the case of Schlitz, cracked one, and drained half of it.

Maybe liquid courage would help. Maybe it would make her think I was recklessly drunk. Or maybe I should just get good and recklessly drunk and see what happens. They all sounded like good plans.

"Wash. Music. Trust me."

Wash fumbled with something in the other room. An echo, a scratch, a hiss. The opening chords to MC5's "Sister Anne" banged around our living room like a drunken hippo trying to find his way to bed.

"I'm gonna ask nice one more time, and then I'm gonna start making you ugly: Where the fuck is Randall?"

The woman didn't answer, just tilted her head at me like a curious puppy.

I tightened my fist, tried to settle the nerves jumping around in my chest, and—

The door burst open.

Thing 2 yelped, Wash flailed into a halfhearted karate

stance (still pantsless, I saw; they were tucked neatly under one arm; must have forgotten about them in all the excitement).

Cops. Of course. Well, about time to start working on the old gag reflex.

They weren't police. Safety Pins shuffled into our apartment, her eyes all hazy and stoned, threw Wash's keys at him, then flopped directly on top of Jezza on his beanbag. I don't think she even saw him there, and he wasn't about to protest the girl-ass on his lap. Thing 1 and Matt the Black Unicorn followed after her. Matt was carrying an open can of Pabst. Thing 1 had an armful of records. Scuffed Flannel stood meekly just outside the door, waiting for a polite invitation.

She'd be waiting a long fucking time.

"Motherfuckers, are you ready to rock?!" Matt yelled, and bounced up and down on our couch.

Thing 1 dropped her records all over the section of floor vaguely near the record player and made her way into the kitchen. She'd gotten all the way to the fridge and actually put a foot up on her climbing chair before realizing it was occupied.

"Oh, shit!" She backed away. Stumbled a little. Been drinking. "Hi, you're . . . wow, you're like a fucking model or something. What are you doing here with these freaks?"

"She's my prisoner," I answered honestly.

Thing 1 laughed. Matt bounded into the kitchen and stood staring at the gorgeous new girl with all the subtlety and grace of a Central Park pervert. The others followed soon after, huddling around the kitchen to watch the spectacle.

"No really," Thing 1 said, "who's your friend?"

"I abducted her. Just by being here, you are all accessories to kidnapping."

Everybody laughed except for Thing 2, Wash, and probably Jezza, who was still sulking on his beanbag.

"I'm being dead serious," I continued. "This is the girl I saw Randall take off with at Fetta. She's pretending not to know him now. Trying to get Jezza to come with her, too."

"Oh, woe is me! The beautiful bird wanted to twirl about on me Johnson. Good thing you were there to rescue me, Carey!" Jezza hollered from the next room.

I killed the rest of my beer and took a breath.

"I'm only going to do this once, so listen up. Everybody look at her. Look at her closely. This is the woman I've just kidnapped. This is the woman they'll be showing on the ten o'clock news if I'm wrong. This is the woman that will ruin your lives and land you all in jail. Take a good look at her, knowing how fucking important she is."

I gave them a minute.

"Now close your eyes."

They did. Matt tried to keep one partially open, and I slapped his round cheeks.

"Somebody tell me anything about her," I ordered.

There was no answer.

"She's really pretty," Thing 2 tried.

"Oh, shit." Safety Pins finally recognized the same strange forgetful aura that I'd felt out on the street with Jezza. "That's totally her!"

"Anything. Any detail. Short hair? Long? Wearing glasses? Anything?"

After another minute of unproductive silence, I let them open their eyes. The mood was decidedly less merry.

"What the fuck do we do?" Thing 1 said.

"We have to call the cops or something," Safety Pins said.

"You're all bloody mental," Jezza said.

"Can I have one of those beers?" Matt said.

I nodded. The others followed his lead and pilfered half my stash.

Fucking parasites.

"Is this everybody?" the unnoticeable woman asked.

She half-stood out of her chair and peered around the apartment, locking eyes with us one at a time: Thing 1, Thing 2, Matt, Wash, Safety Pins, Jezza, and finally, with me. I put one of my Chucks on her belly and pushed her back down into her seat.

"This is everybody," I answered, "and none of them are going to help you."

"That's fine." She flashed her disinterested fuck-me smirk and said, "Let's talk about your friend. He's dead, you know."

That voice was like pornography. She laughed through full, red lips. I slapped her across the face.

"Your friend is alive," she said, still laughing.

I hesitated.

"Nope, now he's dead again." She was almost crying now, it was so funny.

"Where the fuck is Randall?!" I screamed. It shot out of me so fast and unexpected that my voice cracked a little.

"Ask nice, baby, and you'll find me all sorts of willing." She leaned forward and shook her shoulders, her tits bouncing around in that tight T-shirt.

I did my best to shut major parts of my brain down.

"Please." Thing 1 tried being nice, after seeing that I was unwilling to. "Just tell us where our friend is."

"How long would you say you've been here?" the woman asked Thing 1. She still had that lilting edge of mocking laughter in her voice.

"I don't know, ten minutes?"

The unnoticeable woman contemplated something. She was easy on the eyes if you weren't trying to look at her. If you were trying, though, it was like staring through somebody else's prescription glasses. Gave you a focus headache. It helped that I spoke her features out loud to everybody at the start: pale skin like powder, lips like licorice, shampoo commercial hair. Brown. Green eyes.

Remember.

"Listen, love," Jezza said, leaning casually across the counter. "These blokes is mad, of course. But something ain't right, is it? We ain't gonna hurt ya. We're just scared, yeah? Confused like. We just need to know what's going on—a couple little answers won't hurt you none—and then we'll let you go, free as you like."

The woman quivered her lip expertly, and I saw Jezza go weak. Then her face turned cold again and she spat at him. She laughed when he recoiled.

"Ten minutes," she recited. "Sure. Sure, you can have answers now: I took your friend. He's still alive. Probably."

"Can you give him back?" Wash asked with all sincerity.

God bless his little, stupid heart.

"Nooo," the woman answered, thrown. She considered Wash carefully, then slowly said: "I . . . don't think we'll just give him back."

"We?" I was on beer number three. I was hoping that regular, consistent drinking would somehow solve this problem. It wasn't working, but then—I'd only been trying it for three beers now. I was willing to see how this played out.

"There are so many of us," the woman said again, and now her voice was absent of sarcastic glee. It wasn't even the sexy croon she'd been deploying on me and the boys like a chemical weapon. Her tone was soft and even, something like awe.

Reverence. "More than you'd believe. We're right here, in your lives, in your houses, and you don't see us. I've met you before. Every one of you. I go to all the same shows. Carey, you told me you'd build a shrine to my tits last month. Wash, is it? We met earlier this year, at the Dead Boys show in Brooklyn. You asked me if I wanted to ride Go-karts with you sometime."

I saw recognition flash across Wash's face.

"You, the dumb one with the blue hair."

"Hey, don't call my friend dumb," Thing 2 protested.

Thing 1 gave her a sideways look.

"No, I'm talking to you," the woman clarified. "I took your lipstick last week. In the bathroom at Max's."

"Oh, shit." Thing 2 put a hand to her mouth. "I loved that lipstick."

"It's not hard to slip by you. Your perceptions are so small. You're ants, crawling around at the edge of a picnic table and calling it the edge of the world."

"Why can't we see you?" Thing 2 asked. "Is it something you got? Like a Hypno Ray, or Wonder Woman's plane?"

Wash nodded his head like *Yes, yes—good question.* Everybody else rolled their eyes.

"No, sweetie, it's not something we've got. It's something we don't got. You look for humanity in human-shaped things, and when you don't find it, your broken, clouded minds just glaze right over it. We are like you, but missing your inefficiencies. We lack your disgusting internal waste. I don't know why I try. There is no way to parse it that you can process. But don't worry: You won't be fed to the gears. You'll see soon enough. Gus likes you, you know. He wants to meet you. He wants you to see."

"Fed to the what? And who the fuck is Gus? The leader of

your creepy cult?" I demanded, sloshing beer in her general direction.

"Cult! Ha-ha, yes, I guess that is how you'd understand it. That's close, in a way. But Gus isn't a leader; he is the pin that holds our mechanism in place. He is the wheel that turns our belt. He is the piston that pounds inside our cylinders."

"Is it weird that I get hard when she talks about machines?" Matt asked.

"No, it is not," I answered instantly, shifting in my own jeans.

"I like you, baby, to tell it true." She turned those eyes on me, and I ran out of breath. "I'm so happy Gus is coming for you. I'm so happy you get to understand. All of you."

She looked around at each of us, smiling expectantly. When she saw only fear and revulsion, she tried again.

"You think your lives are important. The lives of others. Life in general. That's not what it's about. It's all about something else. It's about existence and movement, about maintaining the engine. Your microscopic little lives could be something grand. You could be used to turn the planets. To fuel the sun. You could be the lubricant upon which the gears of the universe churn, and instead you watch TV and get jobs. But that's at an end now. You don't have much time left here, in the dark. You'll learn." She nodded at Jezza. "You won't need to pretend anymore. Or lie to your friends. Or convince yourself that your decisions are important. You'll know what you are, truly. And what you can be. That's the gift Gus has given me. . . ."

"So this Gus guy, he did this to you?" Safety Pins asked. "He fucked up your head like this? I've seen chicks like you before. I've *been* chicks like you before. He's got you all turned around, is all. You think you owe him something, but you don't. You can get away. Tell us where he is. We'll fuck him up for it. He won't hurt you. Promise."

"I was so small," the woman continued. "I wanted to worship such little things: musicians, celebrities. I wanted them to use me, and in so doing, give me worth. I wanted to suck the dicks of rock stars and have them inject me with meaning. And then I met Gus. When I took him in me I could feel my old life draining out, like pus from a wound. When he put himself inside of me—"

"Gross," Thing 2 said.

"Go on," Matt said.

"When I swallowed him, his energy went to work. Made me like him—no, I shouldn't say that. I can never be like him. He's been touched by the Mechanic! He has seen the machine! That's not something I can ever comprehend. That's not for me. But I was cleaned up enough to uncover my eyes. I can see that there is a problem and that a solution does exist. I see it, and you'll see it, too. Just as soon as Gus gets here."

"What? He's coming here?" Wash asked.

"Bullshit," I called. "Nobody's coming for you."

"Not for me! Oh, no," she whispered rapturously. "They're coming for you. They're coming for you right at this moment, because this is your time, and I am so happy for you all!"

"Oh, shit, Carey. Do you think her friends would really come after us?" Thing 2 said.

"No way," I said. "Nobody even knows you're here but us, standing in this room, lady. Nobody can tell your friends where you are."

"I guess that's appropriate." The woman laughed again. "That's what you think of her. The words you use to describe an absence. Nothing. Nobody."

"What the fuck are you talking about?" Safety Pins slapped the counter.

"Look around you. Carefully. Think. Who is not here that should be? Who is never here, even when she is?"

Now I was looking around, too. I don't know why, this girl was clearly—

Motherfucker.

"Scuffed Flannel," I said.

Jezza's eyes went wide.

The woman laughed again. A tinkling, broken sound. Like wind chimes.

"You don't even know her name!" The woman exulted.

"Yeah, we do," Jezza protested. "We had a thing, she and I. Her name is . . . is . . . Shit. I knew it once!"

I grabbed Safety Pins by the arms and shook her.

"Was she with you tonight? Was Scuffed Flannel here?"

"No . . ." I could see her brain churning, the information slipping around behind her red eyes. "Yes, I think so. I don't know!"

"She was," Thing 1 said. "She was. She was here. She was with us at the park, remember? She turned down the weed, and you said something about her loosening up. We laughed. She came up with us. She was at the door."

"How long has it been now, since you got here?" the woman asked Thing 1 again.

"Twenty minutes," Thing 1 said.

The unnoticeable woman nodded.

"That's enough time," she said. "Gus should be outside."

THIRTEEN

I had my phone out in my lap. I was using the reflective screen to stare at my own bloody eyeball. It was transfixing. It didn't hurt or anything, but it was just so bizarre-looking. At first the red had only spilled across the inner half of the eye, but soon it pooled across the entirety of the white. I looked like a demon. Like a David Bowie demon: one eye normal, one eye bright and terrible and red.

Luckily, nobody in the police station lobby seemed to notice or care. If they were staring at me for anything, it was because I was the only young white girl in here. I felt vaguely racist, just for existing.

"Kaitlyn?" A skinny cop with pointy elbows poked his head out of the door at the far end of the room.

I must have given some unconscious physical sign, because he had singled me out and was waving me over.

Or maybe I was just the only logical "Kaitlyn" in the place: two old Mexican ladies, thick and bent into aged balls. A gigantic white dude with a two-foot beard and stars tattooed over both of his eyes. A homeless guy in intricate layers of stinking rags. A Latino kid dressed like a gangbanger, playing Mario Bros. on his phone. The rest of the age-cracked blue vinyl benches were empty. Looked like they always had been and always would be.

I crossed the filthy white tile, holding my own private white-girl parade. All eyes on me as I self-consciously made my way to the door.

"Room three, please." The pointy kid gestured toward the far wall and vanished before I could ask any stupid questions.

Which, to be fair, I was about to: *Why a room? Like, interrogation room? Shouldn't I be going to somebody's office or desk? I was here to file a complaint.* . . .

But the rest of the office looked busy. The other cops were so aggressively avoiding eye contact that I thought I'd probably get tased just for coughing. I picked my way through the cluttered desks, every one overflowing with papers, fast food containers, half-full coffee cups, and knickknacks. Bobbleheads, action figures, and framed family photos in equal numbers.

Room 3 was a plain white door. A giant faded-blue numeral stamped above the threshold. A fine patina of black smears from generations of shoes kicking angrily at its base.

I knocked, and immediately felt dumb for it.

"Come in!" a cheery voice said from the other side.

I stepped into an unadorned room, the same shade of authoritative white as the door. Billions of little scratches and scuffs marred the hard white plastic furniture. An older man, in his fifties maybe, sat in one of four chairs surrounding a table that had been bolted to the floor. A mirror lined the wall to my left. There was another, unmarked door a few feet away from the one I was uncertainly standing in. So two-way glass, then.

No, seriously. Why are you in an interrogation room?

I pushed the thought aside. I had seen the crowded desks when I was coming in. It was probably too cluttered to meet out there. Or maybe this was standard protocol. Or maybe they just sent me to the wrong place. That was likely it: There was already a guy waiting in this room, and he sure didn't look like a cop.

He was chubby, carrying most of the weight in his gut and sides. An ill-fitting T-shirt with a faded iron-on photo barely covered his bulk. I squinted. The design was shattered like glass, riddled with little cracks and missing pieces that had come off over uncountable washes. The photo was of a vaguely attractive group of young people smiling up from a couch. There were nearly illegible words stamped above it: PARTY OF FIVE.

Yeah, so . . . not a cop.

If the attire didn't give it away, his wild, bulging eyes and nervous smile would have.

Jesus Christ, did they send me to a room with a child molester?

"More the merrier!" he cackled, and drummed excitedly on his own thighs.

No, surely they would have him in handcuffs or something if he was a criminal. The door wasn't even locked.

"What is—" I started, but somebody *harrumph*ed behind me.

I turned to find a police officer waving me forward with a handful of plain beige folders. He waved me all the way inside the room and then down into the chair beside *Party of Five* guy without saying a word. The officer settled, grumbling and creaking all the while, into a much nicer chair across from us. He opened the folders, placed them in front of our respective positions, and stared at each of us in turn.

When I finally had enough of the silence, I opened my mouth to speak.

"You've both filed complaints," he finally began. He was just waiting to cut one of us off before doing it.

"You"—he locked eyes with *Party of Five* guy—"Mr. Fennsen, have alleged that one Matthew Fox has repeatedly attempted to do you bodily harm and even forthright stated his intent to take away your life. Is this correct?"

"Yes, absolutely." Fennsen nodded solemnly, his manic energy temporarily subdued. "He hid in my toolshed yesterday and threatened to chop my Johnson off unless I stayed away from my girlfriend, Jennifer."

"Now, to be clear," the cop said, "we are talking about Matthew Fox, the actor. Who played Jack, from the television show *Lost*."

"I don't know about any of that." Fennsen giggled. "But yes, the actor who played Charlie Salinger on the excellent *Party of Five*."

Fennsen swiveled to face me with googly eyes and pointed at his shirt.

"And to be clear again, Jennifer, your girlfriend, is referring to Jennifer Love Hewitt."

"My little Sarah Bear, yes."

Oh, shit. I just understood why they had me in here.

"Wait—" I said, leaning forward, "I think there's been a misund—"

"Ma'am, please. We'll get to your complaints in a moment. Let me finish with Mr. Fennsen. Now, sir"—the officer slowly flipped some pages until he found the information he was looking for—"last month you were in here alleging that Mr. Fox had the water company cut off service to you."

"The bastard!" Fennsen spat and sniffled.

"And the month before that, you alleged that Mr. Fox had abducted your girlfriend, Jennifer Love Hewitt, and was keeping her in a—and I quote—'rape garage,' until you went on live television and renounced your love for her."

"That is correct," Fennsen confirmed. He shifted around in his chair, writhing and wriggling his hips. "But they wouldn't let me on Channel Six. For all I know she's still trapped there!"

"Mr. Fennsen, you are aware that Ms. Love Hewitt has had a civil harassment restraining order filed against you for several years now."

"It's Fox! He poisoned her against me!" Fennsen squealed. He gripped the legs of his jeans in panicked, twisting hands.

"Sir, you are not allowed within one hundred yards of Ms. Love Hewitt at any time," the officer droned.

"I know!" Fennsen said, "I haven't! I stayed away, I promised! But Charlie is *tormenting* me! He stole my garden hose and whipped me with it! I'll show you!"

Fennsen got to his feet, knocking his chair over, and started ripping his pants off. He tore open the button and yanked down the fly but couldn't get past the belt, which, in his desperation, he had forgotten to undo.

"Sir, please sit, sir! SIT DOWN."

The officer came around the table, audibly groaning from the effort of standing. He twisted Fennsen's arms behind him, secured his wrists together somehow, and then sat him down on the floor. I saw that Fennsen was not wearing underwear. I turned away as fast as I could.

The officer took his seat again, his knees crackling like Chinese fireworks.

Fennsen was wheezing from the struggle but otherwise quiet. I got the feeling this was a routine occurrence for both men.

"Now, ma'am"—the officer closed the other folder and turned to face the one placed in front of me—"you allege that Mr. Luis has been making untoward advances on your person, is that correct?"

"Yes, but I'm not crazy!" I said, and immediately regretted it. Somehow acknowledging the word aloud made me seem crazier than if I'd just sat here like Fennsen and solemnly confirmed the charges.

"Nobody says you are, ma'am," the cop said. He scanned down the page and put his fingertip on some bit of information there. "You state that you met Mr. Luis at a social gathering last week, where he made threatening remarks and attempted to take physical liberties with you."

"Yes." I opted for Fennsen's stoic, official demeanor.

"Then Mr. Luis showed up at your place of work and continued with his threatening remarks."

"Yes."

"And finally, he broke into your home last night and threatened you with rape and other physical harm."

I paused. The other charges were technically true: I was just leaving out the weird parts. The cops would never help me if I insisted that Marco Luis put some kind of life-draining organ into me and threatened me with sexually transmitted nothingness. But forcing himself on me in his car after a party, showing up at my work—that's standard crazy-boyfriend stuff. Totally believable. Last night, though, I had no proof any of that actually happened. The doors and windows were locked, barred, and unbroken. I knew it was real, of course, but . . .

"Ma'am, is that correct?"

"Yes," I said, "sort of. I never actually saw him, only spoke to him."

"But he did force entry into your home?"

"Well, no. I think . . . I think he was outside the window at the time," I lied. But if they checked for signs of a break-in and found nothing?

"You 'think'?"

"It was very dark. I only heard him speak. I know how this looks." I turned and gestured behind me to Fensenn. He looked to be trying to masturbate himself with his feet. He was, of course, failing. He was nowhere near flexible enough. I snapped back to face the cop so quickly I think I pinched a nerve in my neck.

"And do you have others who have witnessed any of this behavior?" the officer said.

"No, I . . ." I thought of Carey. *Yes, officer, an old alcoholic, homeless punk who takes my recycling believes me.* "No, I was alone."

"Ma'am, I'm very sorry, but this is Los Angeles. We get a lot of complaints about a lot of celebrities." The officer's eyes roved to Fennsen. I heard a *squick*ing sound. I opted not to follow his gaze. "Without witnesses, we simply cannot take any action here."

I felt the floor drop away from me. Cold waves broke across my skin.

"Please, he's insane." I knew the desperation made me sound worse, but I couldn't help myself.

"Further—" the officer began, but something had uncorked in me now, and words came spilling out.

"I can't stop him! There's something wrong with his brain. I think he hurt my friend!"

"Furthermore," the officer asserted now, more forcefully, "our records show that Mr. Luis has already taken a restraining order out against *you.*"

"I—what?" I think I physically reeled. I felt myself tip backward in my chair.

"You are not allowed within one hundred yards of Mr. Luis at any time. You are not allowed to contact Mr. Luis by phone, mail, electronic communication, or other means." The cop was dully reciting from the information beneath his fingertip.

"That's impossible," I said. "He must have known I would report him after last night and—"

"Ma'am." The officer sighed. He pinched the bridge of his nose in exasperation. "This order was filed over six months ago."

I tried to push sounds out of my throat. Tried to explain somehow—if not to the cop, then at least to myself—but nothing came.

The policeman fidgeted and began to close the file.

"That's impossible," I finally said. "I only met him two nights ago. At a party."

"We have several witnesses that confirm you have shown up on Mr. Luis's property, uninvited, on many occasions. That you have . . . let's see . . ." The cop flipped my folder out again on the table. He shuffled back a few pages and read: ". . . that you have 'stolen his mail and other personal belongings, have vandalized his vehicle, have made personal threats to his wife and child—' "

Jesus Christ. He has a wife? A kid?

" '. . . have, on more than one occasion, tried to blackmail him with rape charges if he did not agree to impregnate you—' "

"What the fuck?" I moved to snatch the folder away from the officer, but he slammed his hand down atop mine and stood.

"Ma'am, I understand that you may be mentally imbalanced and not entirely aware of reality as it stands—"

"No!" I stood now, too, and yanked my hand back. "He's a psycho! He's deranged! He threatened to hollow me out; he tried to poison me; he can get into my house no matter how many locks I have! You have to help me! He must have paid somebody here, falsified the report—"

"Ma'am." The officer held up a finger to silence me.

He collected the files and composed himself carefully. When he spoke again, it was calm, even, and angry: "I took that report personally. I remember Mr. Luis. My granddaughter loves his work. I asked him for his autograph. Nice guy. He took a picture with me, for her. So I'm only going to tell you this once: Do not come in here again. Do not waste the time of this city's police force. And do not, under any circumstances, attempt to violate the order of restraint filed against you. Confused folks, people like you and Mr. Fennsen here—"

"Hey," Fennsen protested, trying to wiggle his genitals free of his still-belted but otherwise undone jeans, "don't involve *me* with this. That bitch is crazy."

The cop actually laughed, just once, before opening the door and waddling out of the interrogation room.

No. I will not accept this.

I stormed out after the policeman, ready to grab him, scream in his face if I had to; I didn't care what they thought of me. But if Marco had Jackie . . .

He wasn't there.

The man had left the room not one step ahead of me, but

I looked around the office and saw only strangers in crisp blue uniforms. He had to be standing right in front of me. There was nowhere else to go. He was one of these cops here, leaning on their desks or hunched over their papers. He was . . .

He was a big guy. Old. Maybe a mustache. Right? I tried to picture him but could only think of that bald guy from *NYPD Blue.*

I was just looking at him. Why couldn't I remember his face?

Wednesday night, 6:30 P.M.

I was sitting on the edge of my couch, holding my blinds apart with one hand, while the other nervously flicked a Cobra open and closed. I watched the recycling cans.

I couldn't believe it had only been two days since I first talked to Carey. He swore he knew what was happening to me, and I have no idea why I believed him. I'm not entirely sure I did, actually—but I couldn't think of anybody else that would even listen to me right now, much less offer any kind of explanation.

And if the old guy turned out to be crazy, well, that's what the Cobra was for: a telescoping baton comprised of seven inches of dense, hardened steel that, with the flick of a wrist, fluidly extends out to a sixteen-inch hybrid of a blackjack and a spring-coil whip.

It slides out like wet soap. To close it, you flex the shaft while pushing in and down. I don't know what psychological mechanism the repeated opening and closing of it was exploiting inside of me, but the action was intensely satisfying.

With the right permits, you can carry a gun pretty much anywhere in California. But Cobras are straight-up illegal.

I felt much better holding it than the misogynistic devil-girl Mace. I had to dig through my spider-infested outdoor storage for half an hour to find the Cobra. My ex-boyfriend Dean gave it to me after I had a bad scare while out on a jog one night. Some guy with cracked lips and bloodshot eyes tried to drag me into the bushes on one of my laps around the hospital by my apartment. I broke free, ran half a block, then turned around and stormed back. I stomped on his balls until he passed out.

It was a very stupid thing to do, in retrospect.

But it felt *amazing*.

I nervously flicked the Cobra out. Tapped it on my running shoe. Pressed it against the wall and slid it closed. Flick, tap, close.

Every time a homeless person wandered down the alley beside my apartment, my heart skipped a beat. I've never noticed it before, but there are a surprising amount of homeless people milling about my neighborhood on garbage-day eve. It was like watching a migration on one of those *National Geographic* shows.

Yes, Kaitlyn. They're just like animals. Jesus Christ, what kind of thinking is that?

A hunched shape approached.

Flick.

It glanced at the recycling, started to move toward it.

Tap.

It looked around nervously, and I got a glimpse: younger woman, bundled up in a parka. She seemed to reconsider.

Close.

I waited through three more false positives before I finally caught the silhouetted spiked shoulders of Carey's jacket. He sauntered up confidently, a kind of old-school Mick Jagger cockiness in his walk. With equal arrogance, he bent and started rummaging through my garbage.

Am I really going to go out there? Talk to an old, drunk, almost certainly crazy homeless dude because he pinky-swore to believe my own insanity?

The argument was apparently moot. My body was already making the decision. Hand on the knob, deep breath, and out into the surf-and-trash-scented L.A. night. Carey was gently humming to himself as he tossed cans and bottles into a garbage bag.

"Hey," I said.

I wished I had a more appropriate opener.

Hey, so you wanna chat about the inhuman monsters stalking me now, or what? Totally! Let's keep it casual.

Carey grunted and looked up, then spotted the Cobra in my right hand. When closed, the baton just looks like the broken handle of a jump rope, or maybe a light dumbbell. Most people wouldn't have a clue it was a weapon. Carey knew it immediately.

He held his hands up in the air, dropping a bottle of Mountain Dew in feigned terror.

"Take whatever you want," he said shakily, "I've got a few empty beers, a half rack of Coke Zero, and I think there's even a Faygo in there somewhere. Just don't ruin my pretty face!"

I forced a laugh, but the more I looked at his sideways nose, squinty eyes, and cracked skin, the funnier it got. I managed a genuine chuckle; it was the first time I'd laughed since Jackie went missing.

"You look like you've been wearing shit glasses," Carey said, spotting my eye.

"Thanks, just what a girl likes to hear. Burst a blood vessel."

"So, this probably means you want to hear more," he said, and let the lid of the can swing shut. He stashed his recycling bag between it and the wall of my apartment building.

"Yeah, I guess. It's—"

"It's gotten worse," he finished for me.

"Yes. I think my—"

"Friend went missing. Gotcha."

"Is this like your shtick? You're the psychic punk-rock hobo?"

Carey laughed.

"No, there's just a pattern to this. Always seems to go down the same way. Do you want to talk out here or . . . ?"

He surveyed my apartment like a lonely old mutt. My heart tightened a little bit, to see somebody that desperate for shelter . . . then I remembered it was about seventy-three degrees outside and I'd given him free whiskey the last time I invited him in.

Ah, well, not like I'm drinking much of it myself these days.

I motioned to my door with my free hand and followed him a few steps back. I wasn't being as subtle as I hoped—remember, I'm a terrible actress—but Carey didn't seem to mind that I was wary.

I locked the door behind us, never taking my eyes off of him. He may have looked the part in his duct-tape-patched leather jacket, torn and faded T-shirt, oil-stained jeans, and combat boots—but he didn't carry himself like a potential murderer. He stood in the dead center of my living room, hands politely in his pockets, looking like an excited kid waiting for permission to go play.

"Do you want a drink?" I asked.

His eyes lit up like Christmas.

I waved him over to the dining room table and grabbed a dull green bottle from atop the fridge. I poured myself a glass of water. I didn't bother with a mug for Carey; there was only about a third of a bottle left. He was probably going to enjoy it more than me, anyway.

I was right: He took a long swig of the Jameson, swished it about like mouthwash, and then swallowed it slowly and with an exaggerated "Ahh!"

"So . . ." I prompted him, seeing him about to go back in for another gulp.

"Right." He set the bottle aside with some noticeable difficulty and put on his serious face. "Where should I start?"

"What the hell is Marco?" I blurted out.

I meant to play it cool and skeptical, but I was gripping the sides of the table with both hands, and my feet were frantically tapping of their own accord. The Cobra was jammed between my thighs. Even if he did turn out to be a nut job, I doubted Carey would try to hurt me—but I was done making assumptions.

"Marco? That the guy in the car?"

I bit my lip and nodded quickly.

"He's an Empty One." Carey answered the question and took a slug from the bottle as his reward.

"I don't know what that is!"

"He's . . . Shit, this is going to get complicated, scary, and crazier than a bag of wet cats in a big fuckin' hurry. So if we're going to do this, I want you to hold off on calling bullshit until we're finished, okay? When we're done talking, if you think I'm a wacko, I'll leave and you're only out part of a bottle of fine liquor and a half hour of your time. Deal?"

I closed my eyes for a second. Tried to push the logical part of my brain aside.

Fat lot of good it had been doing me lately, anyway.

I took a sip of my water. I nodded.

"Marco . . . Well, things like Marco, they started out human, but something got a hold of them. It emptied out all the parts you and I think of as making a person—nerves, emotions, empathy—hell, I think even their actual insides. The Empty Ones bleed like you or me, but you can stab 'em where the heart should be with a broken mic stand and they won't go down. That one's from personal experience: I've impaled the bastards with fence posts, hit them with Gokarts, thrown them into trash compactors, and drowned them in gasoline then lit it on fire and burned 'em from the inside. I've never killed one."

I exhaled a little. I wasn't sure if I believed it, but it sure as hell wasn't what I wanted to hear.

"Jesus Christ . . ." I started, but he held up a hand to stop me.

Carey swallowed another bulging mouthful of liquor and continued.

"The Empty Ones aren't the only things you have to worry about. Marco is just one half of the shit tornado. The other half is something we call the 'tar men.' I don't know if you've seen them yet, but they're exactly what they sound like: giants sculpted out of used motor oil. Like the sludge that congeals in sewer gutters next to the highway. Only they smell worse. It burns like crazy when they touch you." Carey turned and showed me a vicious, cigar-shaped scar on the back of his neck. "It's like being grabbed by pure acid. They've melted some good friends of mine down to a nasty pink fluid. And near as I can tell? There's no reason for it. They don't eat you, or drink you, or do anything with any part of you. They just wander around dissolving your friends into puddles because they're giant supernatural assholes with nothing better to do."

"That's fucking crazy," I snapped.

I couldn't help myself. I was in too high of a gear. I was laying so much of my hope on this guy making sense of things for me, and to find out he was just off his meds would be too much of a disappointment.

"Hold it until the end—"

"No, god damn it! This is serious. This is my life—my *friend's* life! I know something weird is going on, but oil monsters? Invincible hollow people? No, dude. No way. Marco's on some kind of drug. Or he's a science experiment gone wrong. Or maybe he's an alien or something, I don't know. But—"

Carey slammed his bottle down, shaking the table. I stood quickly, knocking my chair over, and flicked the Cobra out. A quiet shunt and a short click as it locked into place.

"You started this," he said softly, "and you're going to finish it. You got a real nice toy there. You're not going to have to use it. I am not going to hurt you. But I'm not leaving here until we're finished talking. Unless you want to spend the next week cleaning me out of the floorboards, sit back down and listen."

His face was impassive.

I didn't think I could have hit him anyway. He reminded me of a dad. Not my dad—my dad was great—but *somebody's* crazy deadbeat alcoholic father, surely.

I tipped my chair upright with my foot. I tapped the Cobra on the ground and slid it closed. I sat down and sipped at my water like nothing happened.

"There's something else," Carey said, picking up where he was before; "something bigger than Marco and the tar men. They have bosses, kind of. Or maybe gods, I guess. Fucked if I know: I've only seen the things a handful of times. All I know is that they reduce people. They do something to our brains, show them stuff they shouldn't see, and most just up and vanish after seeing it. There's a bang like fireworks, and the floor rumbles like a garbage truck passing by, then boom—a human being is gone into thin fucking air. But some people, they don't disappear entirely. They stand there and scream light instead. They puke black sludge and glow like a bonfire's going on in their skull, then whatever it is slowly hollows them out. When it's all said and done, you end up with two things: first, a smoking, empty husk that looks a lot like a guy you used to know; that's how you get things like Marco. And, second, a puddle of cancer at their feet that gets up and moves; that's how you get the tar men. These bosses or gods or whatever they are—they're using us for something. I don't know what, but when it goes right, we just up and go away. When it goes wrong, they end up with a person split in two, and neither half is anything like human anymore."

I cracked my neck and exhaled some of the tension.

"Thank you. That was a very nice story," I told him with all the forced politeness I could manage.

Carey was quiet for a minute, then broke into a big smile.

"Good!" he said, "That's the smart way to go. You might make it after all."

He chugged the rest of his whiskey—my eyes watered a little just imagining it—and stood to leave.

"Never mind me," he continued. "I sniffed too much glue in grade school, that's all. Just the mutterings of a weird old wino."

Carey moved unsteadily toward the front door, and I could feel stress sloughing off of me like dead skin.

That clinches it: I've gone crazy again. Just like after Stacy died. None of what I thought was happening over the last few days was real. I might actually be stalking a B-list celebrity and blacking it out, and now I just need to see a doctor. They have pills for everything. I remember the pills. I'll take a little blue oval twice a day with meals, and this time next year—

"Just let me leave you with two warnings," Carey said, pausing at the threshold.

"Shoot," I said, positively giddy.

Say whatever you like! We're all crazies here.

"First, if you meet somebody whose face you can't remember—even when you're looking right at 'em—don't trust them."

The room swam around me. I felt like I was standing at the edge of a giant hole, leaning over and spitting down into the dark. A cold wind blew up over the lip. Goose bumps tracked across my legs and arms.

"And two, if you ever see a strange light, brighter than anything should be, making a sound like screaming and singing all at once—if you ever see something that looks like an angel, you run like hell and don't stop until your legs give out. And you never, ever, ever let it touch you. No matter what you think it's gonna do, no matter what's at stake, do not touch the damned thing."

He turned to weave away into the warm, oceanic Los Angeles night.

My lips wouldn't move. My tongue was dead weight. My lungs would not draw air.

The edge of the hole slid away beneath me. I tumbled into the void.

"W-wait." It took all of my energy to force the sound out. Carey turned back to face me. He looked happy and buzzed.

"I've seen them already," I said. "I've seen the angels."

I think I broke his heart just then.

"So they got your sister?" Carey was rummaging around my kitchen looking for more booze.

So far he'd found a swig of ancient tequila hidden in a dusty bottle in a forgotten corner atop my fridge; a Hefeweizen I'd been planning to cook a chicken with, back when I was foolish enough to believe I'd ever learn to cook; and an unopened bottle of blackberry-flavored vodka. He shuddered when he read the label, then opened it and poured the entire thing down the drain while glaring at me.

Carey sat down at the dining room table and carefully nursed the Hefeweizen like a man stranded on a life raft in the middle of the ocean.

"I don't know," I answered. "The cops—they said she might have run away from the fire. But that didn't seem too likely. They didn't find a body or anything, and she never turned up again. They brought my parents in, even. Police thought they had something to do with it at first. But nothing came of the investigation. It's weird. That night should be such an important part of my life, and it's just not there. When I do remember parts of it, they're so vivid it aches— but it's only a second here and there. Part of a song my mother sang while doing the dishes. Stacy messing with her yo-yo. Playing cars in front of the TV in the living room. And something bright, over my bed at night. Stacy said the word, not me: She said 'angel.' Then the fire. Then . . ."

I spread my hands and shrugged my shoulders.

Carey pulled at his beer and swished it around his mouth for a while before reluctantly swallowing.

"So what does it mean? What are they? What do they want with my family?"

"No fucking clue."

"Wait—what the hell? You just said—"

"I just said if you see one, run. I've tangled with 'em before, and all I know is exactly what I told you: The angels do something to people. They 'solve' them—that's the word the Empty Ones use. When it happens, most people are just gone, but some don't go away completely. They split in two. They don't solve right, I guess. They leave behind remainders. Things like Marco and the tar men. I know if you let the tar men get a hold of you, you turn into a meat milk shake. I know if you let Marco get inside of you, he turns you into something like him. But a shittier version. Those people you can't remember, even when you're looking at them? That's what they are. That's what you would've been if I hadn't pulled you out of his car a few nights ago. A faceless thing, following Marco around like a puppy. 'Unnoticeables,' we used to call them. And I know that Marco and the things Marco makes—they serve or worship or maybe just give dainty little hand jobs to these angels. What they do and why they do it is your guess, because that's as far as I've gotten, and I've been at this for decades. For some reason, it's hard to get a straight answer out of a half-solved psychopathic angel-worshiping machine cultist. Go figure."

"What do they do with the ones they take? Is Jackie even . . . is she alive?"

A bundle of nerves pulsed up my neck. My vision blurred and I blinked back the tears.

"Maybe," Carey said.

He didn't seem to plan on elaborating, but then he saw my face and added: "It's hard to tell. They do awful shit to the people they take sometimes. But not all the time. I've gone in after friends and found a pile of bloody pulp being fucked by a coven of monsters. Then I've gone in after friends and found them happily dazed in the middle of an empty subway station. I don't know what the rhyme or reason is to it. I don't have anything more for you."

Carey contemplated his beer for a second, then chugged the rest and set the bottle down hard.

"I wish you had more for *me*, though. Tell you what: I'm gonna return those cans and do a beer run to the Seven-Eleven across the street, and when I get back we'll come up with a game plan to rescue your friend. Fair warning, though: most of my game plans are 'light something on fire and throw it at somebody that looks like they know something.' If you want brains in this operation, you'll have to bring them."

I laughed, and locked the door behind him. I walked down the narrow hallway toward the bathroom, my head lost in daydreams of busting into giant machine temples and rescuing Jackie from angry, faceless natives.

Ha-ha, why natives? TV has ruined me.

I dropped my jeans to the floor and settled against the cold porcelain, forcing the ridiculous fantasies away.

Where do you start looking for a missing person? What would the cops do, if they were helping?

I'd barely started peeing—just a few hasty drops splashed into the water below—when I heard a metallic squeak and felt a hot blast of steam.

The shower.

How did it—?

A man's voice, deep and resonant.

"Getting to knooooow yoooou," it sang. The voice was only separated from me by a ten-dollar shower curtain I'd bought on sale at Target. It was six inches away from my bare knees.

"Getting to know all abooooouuut you."

Marco.

Every muscle in my legs seized at once. It physically hurt to move them, they were so tense. I slowly, quietly, achingly pulled my jeans up just enough to stand, and started reaching for the doorknob. I heard the sliding *clack* of the shower curtain being pulled open. A rush of warmth.

"You can join me," Marco said, his voice casual and friendly. "I don't mind."

I lunged for the knob and yanked it, but there wasn't enough room. The bathroom was so small, and the door opened inward. I had to lean toward the shower to get it open, and as soon as I did, a strong hand wrapped about my naked waist and started pulling me into the stall.

I thrashed, at first just trying to get my bare ass pointed away from Marco, then trying to scramble out of his grasp, then trying to keep my legs out of the impossibly hot spray. I felt it burning me all over, but Marco's skin—and I could see now he was completely nude—wasn't even red. He smiled impassively as I punched and clawed at his face. He didn't even blink when I put a fingernail into his eyeball. His smile didn't falter when I busted my knuckles against his perfectly white teeth. He held me immobile, both hands on my hips, as burning water broke against the back of his neck and scalded my limbs.

Marco started marching us one awkward half step at a time toward the open bathroom window. He repositioned his hands to hoist me toward the opening, and I took the opportunity to twist out of his grip. I kicked off of the toilet and knocked my head painfully against the partially open door. Marco, still smiling, blood streaming down his face from his ruined eye, bent to reach for me. I kicked his knee out, and his bare feet slid on the wet tile. He went down bad. Sideways, and without even trying to catch himself. His neck nearly broke in half when it hit the sink.

Marco lay still. He was a tangled heap of grotesquely twisted limbs on my bathroom floor.

I allowed myself one steadying breath, then yanked my pants up and crawled out the door.

I only made it a few feet into the hallway when something caught my leg. I tried to shake it free, but no luck. I looked back and saw one twisted, tanned hand clutching the hem of my jeans.

Then it started to pull.

I finally thought to scream. My voice was hoarse and ragged. It left me completely when Marco's head peeked around the door, upside down and swiveling loosely on a neck like a boiled noodle.

He smiled at me. That pool-party-poster smile. That smile from my teenage-girl bedroom. And he said, without a hint of pain or discomfort:

"Where you goin', *chica*? We're just getting started!"

I kicked the wall. I kicked the floor. I kicked his hand. I kicked the door, over and over. I thrashed and flailed in a seizure of uncontrollable, primal fear. I did not want to go through that door. I did not want to see the inside of that bathroom. That nightmare of broken limbs. That smiling, inverted face, laughing at me. I kicked again and again and—almost too late, it occurred to me.

I bucked and wriggled backward out of my jeans. They snapped instantly around the bathroom door and out of sight. I crawled backward the first few feet down the hall, then stood and ran. I threw back the deadbolt, yanked open the front door, and sprinted straight out of my apartment and directly into Carey.

He pivoted instantly. His reflexes were strangely quick for a man who looked so broken and worn. I thought he was moving to catch me, but he ducked away at the last second, and I scraped my knees bloody on the driveway. I looked up and found him protectively cradling a twelve-pack of Pabst like a mother with a newborn babe.

Carey blinked in confusion, then helped me up.

"Sorry," he said, nodding at the beer. "Instincts."

"Marco," I said, and my voice cracked. "Bathroom."

Carey gently set the twelve-pack down and bolted for the hallway.

It was a full two seconds before the adrenaline turned on me. Before I kicked over from survivalist flight mode to suicidal fight mode. A huge part of my brain screamed at my stupidity. It offered a thousand other, better alternatives, but I was too far gone by that point to listen to reason. I ran back inside, grabbed my Cobra from the table, and arrived at the bathroom just in time to see Marco scramble up the wall sideways, like a crab, his shattered neck and wobbling face still smirking at nothing in particular. He disappeared through the window and was gone.

A half second later, his hand poked back into view and gave us a jaunty wave, then vanished again.

Carey and I were stunned silent for a long moment.

"Well, that was pretty fucked up," Carey finally said.

It broke the spell. I swiveled about in the cramped hallway, facing my bedroom. I grabbed at the pile of unsorted clothes that always seems to collect at the foot of my bed, and skipped and hopped myself into a pair of black slacks as I ran toward the front door. I emerged onto the street just in time to see Marco's Mercedes fishtail out of the alley and onto Pico Boulevard.

"Fuck!" I screamed, and slapped the wall. "How are we going to catch him now?!"

"Catch . . . ?" Carey turned to me, astonished. Then he smiled so wide I think he split his lip open. "You want to catch him?"

"He knows where Jackie is!" I shocked my Cobra against the sidewalk and collapsed it down into its handle, then tucked it into my waistband.

"I love you," Carey said. Then, more usefully, he added: "I have a motorcycle."

FOURTEEN

I see a man on television, a politician on some local access channel, and I know just by looking at him that he is secretly homosexual and ashamed of it. This is the root cause for much of his behavior: his enjoyment of anal sex and the subsequent shame. It has been the inspiration for a few one-night stands, more than a handful of crying fits, various acts of contrition, several attempts to cover up the indiscretions; all told, he has spent 36,902 hours of his life pursuing various activities and modes of thought that were a direct reaction to his unwillingness to acknowledge his enjoyment of anal sex.

The politician is a living being. He requires energy to function. Those hours he spent actively denying a part of himself were all fueled by calories: enough calories to feed the nation of Namibia for a day; enough caloric energy to augment the magnetic field of Mars for sixteen crucial seconds, thus diverting an asteroid that would otherwise turn a small mountain into a crater. That small mountain endured for 64.3 million years. For the next 23 years, 7 months, 6 days,

4 hours, and 35 seconds, this politician can continue chastising himself for finding pleasure where he does—or I can reach in there and simplify all the decisions influenced by this one petty sexual need, and use that same energy to save part of cosmic history.

Wouldn't he want that, if he knew? Wouldn't he rather his life be used in that fashion?

It makes sense.

It terrifies me that it makes sense.

It terrifies me that I can't conceive of a reason not to apply the politician's solution right now and save the Martian mountain E. Mareotis Tholus. The smell of wood chips; a man's embrace from behind, pressing him into a soft pillow; the tangy sting of poison ivy being burned; his father reading two passages from *Waterless Mountain*.

That is the politician's solution. The catalyst that would reduce him to pure energy.

Incorrect.

I see now that the politician's solution cannot be complete. It will not be perfect. It will reduce his inefficient humanity, but certain base parts of his being are too cluttered. The code is clumsy. I can remove the redundancy, but I cannot rewrite the shoddy programming. There will be a remainder to the politician's problem. It is not like this with most: Most can be reduced completely, shunted away in neat pulses of transmitted energy.

The politician's remainders will not be unique or special. The remainders of all imperfect problems—all human beings too messed up inside to be perfectly solved—are always identical. They are physical manifestations of the core motivations of every living creature in history.

Consumption and creation.

Creation is accomplished through birth or cell division. Progenation.

Consumption is accomplished through digestion. The act of consuming energy and using it to fuel the vital needs of the host.

The by-products of an imperfect problem, what will be left over if I solve the politician, consists of two split entities: a creator and a consumer. What I used to call an "Empty One" and a "tar man." A consumer is a creature that is mindless hunger without purpose or even the biological systems necessary to digest and process the energy it consumes.

It looks like somebody sculpted a giant out of an old smoker's lung, and smells like a road being repaved. Burns like a son of a bitch when it touches you.

God damn it! Snap out of this. Use the nonsense barriers. Free association, song lyrics, blank verse—

A creator is a creature somewhat resembling its old host form (in this case, a pudgy middle-aged man in a brown pinstriped suit) that exists only to procreate: to spread its seed, instinctively attempting to further its faulty code. The remainders are tragic figures. Neither can accomplish their task. The consumer cannot eat. The creator cannot create. Only the angels can fully solve a living being. A creator is not an angel. It is a mistake. It can only hollow out other beings. Birthing what I used to refer to as "Unnoticeables." It can empty them of their inefficiencies, but it cannot solve them.

The creator cannot make more creators. It can only spawn weak, faceless mockeries of itself.

The existence of the remainders plagues the angels. If we could be moved by their plight, we would be—but of course, we cannot.

They cannot.

It is almost within my power to solve the politician. I am still human enough to feel saddened by the plodding damnation of his continued existence, but I see that solving him, even partially, would be for the greater good. All I have to do is let go. Release this last stubborn, stupid part of my humanity, and I will become an angel.

No, "angel" is the wrong word. That's their word. The naive human term for us.

Them.

You're not them yet. Not yet. Hold on.

The angels don't use words, but my human mind goes digging through drawers to come up with a translation.

They call themselves . . . tools. No, *the* tools. The Tools of the Mechanic.

Angels are mere devices, employed by the Mechanic to maintain the ever-pumping engine of the universe. They believe they are the reason that the planets turn in their orbit, that stars burn and galaxies expand.

The Mechanic.

I shuffle through distant files, dig through archives. The words are coming harder now. Concepts are so diluted when they're tied down by these dumb ape sounds.

God. That's the word.

"God" is the closest concept I have for the angels' Mechanic. It is not very close at all. I know this is my own failing: In my human life, my only frame of reference for understanding and defining higher powers was the Bible. I was taught there was information worth processing within that manual and told to apply it to all external stimuli. My mind calls them "angels" because I am using the Bible to interface with and understand these beings. My mind calls the Mechanic "God" because that is the syntax that invokes the existence of a higher power in me.

But their Mechanic is not much like God as I understood him. If the Tools of the Mechanic are on the side of God, then God is an uncaring technician who exists to replace broken parts, not repair them. His focus is on the larger machine, on the universe at a macro scale, and he cares not for the well-being of the rivets and the screws—our solar system, our planet—beyond their ability to hold the machine together.

Why would he care for humanity? Why would the Mechanic care for life at all? We are containers for fuel. To be ignited, consumed, and disposed of.

No, this is not God's will. Our God doesn't behave like this. Our God loves.

Because God is a faulty analogy for the Mechanic. This failure is a result of the lingering human thought patterns within me. They are interfering with my ability to understand and should be abandoned. My old operating system cannot process the kinds of commands that I can now give and receive.

I know the truth. I have struggled so long with the ultimate meaning of life, and now I have concrete answers.

My human mind screams. It misses the warmth of the messy, emotional questions that used to plague it. Only when his presence is yanked away from me do I actually understand the purpose that God served for humanity: He was the knife in our soul. We think the blade hurts us, but remove it and there is only emptiness left. We bleed from the holes in our understanding and we shrivel and we die. I did not know that God was with me until he left. Now the wound has opened, and I have never known a colder place than here, in the shadow of his absence.

This analogy is faulty. The interface must be abandoned.

FIFTEEN

"Oh, God," the woman moaned. She writhed against her chair like an angry snake. "He's close. Gus, baby, I can *feel* you."

"This is some fucked-up shit right here," Matt said. "I don't know whether to stuff a dollar in her panties or run."

"Let's just go, okay?" Thing 1 was blinking hard. Trying to fight off the buzz she'd been nursing all day.

"Yes. I also say we should go. We should not stay, but go," Wash said.

"This is bollocks, though, isn't it?" Jezza was leaning into the kitchen and jabbing his scabby fingers at us. "You all know Scuffed Flannel. We been together for bloody weeks now! That's practically married!"

"Oh, yeah? If you know her so well, where is she? Why didn't she come in with us?" Thing 2 asked.

"Well, I don't—" Jezza started, but I cut him off.

"What's her goddamned name!?" I hollered. "How many fucking times do we need to do this?!"

He opened and closed his mouth a few times. A landed

fish, looking around and wondering where all the water went.

"Wash, you grab one of her arms," I said, gesturing to the faceless, giggling woman practically dry-humping our fridge. "I'll grab the other. We'll walk her out of here nice and calm. It's dark enough now, nobody will see us. And if they do, we just tell anybody who asks she's drunk. But I don't think anyone is gonna ask. It's like they don't see her. We'll head up to Jezza's mom's place and—"

"Like hell!" Jezza protested, but I could see even he was relieved at the prospect of leaving.

"You run ahead and find a pay phone," I said to Jezza. "Tell your mom we're having a slumber party or something."

"A slumber p—? What the hell are you on about?"

"I love you, man. So don't take this wrong, but your mom's an idiot. You're an idiot. Your whole family is idiots. When Randall OD'd last year and we had to crash at your place, we told her he had the flu. She made him fucking Rice Krispies squares. I don't give a shit what you tell her, just let her know we're coming."

Jezza threw his hands up dramatically, but he didn't argue.

"Matt." I snapped my fingers in front of Matt's hypnotized gaze. "Matt! Stop watching that girl pleasure our appliances and focus! You and Safety Pins have the most important jobs, so I need you to pay attention. Are you here with me?"

"Yeah," Safety Pins said, biting her lip in concentration. "What do you need us to do?"

"I need you to carry the beer."

Safety Pins looked a little offended, but Matt recognized the seriousness of his task.

"Thing 2, you run interference in front. Let us know if there are cops or something."

She nodded at me and started heading for the door.

"All right, let's go. Up." Wash grabbed one of the gyrating woman's arms, and I took the other. She licked me from wrist to elbow, then snapped at my ear with her teeth.

Between the two of us, we managed to get her up and into the living room. Thing 2 yanked the door open for us. She was still focused on the girl. She didn't understand why we froze. She tilted her head a little when Wash's eyes went wide. She started to protest when we lost our grip on the girl, who jogged happily toward the open door. It took Thing 2 a few seconds to get the message.

To turn and look into the hallway.

A skinny guy with track-marked arms and cultivated stubble slouched out there. He had long blond hair, high cheekbones, and sunken eyes. He looked like Iggy Pop, and he looked like he knew he looked like Iggy Pop. Like he'd been practicing for years just so he could look as much like Iggy as humanly possible while standing in this particular hallway at this specific time. He smiled at the woman when she leapt into his arms, grinding and pulsing against him. He laughed and motioned her aside, and she dutifully stepped behind one of the massive, oozing black piles that flanked him on either side.

Thing 2 tried to scream, but the tar man was already reaching for her. It was forcing its hand into her open mouth and right down her throat. She started thrashing. Her eyes rolled up into the back of her head. Smoke curled up from between her bubbling lips.

Wash leapt for her, but I grabbed his arm and shoved him backward over the couch. The other tar man was already stooping down to step through the open doorway. Wash would've barreled right into it. You don't get to fight those things. You can't will your way through the pain when they get a hold of you. My neck still screamed at the slightest breeze, If that had happened inside my throat . . . ? No. Thing 2 was gone.

"Window!" I yelled, and Matt and Safety Pins went scrambling for it. Jezza was already on the other side, rattling down the stairs of the fire escape.

He may be a drunk, a poser, and a coward, but you cannot fault that boy's survival instincts.

Thing 1 wasn't moving. She just stood and stared from the kitchen, trying to process. I moved to grab for her, but Wash had gotten to his feet and looked like he might go for Thing 2 again. I lowered a shoulder and charged. I caught him in the chest, knocking the wind out of him and pushing us both toward the open window.

"Grab him!" I said.

Matt reached an arm in, looped it around Wash's waist, and dragged him through the open window. I turned back to find Thing 1. She was frozen, making a broken little humming sound. She was watching Thing 2's face split open and run down the tar man's forearm. She was so transfixed, she didn't even see the other one. The one that was almost on her. I looked around for something to throw, and found nothing.

Stupid. Panic makes you stupid.

I reached into my pocket, snapped my Zippo to life, and whipped it underhand across the room. It went end over end. I could see it, magnified, like it was right in front of me. That tiny flame, flickering in and out of life: It took up my whole world. With each flip it would gutter out, then flare back to life. It was six inches from the tar man's chest and burning strong, when a set of long bony fingers plucked it out of the air.

The Iggy Pop–looking motherfucker caught the lighter, snapped it shut, and pocketed it in one fluid motion. He smiled at me and snaked one skinny arm around Thing 1's shoulders. She was a statue. Still keening and staring at the rapidly widening crimson puddle where her best friend used to be.

"You're Carey, right?" the skinny guy said to me in a voice like broken bottles. "Been hearing a lot about you."

"You Gus?" I asked.

He didn't answer, just gestured at his own body like *Take it all in.*

"I'm going to fucking kill you," I told him.

I wished I had something more clever, or at least more convincing, but hell—you try being six beers deep while you watch your friend get melted. Doesn't do any favors for your wit.

Gus laughed, low and braying, with a touch of a wheeze at the end. Iggy laughed just like that. I talked to him at Max's once after a show. I mean, he laughed exactly like that: It was a pitch-perfect reproduction. Could have been a recording. Gus snapped the laugh off clean. He straightened up, losing the junkie slouch, and instantly lost every ounce of sleazy charm. His eyes went wide and unblinking. His neck jerked painfully at an inhuman angle.

"I do not think you can do that," Gus said, and his voice was still water. Deep and flat and unfathomable. "It will be interesting to watch you try."

He gestured and one of the tar men stepped forward. The brass gears in its face clicked together and whirred. That nauseating, balance-shattering whine started building. I dove backward through the open window. I hit my head on the iron railing of the fire escape and went somersaulting painfully down the steep, sharp stairs. I crashed into the landing and my vision swam. I fought it back. I could hear the noise growing, even from here. I didn't have time to take the ladder the rest of the way down to the ground, but we were only on the second floor and I'd fallen half that already. I vaulted over the railing without looking.

I landed sideways across Jezza's shoulders. He started to call me an asshole, paused, began correcting it to "arsehole," and then just gave up entirely. He was looking at me with searching desperation. So was Safety Pins. So was everybody.

They stood quietly for a moment. The only sound was the distant but building metallic whir.

"Well, fucking run!" I told them.

They scattered like kids who'd just hit a baseball through a window. Safety Pins and Matt hauled ass up the street, toward the corner store. Toward people.

Smart.

Jezza and a still-in-shock Wash hobbled the other way, toward the alley. Toward the filthy, darkened alleyway.

Less smart.

I thought for a second and decided on the alley. If Daisy was still there—if nobody had stolen her or thrown her away since I last stashed her—we might need her. I sprinted down the block and ducked around the corner, hoping to get out of sight before Gus got to the window.

I was too hopped-up on adrenaline to feel it, but I knew I was in a bad way. I'd likely have some wicked bruises. Probably busted a rib. I wheezed painfully, but tried to keep it quiet. Like Gus could hear me from a second-story window a block away.

Shit, I don't know—why couldn't he?

I nearly pissed myself when a raspy voice in the darkness said: "Only six."

"Bloody hell!" Jezza yelped.

"Only six now," Sammy Six repeated loudly. "You can count them one two three four five six, it always lands on six."

"Sammy!" I grabbed him by the shoulders and looked him in the eyes. "Shut the fuck up."

"Six standing, six angels, six steps. Carey, you're not the six. I'm not the six. We're not the six! Sixty sixty six! You can't choose your friends. Choose me. Please choose me. Some-body's gotta choose the old guy—"

I shook him but it just seemed to rattle him more. He grew louder. Frantic.

"It's all there! It's a codebook! Watch the sixes: Ezekiel 16:6—'And when I passed by thee, and saw thee polluted in thine own blood, I said unto thee when thou wast in thy blood, live.'"

"Sammy, listen man." I let him go and held my hands up in front of his face so he could see I wouldn't shake him any-more. "Some serious shit is going down. Just hold it together for a minute, just be quiet—just for a minute—and I will give you all the money I have in the world."

He looked at me skeptically, whispering multiples of six to himself.

"Here"—I held my wallet out to him—"this is everything I got on this planet. Take it. I got a feeling I won't be need-ing it much longer, anyway, and you can maybe get a roof over your head or something. All you have to do is leave, okay? Just take it and go. Get out of here. Now."

"No." He slapped at his head. "Made a mistake. I took too much away. I forgot too much. There's a reason why not. "

"There's no reason why not, Sammy. You can take it. It's fine. Please, for the love of jumping Christ, take the wallet and get the fuck away from us so I don't have to knock you out."

Sammy took the wallet like it was communion. He was equal parts reverent and dubious. He wasn't used to lucky breaks and he didn't understand charity like this. He had no way to process his good fortune. He looked inside.

"All you got in the world is twenty bucks?" he said, already wandering off.

"Bollocks!" Jezza's eyes were rolling around in his head like loose marbles.

"They have killed her," Wash said, then looked to me. "Is that right?"

"Yeah," I confirmed. "I don't think Thing 2 made it through that."

"So we should kill them," Wash said, then looked to me again. "Is that right?"

"Bloody bally bollocks!" Jezza slapped at Wash's arm. "Bollocks to that, to them, and to you! B-boll-b . . . bullshit! Fuck this!"

Jezza's faux accent dropped away. He seemed smaller without it.

"We don't even know what those things were! How could we possibly hurt something like that?"

"They were tar men," Wash answered.

"And tar will burn," I supplied. "Why do you think I bought everybody those lighters?"

I put a hand on Jezza's bony shoulder. He was five and a half feet on a good day, a hundred pounds on a bad one. He was shivering and wild-eyed and sweating.

"No way. I'm done," he said. "I just want to go to shows and fuck girls and maybe throw a beer can at a cop car if shit gets crazy. How the hell did this happen? How is this insanity on us?"

"It wasn't," I said, "but now it is. You saw it, Jezza. They killed Thing 2. They took Thing 1. They know our names and where we live. They're fucking targeting us!"

"But why?!" Jezza screeched. I closed the distance between us quickly and clamped a hand over his mouth.

"Quiet. I don't know if they can hear us or if they're even still after us, but keep it down until we get mobile."

"Why?" Jezza asked again, softer. "Why us? We're fucking nobody. We're nothing. We're the pieces of shit that pieces of shit shit out."

"That is probably why," Wash mused. "Vanessa—Thing 2—she ran away from her home last fall. She crashes at the place of whatever guy she is with at the time. I don't even know her last name. How am I going to file a police report about this? Who even knows she was here?"

Me and Jezza stared at Wash like he'd just grown wings.

"What?" he asked.

"The fuck did that insight come from, buddy?"

"It makes sense, is all," Wash said.

I gave him a skeptical glare and went back to rummaging through the trash cans as quietly as possible. I had stowed Daisy here a while back. It was always an adventure, going to find her: I never knew if this was the time she'd be gone. Ordinarily it wouldn't be a big deal: I didn't pay a dime for the motorcycle in the first place. I found it knocked over beside a Dumpster in Queens while looking for a place to crash after some shitty house show. I used her seat for a pillow to sleep it off for a few hours. When I woke up, I pulled the little lever on her left handlebar and coasted her downhill for about a mile. It was four in the morning, and only a handful of cars were on the street. After the road leveled out, I pushed her for a bit, thinking I could sell her for scrap or something, but I was tired and still hungover-drunk, so I laid her in a drainage ditch and walked home. Two weeks later I was back in the neighborhood trying to score pot, and I checked in on her, just out of curiosity. She was still there. I couldn't feel my legs anyway, so I pushed her back to my friend Boxer's place. He was always fucking with old cars and shit. I gave him the rest of my bag to get her running again. Only took him a few hours. He gave me a crash course in how to work her, which turned out more literal than he probably intended. I rode the bike all the way home at ten miles an hour, my rashed-up legs held out to the sides like training wheels.

I never knew when I'd need Daisy, and I didn't want to get too attached, so I just hid her as best I could when I was done, and left the keys in the ignition. If somebody took her, well, they probably needed her. Just like I did once. But nobody ever took her. She wasn't much, and I didn't know fuck-all about riding her, but nobody else seemed to want Daisy. So I guess she was mine.

And every once in a while, like right now—peeking out from behind a busted mattress frame, her handlebars draped in old noodles, smelling like somebody peed on her wheels— she was the most beautiful fucking thing in the world.

I wrestled her out from her hidey-hole and wheeled her to the end of the alleyway, where Wash stood staring at his feet, and Jezza shivered into his own crossed arms.

"What the fuck is that?" Jezza asked.

"This is Daisy," I answered, "and I'll thank you not to speak to a lady like that."

"She smells of urine and chow mein," Wash said.

"Most of my ladies do." I grinned.

Jezza laughed a little. His death grip on his own elbows loosened.

"What are you gonna do, chase them down?"

"Shit, of course not."

Jezza looked relieved.

"*We're* going to chase them down," I finished.

He gaped like a dirt farmer at a carnival.

Wash nodded once and wordlessly mounted up behind me. He patted the extremely small patch of seat remaining to his rear. Jezza shook his head.

"No," he said. "I'm sorry, I just can't."

"Jezza." I looked at him levelly and tried to keep my voice as somber and even as possible. "Scuffed Flannel came around with you first. In a way, you brought them to us. You owe for that. She never tried to take you, so I guess she was just here to keep tabs on us. But then there was the brunette at the bus stop. She was trying to take you. That means they obviously know who you are, and they want you. Do you think they're going to just leave you alone now? Ask yourself: Where are you gonna go? Who's going to help you? What are you gonna do?"

Jezza's face grew darker with every question.

"Doesn't look like you have answers to those questions," I continued, "so try this one: *What would Johnny Rotten do?*"

He laughed at first, then thought about it. He shrugged, shook the cold out of his shoulders, and straightened up.

"Shite," he said, the accent finally returning in all its ridiculous glory. "What's the bloody holdup, then?"

He threw a leg over the seat and tucked in behind Wash. I kicked the bike over once, twice, three times, four.

"Uh . . ." Jezza said uncertainly, "you're kind of ruining the moment here, mate."

Five. Six. Come on, baby, god damn it.

"There's a red button with an *x* here," Wash supplied, pointing to the handlebar. "Do you want me to push it?"

"Couldn't hurt," I replied. "I don't think this has a self-destruct."

He pushed it. I kicked again, and Daisy blared into life like an angry drunk getting splashed with cold water.

I eased us out into the street. The bike jumped with every gear shift, wobbled with every turn, and nearly stalled every time I tried to brake, but eventually I got us the half block back to our apartment building. Wash had his arms wrapped tightly about my midsection. Jezza had his encircled all the way around Wash and was grabbing onto my shoulders. His fingernails were digging into my flesh through my jacket.

When we rounded the corner, Gus was standing in the middle of the street with an impatient smirk, his low-slung jeans cocked perversely on his hips. He lifted a single bony finger and curled it. Then he laughed that Iggy rasp and hopped into the back of a nondescript white van. I got a look inside, just before he slammed the doors shut. Thing 1 was kneeling on the floor, one side of her face swollen and red. A girl it took me a while to recognize as Scuffed Flannel was whispering something vicious at her from the bench seat. Thing 1 flinched with every syllable.

I squeezed the lever and twisted the grippy thing, but I must have done it in the wrong order, because Daisy just lurched and stalled. The van was moving now, easing away.

"Carey, get a move on!" Jezza said.

"We should try to catch that van," Wash reiterated.

A few kicks and the bike spasmed into life again. With much twisting and lever pulling, I got her moving. The van took a wild, swaying right turn up ahead, nearly clipping a fire hydrant. I urged Daisy on, but her load must have been too heavy. I could feel the bottom of the seat scraping against the rear wheel with every bump. I pushed the foot lever on the left, and she got louder, which I assumed would mean faster, so I pushed on the one on the right, but she began to slow.

I tried to remember what Boxer taught me about riding that first day, but I had tuned out as soon as he got to "Twist this grip and ease this lever out to go. Pull this lever in to stop." I pretty much only used Daisy to get home when I was too drunk to walk very far. I never got her much above a casual jogging speed. Why would I need to?

But now I was a swearing flurry of feet and hands, trying to coax any amount of power out of the neglected little motorcycle. And then trying to get all that power right back out of her because we were going into this turn way too fast.

Upward of twenty miles per hour.

I got this awful feeling we were going to hit that fire hydrant. I couldn't take my eyes off of it. I tried to point the bars away, but the more evasive maneuvers I took, the more inevitably we careened in that direction.

"We are heading for that fire hydrant," Wash observed.

"I fucking know!" I snapped, wrestling with the bars.

I held the brake in, and we slammed to a stop inches from

the sidewalk. Wash's nose collided painfully with the back of my skull. I turned the wheel and gave Daisy some throttle, but it was no use: We were too close to the curb and too heavy to get over it. I tried to push us back, but we were pointed slightly downhill and I couldn't get any leverage.

"Get off!" I yelled.

"What the bloody hell?"

"We're not there yet," Wash said. "We still have to chase them."

"I know! There's no reverse. You have to get off so I can turn the bike around. Hurry the hell up; they're getting away!"

I heard Jezza eat shit while trying to dismount, but Wash managed it a bit more gracefully. I heaved back on the bars with all my strength and got the bike moving for a few inches, but then the worn soles of my Chucks slipped on the pavement and I fell over sideways.

Daisy went down right on top of me.

Jezza had the audacity to laugh.

"Help, you cunt!"

"Bloody hell, Carey." Jezza grabbed the seat and tried to hoist Daisy up. "This is the worst motorcycle chase in history."

"There is no way we are catching up to them now," Wash snapped.

The bulk of the bike's weight was off me, so I scuttled out from under it and went about helping Jezza get her upright again. We heard a mechanical whine from the next block up and stared numbly as the white van reversed into the street. The rear doors opened and Gus poked his head out.

"What's the holdup, man? Are you guys coming or what?"

Jezza held up a backward peace sign and spat on the street.

"Fuck you!" I screamed. "You try driving this piece of shit! It's like riding a goddamned sausage!"

Gus laughed and slammed the doors. The van idled impatiently a few hundred feet away. Wash started running for it, but it pulled away when he got close.

"It's just waiting there," he hollered, "down the next block."

I hefted, shoved, and wiggled Daisy straight again, then motioned for Jezza to hop on behind me. A few kicks to get her going and we wobbled up to Wash. He threw a leg over the back, grabbed onto Jezza, and we were moving. I had to come to a near-full stop at every corner, putting both feet down and waddling the bike into the turns, but it didn't seem to matter. The van politely waited for us at every intersection.

We weren't chasing them down. They were leading us like a big white duck guiding her clumsy, angry ducklings.

SIXTEEN

"Behold!" Carey did his best carnie impression and whipped a stained drop cloth off of a rusted, dented tangle of metal.

The motorcycle was the color of a storm drain after a heavy rain. The seat was an indistinct wad of faded duct tape. The grips were filthy rags secured with baling wire. The clutch lever was a set of vise-grip pliers clamped onto the end of a fraying cable. A thick pool of oil was curled up on top of the engine like an old cat in a sunbeam: It looked like it had always been there and had no plans to ever leave.

"Wow," I said, "that's . . ."

"Daisy," Carey finished, patting the seat by way of introduction. A seam of tape cracked open at his touch. He did not seem to notice.

"Wait—is this a Samurai?"

"No," Carey said, eyeballing me warily, "this is a motorcycle. You're thinking of those guys with swords."

"It is!" I pushed Carey aside and wheeled the bike out from

its hidey-hole, wedged between the Dumpster and the apartment building's outer wall. I backed it into the street, and the high pipes confirmed my guess. "It's even the SS!"

"My bike's a Nazi?" Carey was throwing a leg over the seat and fiddling with the controls. He gestured for me to jump on behind him.

I looked at the thick patina of scratches and dents that had once been a gas tank. I have never crashed a motorcycle that hard in my life, and it is literally my job to crash motorcycles.

"No." I pushed Carey backward on the seat and mounted up in the space in front of him. "You look like you don't so much ride this as you repeatedly crash it until you reach your destination."

"Hey, that's . . ." Carey contemplated it for a moment.

"Fair enough," he finished. "Like you can do better?"

I turned the key, which Carey apparently just left in the ignition, pointed the bike downhill, and pushed off. When we got a little momentum, I shifted up into second and dumped the clutch. The engine coughed into life with a sound like the laugh of a career smoker. A black cloud billowed out of the pipes. I leaned away from the turn, locked the bars, and pinned the throttle, fishtailing us into a 180. I fought the front wheel back to the ground as the torque threw the bike into a wheelie.

"Balls!" Carey swore and grabbed at my hips like a nervous prom date.

"My dad had one of these when I was a kid," I hollered over my shoulder. "First bike I ever jumped."

Carey's grip loosened. He stuck his legs out to either side and whooped.

"I didn't know she could do this!" He giggled. "I thought she was too weak!"

"There are no weak bikes"—I quoted my dad, the first time I complained about the little 125 he bought me for my fourteenth birthday—"only weak riders."

"Hey," Carey protested.

"You're not even leaning into turns. Lean with me—now!"

I pushed on the grip and ducked us around the line of post-rush-hour, pre-dinner-hour traffic gathered at a stoplight. It's always some kind of rush hour in L.A. The only real difference is in the attire and sobriety of the people caught in it. A motorcycle is the only thing that moves here, because you can split between lanes of stopped cars. It's not illegal in California . . . though it's not entirely legal or safe or really all that smart. But it is fast: We cut down the space between two lanes of jammed cars. It was like riding a lawnmower down a cramped hallway. Carey yelped and pulled his legs back in, narrowly avoiding clipping a bright green Prius's side mirror. The owner honked. Carey shot an instinctive middle finger up in the air. I stood on the pegs and checked the cross traffic up ahead. Nothing. I opened the throttle and shot us through the red light.

The Samurai was small, old, and weighed down too much. There was a flat spot in the throttle that told me her air-box wasn't totally sealed, but she was still running surprisingly well. Even so, we'd never be able to catch Marco in his souped-up Mercedes.

Or we wouldn't have been able to if he'd been in any other neighborhood at any other time of day. But my apartment was four blocks from the on-ramp to the 405. Cars didn't so much drive on these streets as they just parked in rapid succession. Every traffic light was a line at Disneyland: just a bunch of bored people waiting for the brief, giddy thrill of movement.

"Are you looking?" I let off the gas at every cross street, scanning the queued traffic on the adjacent roads for Marco's car.

"I was having too much fun," Carey said. "You have to teach me how to do that."

"You take left, I'll take right. Yell if you see him."

It was tough, even for me, to lane-split like this at speed, all while running traffic lights, standing on the pegs, and scanning the parallel roads. It was made tougher still by the sheer abundance of cars that looked just like Marco's. Those Mercs—I was never good with newer cars, much less European models—probably cost hundreds of thousands of dollars. And yet in every fourth vehicle in West L.A. was a yuppie with perfect teeth and a button-down shirt open to the chest, doing six miles an hour in a German supercar.

"Shit!" I stomped on the rear brake and locked the wheel. An old Mexican lady just materialized into existence right in front of me. I guess she must have stepped from the space between two idling cars and started walking across the street, not even checking for traffic. The back tire of the bike squealed and darted from side to side. I rode out the slide to a full stop, not wanting to risk a high side crash in this traffic. Carey immediately set about flipping her off, but she beat him to the punch. They both yelled obscenities, waving middle fingers around and grabbing at their crotches. I planted a foot, held the brake, turned the bars, and opened the throttle: The rear of the bike spun out as I dropped into gear, shooting us into the gap the old lady had spawned from. I blipped the throttle and yanked up on the bars to hop us over the curb, then hammered it down the sidewalk. Two ripped guys in half shirts released the hands they'd been holding and hopped to either side as we rocketed into the crosswalk.

"Look left, god damn it!"

"I'm a little fucking distracted by my own impending death!" Carey protested, but I felt his death grip on my hips slacken as he turned his head.

Intersections, alleys, and driveways whipped past, but no sign of Marco.

"There!" Carey yelled. "Back there. I think that was him."

I hit both brakes and steered us into a tight U-turn. We made the last intersection just in time to see Marco run down a kid on a skateboard while trying to nudge his way through a red light. Luckily there was no space for him to get speed; the kid was up and hollering almost instantly. I leaned into the turn hard, and we cut wide through the light. My stomach dropped to my knees from the g-forces. The little bike's old suspension sagged, bottomed out, and then slowly rebounded. I slipped us right into the space between lanes and kept as much speed as I could. I stood on the pegs and saw Marco riding the shoulder a block ahead of us. He floored it through the clear spaces until he reached a parked car, then yanked the wheel back into traffic whether it was clear or not. The crash of plastic on plastic, long honks, and angry shouts followed in his wake.

"This might be the best day of my life," Carey said. "I get to be in a bitchin' motorcycle chase while a beautiful girl repeatedly sticks her ass in my face."

I sat down, just now realizing where my rear end was positioned whenever I stood on the pegs.

"Heads up!" Carey said.

I snapped my attention back just in time to see a chubby lady in a PT Cruiser open her driver's-side door. Luckily the feathered-hair dude in the next lane was too busy texting to notice that traffic was moving again. He had accidentally left the slightest space between cars. I weaved into it and angled us down the center divider.

"No cuts!" PT yelled after us. I hoped Carey was giving her the hardest finger possible.

A pair of bright red Hummers were stopped in the middle of the intersection at the next light, blocking every inch of road space. They both had personalized license plates and Ayn Rand bumper stickers.

We would not be passing through here.

I honked, but the bike only emitted a nasally gasp, then a snap, and the horn clattered to the street. Annoyed, I revved the throttle, and a thick, tattooed arm emerged from the passenger-side window of the Hummer directly in front of us. It casually tossed a latte at my face. I ducked out of the way, but it must have clipped Carey, because he was already starting to dismount.

"No time." I reached back and held him in place. He reluctantly settled back onto the seat, but when traffic started moving again, he held up a fist and punched off the driver's-side mirror as we passed.

We caught up to Marco six blocks later. I swerved around a FedEx truck just in time to see Marco's reverse lights flick on. He came rocketing backward at us from the opposite lane of traffic. I locked the bars and spat us up onto the sidewalk right as he slammed into the grill of the delivery truck.

Marco laughed, threw the Mercedes into gear, and squealed away. There was music thumping from his open windows.

> *No matter how far you might roam*
> *It's still your home away from home*
> *Home Room!*

The theme song to his show.

I got the message. Cars beat motorcycles. I couldn't rescue Jackie while lying in a pool of blood and oil on Sunset. I fell back and settled for just trying to keep the Mercedes in sight. It didn't seem to matter to Marco. He didn't speed up or slow down, now that we were off of his tail. He kept right on running lights, jumping lanes, and clipping pedestrians. He didn't even think we were in a chase: This was just how he drove.

Twenty minutes later, we had wrestled our way up into the hills. Traffic had let off a little bit, and I had to keep the throttle wide open just to keep up with Marco on the winding, narrow streets. I carved easily through a set of neat S curves. I could close distance on the corners but lost it in the straights. Every other block, a car reversed obliviously out of its driveway; a jogger blindly plodded into the crosswalk; a dog chased a cat into the open road. I have never been that close to death in my life.

Carey laughed the entire time.

When we finally pulled into a cul-de-sac overlooking West L.A. and killed the engine, I glanced back to find him bright red, still trying to catch his breath, tears welling up in his eyes.

"That was the most fun I have ever had," Carey said, "and I once fucked a girl on a roller coaster."

Marco had pulled into a long, snaking driveway that led downhill. It was packed with cars. He opened his driver's side door, stood, and stretched—like he'd just left behind a long commute instead of a swath of destruction. He was still completely naked. He strode toward an eggshell-white mansion the size of my entire apartment building, his butt flexing and rolling like the angry sea.

*I mean, I know he's a demon yanking strings inside the rav-
aged shell of a human being, but there is just no denying that
ass.*

When Marco reached the door, he turned back and hit a
button. The Mercedes beeped once and flashed its lights.
Locked.

Every inch of the driveway's absurd length was utterly
packed with Ferraris, Bentleys, Lotuses—even a few old Spy-
ders. There must have been ten million dollars' worth of car
down there. Every single one with broken headlights, bashed
fenders, or deep scratches.

Did Marco own all of these?

No—all of the lights inside the house were on. Muffled
bass emanated from somewhere deep within the mansion.
The gabble of distant conversation floated from an unseen
deck.

It was a party.

He took us to a party.

"No, no. Here's the plan." Carey was drawing diagrams in
the dirt by the side of the road with a broken stick.

"I'll move up to the front door . . ." he continued, sketch-
ing an arrow leading from the little *x* that represented our
current position to a lopsided square in the upper corner.

"Then you"—Carey drew a wide, curvaceous *w* and put
two dots toward the bottom of each arch—"take your top
off and bounce around some—"

I tweaked his ear. He swore.

"What? It's a distraction!"

"Take this seriously, jerk. We're trying to find my friend."
I ducked my head back around the hedge and tried to spot

an open window or something. Like most of these modern-style hill mansions, the building was a series of large, flat rectangles stacked atop one another. The bottom one was featureless. The second story had narrow slit openings—but they weren't wide enough to slide through, even if they had been low enough to the ground to reach.

"It's a joke," Carey said. "We're squatting here plotting out war games, when we're just going to go through the front door."

"Oh, are we? We're just going to walk up and ring the doorbell? That's great. How are we going to explain to the other guests what we're doing?—'Hey, sorry to intrude, everybody, we're just here to torture a former teen-heartthrob because he's actually a hollow, indestructible monster who kidnapped my friend. Party on!' We'll be in a padded room come morning."

Carey gave me an arch look.

"Look at the cars," he said.

I did.

I've been through Beverly Hills during rush hour; I've seen million-dollar supercars being abused and neglected by douche bags before. But never so many all together like this. Must be some serious money at this party.

"What about them?" I asked. "They're a little dinged up. . . ."

"And that's not strange to you? That every single one of these extremely expensive cars is smashed to pieces? Look at the pointy red number with the white stripe—"

"That's a GT-Forty," I supplied.

"The pointy red one," Carey insisted; "the bumper's gone. You think anybody who drives a car like that would be caught in public with it looking that shitty—much less out here at a nice party? Look at the curvy silver one: both headlights knocked in. The little gold convertible. Check out the grill. That's blood."

"What the hell?"

"There are no 'guests' at this party, darlin'. They're all like him. They're all Marcos. They're Empty Ones."

Both of my feet went numb.

I tried to say "holy shit" and "Jesus Christ" at the same time. It came out "hosus."

Carey didn't even notice.

"You were pulling some true Evel Knievel shit on Daisy earlier. I gotta give it to you. But the two of us on that little bastard, even riding like the devil himself—you honestly think we could catch Marco's big German cock-rocket if he didn't want us to?"

"He . . ." I didn't even want to say it. I didn't want to validate it. But Carey was right. "He was leading us here?"

"Might as well use the front door then."

"Why did you let me waste time planning, if you knew?"

"Jesus, girl. Gotta be a hundred of those fuckers in that house. I'm just trying to get up enough balls to go in there."

I straightened and started moving before I could give myself a chance to think about why. Careful consideration could only reveal that this was a terrible idea, and I had to be stepping through that door well before logic caught up with me. I had no other way to find Jackie. It was walk straight into the fire smiling, or do nothing at all.

After a few seconds, I heard Carey crunching along the gravel behind me. It helped, having him here, but it was a slight comfort. He was a thin, ratty blanket thrown over your shoulders in the middle of a blizzard. Marco had plainly shown we couldn't hurt him, no matter what we tried. A crowd of those monsters could tear us apart without breaking a sweat, and here we were walking in unannounced—

"Miss Kaitlyn Barr and Mr. Carroll Horton," a tremendous black guy bellowed, swinging both of the front doors open just before we reached them. He must have been seven feet tall and four hundred pounds. It looked like somebody had stuffed the night into a suit.

The announcement caught me off guard.

"C-Carroll?" I stammered.

"Oof, don't call me that. Only my mom calls me Carroll, and that's because she's a spiteful bitch."

I started to ask him a question, but he was being spirited purposefully along by a sharp-faced woman in a little black dress. I followed and heard the distant music of glasses clinking. Laughter. The rustle of a hundred simultaneous conversations. I don't know what I was expecting—a great black altar and a bunch of naked people in animal masks, I guess—but on the surface, this looked like just another industry party. A high-end one, sure, but—was that the guy from *Skater Caveman*?

I tried to get a closer look, but he was turning his head away to whisper something into a thin blond woman's ear. She laughed, showing a large set of perfect white teeth.

Wendy Palmer. I almost doubled for her once, in one of those blurred-together romantic comedies she was famous for. Her character was clumsy. I would have had to do two dozen pratfalls.

"I have gone mad," I muttered.

"Haven't we all?" A short fellow in a crisp blazer casually took my arm. He smiled up at me, and I swore he had the exact same set of teeth as Palmer. I scanned the crowd. Dozens of familiar, smiling faces.

One mouth.

I tried to shake him off, but he clung to me like a smarmy limpet. His tiny fingers dug painfully into my arm, but his expression stayed friendly. Unshifting. His smile was charming but carefully constructed. The mischievous twinkle in his eyes was painted on. When he looked at you, he didn't quite focus all the way—like you were just an obstacle obstructing the view of what he really wanted to see. He was moving now, and I was moving with him, because if I didn't, those vise-grip fingers tore into my flesh like talons.

"Let me introduce you," the little guy said, and gestured around the room.

We approached a familiar-looking woman with thick hips and olive skin. I knew her from somewhere. I think she had a sex tape. I couldn't place her name—something with too many consonants.

"I love your look," she said, downing a thin flute of champagne. "It's so *accessible*."

She said the word like it was the vilest of profanities.

A guy that looked like Asian Dracula asked me where I got my teeth done. He laughed and turned away before I could answer. A gorgeous old woman in a pristine pink pantsuit gave me an assuring smile and told me not to listen to the rest of these bastards. She thought I was perfectly lovely. I reminded her of her dog. A pug. "He's gorgeous," she said.

A handsome guy with carefully nurtured stubble and perpetual bed head introduced himself as "*People* magazine's current Sexiest Man Alive." He rolled his eyes when I tried to tell him my name.

Another good-looking dude in an immaculate white tuxedo informed me I could be in movies—somewhere in the background, at least. He gnashed his teeth as the little man guided us away.

"My friend has that same shirt!" proclaimed a red-haired, pale-skinned woman I recognized from . . . something. Insurance commercials? "At least she used to have it. I think she might have given it to Goodwill a few years back. Hey, it might literally be the same one!"

A fight choreographer I recognized from a straight-to-video sequel we'd worked on together was talking to the faded action star who graced the production with a brief cameo at the start of the film. He must have starred in the first one but gotten too big to do the second. He was only on set for a day—just long enough to die in the opening sequence. I'd never actually met him.

"You've got a great body," Faded Action Man said, after scanning me thoroughly. "It seems very functional."

A river of faces and voices swept past, each with some cutting passive-aggressive comment or scathing assessment. I got the sense that we were rudely interrupting these people's conversations when the little guy had first started parading me around the room. But after a while, I noticed they weren't really talking to each other. They made words, they laughed, they smiled—but nobody was responding appropriately. Somebody would mention the traffic, and another would laugh, then start talking about a new project he was working on. A brunette called me "definitely passable," then turned to resume her conversation, which consisted of loudly insisting that she drove better drunk. Her conversational partner replied that he thought it was supposed to be muggy tomorrow, and he was happy to live by the beach.

They weren't talking. They were practicing.

I watched the eyes of the partygoers across the room. Their

faces pointed at each other, but their eyes were in constant motion, keeping me in view at all times. The entire room was just waiting for me to get close enough to criticize and insult. After a solid hour of being called "exotically ordinary" and "the perfect supporting type," the little man guided me to a relatively empty section of hallway, released his painful grip on my arm, turned, and left without a word. I nursed the tiny purple bruises already welling up there. It looked like I'd been attacked by a superpowered baby.

I leaned against the wall and tried to keep my hands from shaking.

"I'm not saying he's right for the part," a younger, red-faced man in a tight white T-shirt said. "I'm saying the part is right for him."

"I get you," another, older man replied, this one dressed in a rumpled but finely tailored charcoal suit. "I get what you're trying to do: I know you're using me here, and I love it, and I love you for it—but buy a girl dinner before you throat-fuck her in the bathroom, all right?"

White T-shirt laughed. "Geoff, I'd be happy to put a steak and a baby in you. You saying you want to be wooed?"

"I want to be wooed," Geoff confirmed. "Is that too much to ask, Chaz? A little song, a little dance, a little reach-around . . ."

"I love when you're coy. You know that. Makes me feel like a sexual predator. But there's a limit, baby. Be forthright. Just tell me what you need to make this happen, and I'll make *that* happen."

"My wife's shithead brother's shithead kid wants to break into the biz—his words"—Geoff made a wanking gesture with his hand—"so I need a major film, but a minor part.

Something action-oriented. Maybe sci-fi. Make that a reality, and I'll get Nic into the tights for you."

"Is that it?" Chaz laughed. "I thought I was gonna have to buy you lobster and take you dancing, and all you're asking for is a McRib and the bowling alley? Consider it done! It's already happened, baby!"

On the table across from me, I spotted a framed photo: Marco, his arm wrapped around an old Asian man in a maroon robe. Eyeglasses in large square frames.

The fucking Dalai Lama.

Marco was making bunny ears behind the man's head with his fingers, all with that same plastic smile and those glinting shark eyes.

This is his home. You are in his home.

My head was swimming. My breath came shallow. I was in way over my head here. I needed help.

"What are you thinking?" Geoff asked Chaz.

"Shit, I don't know. How about the next *Transformers*? He can be, like, a fucking GoBot or whatever."

"There's a next *Transformers*?"

"There's always a next *Transformers*. It's like the tide."

I decided to chance it.

"Excuse me?" I stepped up between the two men, and it took a full minute for them to get their heads pointed at me. Their nostrils were red and inflamed. White T-shirt—Chaz, I gathered—still had powder on his upper lip. They didn't look like they'd be much help, but they were the only people here having anything resembling a human conversation.

"I'm looking for my friend," I continued.

"Oh, yeah. Busted-up old guy?"

"Right!" Geoff said. "I saw him come in, and I thought,

That's Mickey Rourke, if nobody fed him for a year. Love the look. Totally unique."

"I don't know, I feel like haggard old dudes are out this year. It's due for a swing back to young and fit any day n—"

"I was actually talking about another friend." I waved my hand in front of Chaz's face, trying to get his focus back. "A girl. Short hair, brunette, thick cat's-eye glasses . . . Maybe she was wearing a kind of tuxedo thing?"

"Oh, her?" Geoff's head executed a lazy orbit around his own neck. "Yeah. I seen her. In the back, I think."

"Jackie something?" Chaz asked.

"Yes!" A surge of adrenaline shot through me.

She was here!

"This way." Chaz snapped his fingers and stumbled down the hallway.

"I saw her, and I thought, *Oof, not another one of these chicks.* This hipster thing is played out," Geoff droned behind me. "Like, we got over Ally Sheedy when Ally Sheedy was still around, you know?"

"I disagree," Chaz said, swinging open a door and motioning me through it. "I'll never get sick of banging girls that dress like my grandma. It adds a much-needed element for me."

My eyes took a few seconds to adjust to the dimmer light. Wan yellow shapes swam around the room, making wet slapping sounds. When my sight returned, I saw that they were girls, mostly. A few pale, skinny Asian boys mixed in. All naked. All screwing. All in a nearly catatonic, drugged haze. My chest clenched. I looked for Jackie's face, her hair, the Steamboat Willie tattoo on her butt—but she wasn't there. I sighed with relief.

Then I heard the door lock behind me.

I turned and found the two men blocking the exit. From the way they'd been talking to each other earlier, I thought they were human. Douche bags, certainly—but human ones. Some oblivious bystanders attending what they thought was another industry party. Now I realized they weren't people at all—they were just well practiced. Standing this close, I now recognized the vacant, unfocused stare of the Empty Ones.

"I don't see my friend here," I tried, knowing it was futile.

"She's got a vibe to her, doesn't she?" Chaz asked, gesturing vaguely in my direction.

"Yeah, kind of a Buffy-meets-young-Linda-Hamilton feel," Geoff responded, sliding out of his blazer and slowly unbuttoning his shirt. "But that finger will have to go."

"I disagree," Chaz said. He wrenched his jeans down over his hips and kicked them across the room. They landed on the face of a writhing blond girl with a buzz cut and dull eyes. She didn't duck. She didn't even pull them off her head.

"Ha." Geoff laughed. He was down to his purple silk boxers. "Now I know you're just twisting my dick. Mutations will never play with the flyover states."

"She's a niche demo for sure, but niche is the new mainstream."

Chaz was naked from the waist down. He didn't bother removing his T-shirt. He closed the distance from the door to the bed in a few loping strides, then seamlessly slipped into a redhead with milky white skin grinding absentmindedly against a bedpost. With every thrust, he brought a closed fist smashing down on her breastbone. She didn't so much as flinch.

"I don't deal in niche. If niche wanted to be mainstream, they shouldn't have been so fucking niche in the first place."

Geoff stood immobile. He distractedly pawed at his own crotch as Chaz hammered on the redhead.

They hadn't looked at me once. I wasn't even here anymore. I took a few steps to the side and tried to blend in with the shadows behind an overturned armchair. They stayed like that for a while—Chaz bashing in the impassive girl's chest as Geoff pantomimed masturbation. When she finally stopped moving, Chaz straightened and peered around the room. His posture was that of a snake, waiting for vibrations. From the shadows in the corner opposite mine, the slightest whimper.

Geoff flew across the room and over the bed faster than my eyes could track the movement. If there was any doubt the two men were something like human, it ended there. He thrashed at something I couldn't see, making short, sharp barking sounds in the back of his throat. Chaz laughed, pulled out of the unconscious redhead, and danced a perverse jig across the bedspread toward the commotion.

I didn't see what they did to that whimpering shape in the shadows. I was thankful for that. I could only hear the muted whining, the wet sucking noises, and a few vicious snaps. When the noises stopped, the two men reemerged, both covered in blood from the waist down. I froze completely. I couldn't have twitched a finger if I'd wanted to.

"I'm thinking about remaking *Ghostbusters*," Chaz said, in a voice utterly devoid of tone.

"The blond kid from One Direction wants to get into acting," Geoff replied. "He'd make a killer Egon."

I could only tell there were two voices speaking by the

distance between them. They had become identical in every respect.

Chaz shuffled sleepily to a nightstand, opened a drawer, and withdrew a bag of white powder.

The other door, Kaitlyn. Look. They forgot all about you. Go. Go. Go!

My useless limbs would not respond.

"I was thinking Shia LaBeouf," Chaz said, seizing a small Asian boy by the back of the head and dragging him up onto the bed. He yanked on the kid's hair, tipping his chin back, then upended the bag over his face. The boy coughed and spasmed, but Chaz clamped a hand over his neck and held him fast.

"Thinking Shia LaBeouf for what?" Geoff asked, though there was no inflection to mark it as a question.

"For anything," Chaz said. He bent and snorted powder from the boy's twitching face, his hand still white-knuckling around the kid's throat. "I was just thinking Shia LaBeouf."

Chaz motioned to Geoff, and the portly older man took a deep huff from the thrashing boy's mouth just as he threw one last frantic kick and lay still.

"You cashed this one," Chaz noted.

"I'll get you another," Geoff said.

He reached down and hauled up a thick-hipped girl with a teardrop tattoo on one cheek. He threw her down atop the Asian boy, mashing her face into his. She didn't protest. She didn't blink. She didn't make a sound, even when Geoff entered her from behind and Chaz leapt up on the bed to put his foot on the back of her neck.

The girl was looking right at me the entire time. I could

see her eyes with perfect clarity. There was nothing left in them.

Survival finally won out over fear, and my legs freed themselves. I bolted for the door, stupidly yanking at the handle. I could see it was locked, but it was like panic lived in my fingers now. I willed them to stop scrabbling uselessly at the handle and to just twist the little switch, but they wouldn't. They would only pull and pull and pull.

"She tries to flee," a voice droned behind me, each word punctuated by the slap of skin on skin.

"She thinks there is somewhere to flee to," the other voice answered.

"Does she know we have a role for her."

The slapping increased in tempo.

"Perfect casting. She was born for it."

"Like fuel is born for fire."

"She comes to us freely, as they all do."

The slapping came faster and faster. There was a sound like wet paper tearing. I pried my hands from the handle. Held them out in front of me. Focused on making them still.

"Yet they wonder why they are here."

"They are drawn to this place. They are flawed, weak, and stupid. They are human. Yet through systematic degradation and avarice, they are reduced. Cleared of pretension."

"And here, at last and for the first time, they are rendered useful."

"They walk proudly into this place. They speak of it in hushed and optimistic tones. They dream all their lives of the refinery."

"And still wonder why we burn them when they arrive."

There was a sucking pop and the sound of liquid splashing to the floor.

I set my fingers around the lock and twisted. I pulled the door inward toward me, trying not to think that, as I did so, I was taking a step backward toward the two men and whatever they were doing to whatever was left of that girl.

I was out. I was gone.

And then, to my own horror, I found myself turning around. I was operating purely on muscle memory, and muscle memory was turning to politely close the door behind me. I caught a glimpse of something like a man, bent grotesquely out of shape. He crouched with his knees to either side of his head like a grasshopper. A pile of gore lay in front of him. He was still thrusting. My eyes flicked away before they had a chance to take in any more details.

And they landed on a familiar image.

A young, muscled Latino man smiling up at the camera, waist-deep in crystal blue water. The words J. C. SABLE across the top in bright pink letters.

Marco wasn't kidding when I first met him. He really did have the same poster above his bed.

SEVENTEEN

We followed Gus's van for a full hour before it finally pulled up in front of an unsigned building on the East Side. Along the way, I drove us into an open manhole, a mailbox, an ice cream truck, and a Puerto Rican.

Didn't catch his name.

I busted my lip, and Jezza did a full headstand on the street that fucked up his pompadour pretty bad, but Wash came out mostly unscathed. Well, shit, I don't know that: The Puerto Rican guy called him a homo as we sped off. Maybe it hurt his feelings.

"I believe the best strategy is no strategy: I will hit that guy in the face," Wash said, pointing to a fucking monument of a man hovering like an overprotective boyfriend around the front door of the building.

A bouncer, a hopping club booming live music nine o'clock at night in Manhattan, and no line? These bastards really didn't understand people.

Jezza and I waited for Wash to continue his thought, but I guess that was it.

"I don't think that's gonna work, mate," Jezza said. "Bloke's got ten stone on you, easy."

"Maybe we can cut down through the sewers," I said. "There's got to be, like, an entryway up into that building from below."

"Why?" Jezza laughed. "Why would there be an entrance from the sewer into there?"

"Well, I don't fucking know; there always is on the TV."

"Is there an entrance up from the sewer into your apartment? It's not a bloody sidewalk. You know what's in the sewer?"

"Poop," Wash offered.

"He's right," Jezza confirmed.

"What else do they do in situations like this, on the television?" Wash asked.

"Distraction?"

"Yes." I punched Jezza in the shoulder by way of congratulations. "We need a distraction. I think I've got enough fluid left in my lighter to soak Jezza's shirt, then we can light him up, and while they're over there stomping him out, me and Wash will—"

"Hold on, now!" Jezza cried, "I see a great big bollocking problem with this plan."

"Shit." I snapped my fingers. "He's right. Gus still has my lighter."

"That wasn't the probl—"

"My first plan still seems to be our only reasonable course of action," Wash cut in. "I shall hit that man in the face."

Jezza and I tried to think, but we weren't great at it.

"Okay," I conceded, "you coldcock the guy, and we'll try to jump him from behind while he's beating the holy shit out of you."

Wash nodded somberly, then stood and walked off to punch a man the size of a car straight in the head. I took a breath. Jezza muttered a long stream of worried profanities. We reluctantly followed.

"Name?" the man asked Wash, when it became apparent he was heading toward the door.

"This is my name," Wash said, and heaved the most gorgeous uppercut I have ever seen. He sprinted a few steps, dropped all the way to the pavement, then came bursting up like an industrial spring. It was perfect. It was like ballet. It didn't do a goddamned thing.

Well, that's not strictly true. I'm pretty sure it broke some of Wash's knuckles.

The bouncer didn't so much as blink. Wash was dancing around, holding his busted hand to his chest and waiting for a beatdown. The man simply checked his notepad.

"You're not on the list," he told Wash, without a hint of malice.

That ham hock of a head swiveled to acknowledge Jezza and me.

"Name?" he asked us.

Jezza whimpered something I couldn't make out.

"Carey," I answered, too stunned to do anything but exactly what the human cliff told me.

The bouncer checked his notepad. Every movement was like a statue coming to life. You just didn't think something that big could be mobile. It defied nature.

"Here you are," he said, crossing a line off on his little pad. "Head on in."

He swung the heavy steel door inward, and a furious clash of mistuned guitars washed out. Still in obedience mode, I headed into the club without another word. Wash followed, eyeballing the hulk warily. Jezza didn't move. I had to go back out and physically drag him in with us. His eyes were locked solidly on his feet until he was sure the door was shut behind us and the bouncer was out of sight. Then he looked up—and probably wished he hadn't.

We wouldn't have noticed, a week ago. We wouldn't have spotted anything wrong with the scene in front of us: just a bunch of mediocre punks in an anonymous dive bar with a six-inch stage in one corner. Some amateur band failing to produce music while everybody ignored them in favor of building a foundation for a nice drunk. But I knew, by the silence behind me, that Wash and Jezza saw it, too. The crowd's clothes were torn and shabby, but it was all done in this careful, uniform way. You could see repeating patterns if you looked hard enough: three little tears at the right hip, one big rip under the left armpit. Their stained Chucks were suitably filthy, but the seams were still crisp, like new. These weren't shoes that had been stomped on a thousand times in crowded venues, thrashed through puddles and puked on after the last shot of the night. They'd barely been used. The whole bar had bought their footwear within the last month, and torn their clothes according to some preestablished punk-rock template. I scanned their faces and came up blank. I couldn't tell you what a single one looked like, even if I focused. Even knowing the trick, I just couldn't get through it. There were too many of them together. It was like trying to recognize one grain of sand out of a beach full of them.

There was one distinguishable face in the crowd. It stood out from the anonymity like a lighthouse in the sea. Flat and impassive. Viking cheekbones. Blank blue eyes. Long unwashed hair. It turned its thousand-yard stare vaguely in our direction and beckoned with one hand.

Gus wanted us to join him at his private table.

"We have to get out of here," Jezza said, backing away.

"Bullshit." I grabbed his sleeve and hauled him over to me. "We're here for Thing 1, remember? Fuck, maybe they even have Randall. If it was you they had, we wouldn't just cut and run."

"Yes, you bloody would!"

"All right," I conceded, "probably, yeah. But they don't have you. They have her, and him, and so we're not going any-where. Besides, you think that fucking Grizzly Bear out there is just gonna let you walk? He's gonna use you to pick meat out of his teeth."

"I'll take my chances! You might have a stiff willy over that blue-haired bird, but me and Wash are . . ."

Jezza scanned the room frantically. His eyes went wide. I turned to look for what had gotten him so riled up, and saw Wash shoving his way right through the press of Unnotice-ables. He was making a beeline toward Gus. I dropped Jezza and ran.

Like hell I'm getting showed up by fucking Wash.

I raced into the crowd, shoving through an indistinguish-able block of leering faces. Every goddamned one of them had some snide comment for me:

"Nice hair," one said. "Did it come with the punk-rock starter kit?"

"Jesus, but you got a face like a bulldog's ass," another said.

"Oh, hey, it's Carey! Thank God you got here. I was won-dering who was going to fuck my ugly friend tonight."

And on and on. Some just spat on me. One—a girl, I think—reached out and grabbed my dick and twisted pain-fully. I was lost. Sweating. All turned around. I couldn't see beyond the blur of faces to get my bearings, and I couldn't even pick out their features to tell them apart.

I was lost in a forest of assholes.

Then the curtain of bodies parted. It happened so abruptly that I caught my foot on the step up to Gus's booth and went sprawling under the table. I rolled with the forward momentum, crawled over his feet, and slid up onto the leather bench like I'd meant to do the whole thing.

"What are we drinking?" I asked him, throwing an arm across the seat beside me.

He almost registered surprise.

"I am going to kill you," Wash said to Gus, appearing out of the crowd a few inches from the table.

"Your friend said that already, man. You guys gotta get a new catchphrase."

Gus smiled lazily and motioned for Wash to sit.

He did.

I don't know why. If the bastard had just burned my woman from the inside out, I like to think I'd at least turn down his hospitality. Maybe Wash had a plan, or maybe he was hoping I had one, or maybe he didn't want to risk pissing off the Unnoticeables this early in the game. Or maybe Wash was just dumb as a brick.

Jezza staggered over last, obviously more scared of facing the bouncer alone than pushing through a crowd of monsters with some backup. He looked back and forth between Gus, Wash, and me like a rabbit faced with a hawk, a snake, and a stewpot. He finally decided on a path of least fuckedness and motioned for Wash to shove over.

For a few seconds, it all felt weirdly normal. Me, Wash, and Jezza crammed into a smelly booth in the corner of a ratty club, marveling at the audacity of some asshole or another. Just a Saturday night. But if you looked out of the corner of your eye, you could see the entire bar was watching us intently, trying to look like they weren't. Gus slid his dopehead smile back in its holster. His face went blank and his voice lost all humanity.

"Why do you follow, even when you know you are going to die?"

After ten seconds of awkward silence, I realized he was waiting for a response.

"You have our friend," I said.

"I am going to kill you," Wash said.

"We was bored," Jezza said.

"It is interesting. You possess survival instincts. You practice risk aversion. You nurture phobias and cultivate fears, trying to stay alive. Survival is so important to human beings that entire cultures"—Gus gestured around at the room full of pseudopunks—"crop up, basing their identities solely on the bucking of traditional survivorship practices. And here you are. You are sitting with a predator. You are in a room full of predators. You realize you are prey. You know that, should we choose, we could tear you apart in an instant. You could not realistically expect to rescue your friend. Why did you come? Because you were expected to. Because you were asked."

Another long silence. A teacher, patiently waiting for somebody in class to raise a hand.

"Well, maybe we just ain't that smart," I answered.

Gus's face crinkled into a smile. He clapped his hands.

"You got balls, man. I love the balls on this guy!" he yelled to nobody in particular. "So all right, then. Let me tell you what happens next—"

Wash cut him off. Cut off the artery in his neck. Cut off part of his ear too.

With one fluid motion, Wash reached out, snatched Gus's drink up, cracked it on the table, and then went digging around in his neck like he was looking for prizes. Gus coughed and gurgled. He tried to make words, but only blood came out. After he'd sawed halfway through the neck bones and got the glass stuck in Gus's spine, Wash sat back down.

"Bloody fuckin' . . . shitting . . . hell!" Jezza sputtered.

I clapped Wash on the shoulder.

"Well done," I said.

"No! Not well done at all!" Jezza screeched. "We're bloody trapped! They're going to shred us to bits!"

Wash scanned the crowd impassively.

"I think that they would have already done that," he observed, "if they were going to do that."

"I . . . I think Wash just said something smart," I said.

Jezza started to protest, but I pointed behind him. He turned slowly, expecting a blow to come crashing down on him at any second. The whole bar had frozen in place. Still life with gutter trash. Every single face was pointed our way. All eyes watching, and not a sound. Not even from the band, who I noticed now was just as unnoticeable. They stood, holding their instruments slack, heads cocked like inquisitive puppies. Just waiting.

"It is good that you did that," a flat voice said from across the table.

We all jumped. Don't ever tell anybody, but I even peed a little.

Gus was holding the shard of glass that had been inside of his neck a moment ago up to the light. He regarded it with distracted interest, like a scientist watching moths mate. He dropped the glass to the floor, and it shattered. I could see inside of his neck. I could see the meat latching onto itself. Knitting back together.

"Now," Gus grinned, "we can get this party started."

Wash said: "Oh."

I said: "Fuck me."

Jezza said: "Kerble."

No idea what that meant. I expect his brain just up and broke for a second.

Gus reached across the table. He moved like cold molasses, his expression frozen in calculated idiocy. He grabbed Wash by the collar and slammed his face down into the table so hard it nearly flipped over. I hopped to my feet, standing on the bench, and planted a sneaker in Gus's face. It was like kicking a brick wall. He didn't move an inch, but I fell backward from the force of it, right onto Jezza's face.

Gus grabbed for Wash again, who was still too stunned to move. He just blinked at me, an expression more of curiosity than pain, like he was just really intrigued by the mystery of his own bashed-in head. I huddled up against Jezza, put both feet on Wash's side, and shoved him out of the booth before Gus could get a grip on him. I rolled myself under the table right after, and hit the beer-soaked concrete with both elbows. It sent lightning bolts of pain up the long bones in my arms.

"What do I do? What do I do?!" Jezza screeched from somewhere above. His voice cracked and wobbled.

"Run, dipshit."

I army-crawled backward from beneath the booth. Gus wasn't concerned about Wash or me anymore: Now he was focused on Jezza, who was slapping at Gus's face rapidly, like he could dog-paddle through the guy's head. I put my hands beneath the lip of the table and heaved. It tipped up between the two of them, giving me just enough of a window to grab Jezza by the sleeve and yank him into the crowd with me. I couldn't see Wash. I hoped he was making his way back to the door and not just wandering around somewhere in a concussed daze. If he could just keep his bearings, he should be okay. The pseudopunks all seemed to be on pause. They weren't even looking at us, just staring back at Gus's booth, immobile. Waiting for something. We'd gotten maybe twenty feet, when Gus said:

"Who turned off the fucking music, man?"

And the band launched into the worst version of "30 Seconds over Tokyo" I have ever heard.

Gus laughed, wild and braying.

"You can't dance without music!"

The Unnoticeables surged into life. The one nearest me put his entire hand into my mouth and started to yank on my tongue. I bit down hard and the hand withdrew. A solid kick to my shin came next, then a punch in the guts. I doubled over, and somebody behind me took the opportunity to force their pointed fingers halfway up my ass, straight through my jeans. I yelped like a fifties housewife spotting a mouse, and instinctively flailed my legs. I connected with something fleshy, and the pressure eased. I straightened up and threw a wild haymaker. Another connection. I couldn't even distinguish the faces to aim for a specific one. It was like fist-fighting a fogbank. I dished out elbows, knees, and wild headbutts in every direction. I was so intent on beating the shit out of everything in the world that it took me a few minutes to realize I wasn't the only one fighting. I assumed the Unnoticeables were trying to kill me, Wash, and Jezza—but they weren't targeting us. They were just fighting.

They tore at each other's skin with their nails, bit off ears, gouged at crotches. The ones that had attacked me just happened to be close enough to do it. I dropped below the riot's line of sight and crawled on my hands and knees.

I heard an oddly pitched moan beside me and looked over right into a half-naked girl's face. She was maybe six inches away from me and being fucked from behind by another Unnoticeable. The girl opened her eyes, saw me, and tried to bite for my nose. But her partner wouldn't release the death grip on her hips, even though two more Unnoticeables were busy kicking his face in. The girl snapped at me over and over again like a dog on a leash. I backed away and looked for an exit point, only to find the scene repeating: The Unnoticeables were fighting and screwing in equal measure, some at the same time. I spotted Jezza trying to crawl around two men giving each other the most violent hand jobs in history. He caught my eye and desperately crawled in my direction, Wash following after him.

I couldn't hear a thing over the flesh slapping, the moaning, and the furious screaming—not to mention the unfocused guitars and sloppy drumming of this bullshit house band completely butchering Rocket from the Tombs. So I just pointed to where I thought the door was, and shuffled off in that direction. It was slow going. The floors were slick with blood, gore, and other fluids I didn't want to think about. And though most of the Unnoticeables were too busy tearing each other apart to bother with us, sometimes one would get knocked down, spot us, and come slithering over with murder in its eyes.

After busting a few dozen noses and gouging as many eyes, we finally made the door. I wriggled up against the wall and hauled it open, shoving against the press of bodies. I held it there while Wash crawled over me and outside. I motioned for Jezza to follow, but he only got one arm out before he started screaming.

Something was dragging him backward. He clutched at my jacket, but it was too wet with blood and sweat to get purchase. I grabbed for his hands, but I was just too fucking slow. Jezza disappeared in a forest of legs. I tried to go after him, but whenever I moved my arm, the door just started slamming shut on me. I couldn't get the leverage to haul myself all the way back inside.

"What is it?" Wash yelled.

"They got Jezza. Help me get—"

Something big, pale, and fleshy covered my entire face and started to squeeze.

What the fuck? Did they have a giant squid at this punk-rock club?

I tried to pry it off of my face, and my fingers wrapped around a thick stalk at its base.

An arm. A hand.

The fucking bouncer.

His grip, impossibly, tightened. And then it started to twist. I was hauled up in the air and hurled to one side. He was dragging me somewhere.

Outside. He was dragging me outside.

I tried to scream, but the man's flesh was sealed around my face like a plastic bag. I tried to kick, but it only seemed to make the bastard mad. I tried to bite but couldn't get my teeth around his massive palm. I was desperate. I needed free of this suffocating, crushing darkness. I did the only thing left to me. I poked my tongue between my lips and I licked. I hoped the bouncer would be surprised enough to drop me. Or maybe just grossed out enough to recoil in disgust. But mostly, I hoped I wasn't going to die licking another man's sweaty palm.

Air.

I hit the ground butt-first, and pain shot up through my tailbone, but it didn't matter. Oxygen was burning through my lungs like a beautiful wildfire. When the stars cleared from my vision, I saw that my clever tongue-based defense had not, in fact, freed me. I owed my life to a dented metal trash can and Wash, who was repeatedly and furiously bashing the bouncer's face into tapioca with it.

As soon as I could stand, I ran to the door and threw my weight against it. It gave an inch, then slammed shut. I tried again and it didn't budge in the slightest. Same for the next attempt. And the next. And the next. I had to get in there. I had to, because I could hear Jezza inside. I could hear him screaming.

And then I couldn't hear him at all anymore.

I ended up on the ground somehow. I guess Wash must have tackled me at some point and dragged me away from the club. We were sitting in a parking lot across the street. I was propped up against Daisy. My shoulder throbbed. I was having trouble moving my arm. Wash was saying something to me, but I couldn't make it out. His lips smacked around stupidly, and dumb noises poured out of him.

Then he hit me. Twice. And he started to make sense again.

"The sewer," Wash said. "Remember? We can try the sewer."

EIGHTEEN

I stood with one hand on the doorknob. Shut down. My brain refused to latch on to the images I had just seen. It did not process the limbs bent at broken angles. The viscera that used to be a girl with a teardrop tattoo. The smell of blood and cum and cocaine in the air. My mind went looking for logical explanations:

This is Punk'd. *This is* Candid Camera. *This is some kind of elaborate, high-budget prank somebody is pulling on me. I'm Michael Douglas in* The Game. *Somebody is* The Game*-ing me.*

Jackie. Of course!

She's been busy lately. Kept talking about her spot in that improv troupe. I bet that was a cover story. I bet she got a part on one of those prank shows and convinced them to come after me. Right now she's . . .

Behind me, there was a gentle commotion. Cloth rustling, glass clinking, muffled footfalls.

I turned slowly, thinking that if I just moved cautiously enough, I could slip away unnoticed. Maybe these freaks worked like the T. rex in *Jurassic Park*? I don't know. I was

probably in shock. Certainly not in a place for sound strate-
gizing, so I just continued with my ill-advised orbit, keeping my neck stiff and my eyes straight ahead. The plain white
wood of the bedroom door slid out of view, replaced by some
tasteful slate-gray walls. Then a framed photo of Marco shaking hands with his stunt double.

*God, you can really see the difference there, side by side. Only
one has life in his eyes.*

Another door, closed—*is the same thing happening in all
these rooms?*—and finally the hallway. There was a woman
standing about ten feet away to my left, regarding me with
unsettling enthusiasm, a big red-carpet smile hot-glued to
her face. A man in a paisley vest stood beside her. Across from
them, a chubby guy with thick horn-rim glasses. A dude with
a thin, ironic mustache. A girl with bright purple collagen
lips. There were dozens of them, lining either side of the hall.
They were all pushed up against the walls, intentionally leaving a space for me to walk . . . right between them.

Red Carpet raised her glass, by way of a toast. One by one,
the others joined her.

*There were only two of the bastards in the room behind me, I
could—*

No. I knew I would never go back into that room. I couldn't
confirm those half-seen details in my mind. Not if I wanted
to stay sane. Forward was my only option.

I took a step, trying not to meet the countless eyes tracking my every movement. I passed within an inch of Red Carpet. She was perfectly, unnaturally still. Horn-Rim Glasses
was like a fat wax figurine of Buddy Holly. Paisley Vest was
frozen, too. Twenty feet into the procession, I realized what
was so unnerving about it: They weren't just still. Their hands
were not wavering as they held their glasses mockingly in

the air. Their eyes did not blink. Their chests did not rise and fall.

They weren't breathing.

I concentrated on making my legs move. Maybe if I didn't acknowledge the situation, it would stop existing. Willful denial isn't exactly a brilliant defense mechanism, I know, but—

I saw a familiar face, and I couldn't help it. I locked eyes with the stunt choreographer. The one I had worked with, briefly, in—what was the name of that movie? *Double Vision? Double Indemnity?*

The second I caught his gaze, the choreographer gave me an exaggerated wink, then reached over and tore a small piece of my sleeve away. I wanted to flinch, but it was over too fast. He moved in the space between blinks. I felt a brief tug on my opposite side and saw a patch from the knee of my pants missing. A thick-faced guy smiled at me, holding up a swatch of black fabric. He looked familiar.

He was on that teen show that was big a few years ago. Cherry Lane?

Cherry Lane twitched. When he moved it was like reality skipped frames: His neck bent ninety degrees and then snapped back in an instant. He seemed to lose control of half of his face. One eyeball rolled and spasmed. The right side of his mouth gnashed its teeth, while the other stayed fixed in a friendly, approachable smile. I jumped and recoiled but didn't make it far. Somebody was behind me. I felt a sharp pinch on my ass, and then another strip of fabric was gone. I turned around to find a thin girl with spiky pink hair grinning at me. She held a scrap of torn cloth between her fingers. She waggled it at me playfully, then put it in her mouth and swallowed it.

Somebody laughed, and then hands were all over me. They

swarmed like piranha; nipping, tearing, pinching, and scratching. Minor wounds. Little pains that were over before they started. I was becoming naked by inches. I struck out with my elbow and caught a girl that I recognized from daytime TV squarely in the boob. She didn't register the blow. I planted a foot in the groin of an aging hipster, still dressed like he was in a grunge band. No response. I accidentally stabbed a finger through a beautiful Asian woman's eyeball, just trying to shove her away. It sunk in a full inch, loosing a gush of ocular fluid. She hungrily devoured the strap of my sports bra while the discharge ran down her cheek.

I fled.

And to my surprise, they let me. I bolted down the rest of the hallway and encountered no resistance. The crowd parted as I came near, still snatching and clutching, taking little pieces of me as I passed.

I tripped and fell out of the claustrophobic hall into the huge, relatively empty living room. I spun around to kick at the press of people I assumed would be chasing me, but they seemed to have lost interest. Dozens of Empty Ones were filing out of the corridor, not even glancing in my direction as they took their places around the perimeter of the room. I used the moment to take stock, and found myself left with half a pant leg, something like a ragged halter top, and no shoes. I was bleeding from a hundred tiny cuts. Angry red welts were already forming on my exposed skin.

"Hey, *chica!*" a voice bubbled behind me.

Marco was standing atop a red leather ottoman. He was no longer naked, but dressed impeccably in one of those suits that always remind me of Miami. Sharp, thin lines. Dark jacket. Bright colored silk shirt, two buttons open at the chest.

He was pointing his sitcom-sex-symbol smile at me, holding a glass of champagne above his head.

"Glad you could make it to the fiesta! *Fiesta* means 'party' in *español*!" he shouted.

There was an answering groan from his feet. A ragged, bloody scarecrow was curled up on the floor beneath him. It was roughly in the shape of Carey.

"I'm done with this!" I shouted, trying to keep my voice from cracking. "I'm not playing anymore. Just give me Jackie and let us leave, or I'll . . ."

Call the cops? Kick your ass? Kill myself? Write a scathing review of your newest film on my blog? What possible threat could I make?

"I'll . . ." I had nothing. "Do fuck-all, I suppose."

"Ha-ha! There it is! That's the spirit! I think she's finally ready! *Amigos y amigas*: We have broken the candidate!" Marco clapped, and the whole room joined in.

Raucous, enthusiastic applause. I guess I'd just won the coveted Seriously Fucked Award.

"You are ready," he repeated, his voice dropping all pretense of humanity. It was like listening to the wind form words.

He beckoned me forward, and I flipped him off before I realized I was doing it.

"No." Marco shook his head, then leapt off the ottoman and landed squarely on Carey's back. He barked and twisted in agony. "That is going backward. It is time to move forward. Come with me willingly, or we will stomp on your friend until his teeth shatter in his skull."

I tried to come up with a response but could only make a sound like a squeaky hinge.

Marco lifted one finger and pointed it toward the door.

I stood and obeyed. As I walked, the Empty Ones broke

off from their positions around the room and fell into step behind me. I tried not to look back.

Marco's phallic silver Mercedes was idling in the driveway with its doors open. I moved to the passenger side and got in. Somebody slammed the door behind me, nearly catching my fingers.

Looking out of the windshield toward the house, I saw something crawl onto the deck and roll off the edge into the bushes below.

A few seconds later, Marco eased into the driver's seat, closed the door, thumbed the ignition, and hit a button on the console. The theme from *Homeroom* blared out of the speakers.

> *Rolled out of bed*
> *Feeling half dead*
> *Can't seem to catch a break today*
> *Just got to school*
> *Tryin' to play it cool*
> *But you can't think of nothin' to say*

Marco fixed me with his plastic grin, and said: "This is my favorite song!"

He stomped on the pedal and we fishtailed out of the driveway. In the rearview mirror, a single weak headlight flickered into life. The Mercedes was sealed up so tightly, I almost missed the sound—like a squirrel caught in a hive of angry hornets—of Daisy's engine turning over.

We drove for hours, past night and into early morning.

Every time I turned my head, I found Marco staring at me.

His face was aimed forward, pantomiming intense focus and attention to the road ahead, but his eyes were shifted completely sideways in his skull, wide and unblinking, locked onto my every movement.

I tried not to turn my head much.

At first, I made up my mind to ditch out of the car at the earliest opportunity. I have a very select, specialized set of skills that practically never come in handy in real life. I can't fix a toilet or a computer. I can't build a chair. I cannot, for the life of me, bake a decent cake. But if you need somebody to fall down a set of stairs without getting hurt, or roll out of a moving car at fifty miles an hour—shoot me a text. I'm your girl.

I had my fingers wrapped around the door handle and my left foot planted, preparing to spin myself out and away from the wheels, when I remembered the first night I met Marco. He had done something to his car. Modified it with that rapist kit that prevented my door opening from the inside. I thought about clocking him. I thought about grabbing the wheel and yanking it, hoping to escape in the chaos of the wreckage. But I kept flashing back to Marco's head in my bathroom—dangling from a shattered neck and still smiling.

I don't get hurt.

That's what he told me. Even if I could wreck the car, I'd probably only hurt myself. I thought about subtly trying to contact the authorities—*you can text 911, right?*—but I'd left my phone back at my apartment in my haste to go after Marco. I thought about the Cobra I'd stashed in my waistband, but I guess one of the Empty Ones took it as a trophy back in the hallway. And even if they hadn't, it seemed laughable now. *Did this bitch just bring a stick to a monster fight?* I thought about waving at passing cars, in case they could see me. I thought about tapping out rapid Morse code on the window in case there was a helpful, keen-eared sailor standing by the side of the highway. I had wracked my brain for the first ten minutes of the drive, and every plan came back with a big fat red REJECTED stamp on it. And then I just tried to stop thinking. When I did, I thought about Carey:

Was that him, rolling off the deck? Was that him, starting up his bike to come after us? Or was that one of the Empty Ones, just getting the motorcycle off the street so nobody would come around asking questions? I tried to spot the single flickering light of Daisy's headlight in the rearview mirror, but I couldn't make it out. Was Carey too far back? Did the headlight give out? Was he even still there, or did he take off to call the cops? Would they even help? Was I going to die tonight? What difference did it make? What could I do about it?

It happened or it didn't.

Tepid apathy settled over me. Whatever came next, it was fate's problem.

I spent an indeterminate amount of time watching highway reflectors shoot past in a blinking line. I could see the clouds on the distant horizon starting to fade from black to blue. Sunrise soon. Probably my last, and I wouldn't even get to see it.

Eventually, we slowed and pulled up to the gate of a massive complex situated at the base of some looming black mountains. Marco gestured at the guardhouse, and the blockade slid away of its own accord. As we passed, I noticed that the fences bulged out oddly: They seemed to grow wider and flatten out toward the top. I didn't understand, until Marco's Mercedes eased into the compound, and his headlights revealed the truth: They weren't flat at all; the tip of each side of the fence was lined with thick, shining, six-inch-long steel blades running parallel to the ground. I'd never seen anything like it. It wasn't just defensive. It was sadistic.

After the vicious fence, I expected to be driven through a prison. Or maybe some great industrial complex populated by vast and incomprehensible machines chugging away with sinister purpose. Instead, I got a golf resort. Rolling hills with immaculately trimmed grass. Meticulously raked gravel paths. Tennis courts. A swimming pool.

Either the heart of evil wore a cardigan tied about its neck, or Marco had accidentally taken me to a Sandals by mistake.

We pulled up in front of a small brightly lit chapel with an old-fashioned stone facade. Its steeple sported a set of interlocking gears and a blinding, brilliant searchlight that raked the sky without pause. Marco came around to my door and held it open.

Such a gentleman.

I kicked him in the knee and went to use my momentum to shove past him, but he barely staggered from the blow. He had his hands on me before I even got to my feet. He swung me down hard and bashed my forehead into the dash. My vision swam and nausea seized my stomach.

Somebody was pushing me, saying something, and I could only nod and make foggy attempts at words.

By the time I could see straight, we were already inside the chapel. There hadn't been any others cars parked where I could see them as we pulled up, but the place was packed. Standing room only. I didn't recognize any of the faces, but I could tell by the white teeth and complete absence of

wrinkles that these were all industry folks. And by the un-
seeing gaze and preternatural stillness, I knew they were all
Empty Ones.

All eyes on me. Through me. Star of the show again.

But I had a supporting cast this time. Two lines of beaten,
bloodied, and broken girls stood to either side of a low dais.
A gargantuan machine dominated the platform. I couldn't
even guess at its purpose. It just looked like a thousand mean-
inglessly interlocking gears, each plated in gold and studded
with jewels. There was no drive that I could see. No point
where the gears met and worked some kind of device to
achieve a result. I wasn't even sure if it functioned. It might
have been just decorative. But something about the huge silver lever jutting out of the floor next to the burnished-steel
pulpit indicated otherwise.

Distant shuffling. A *thunk*. An unseen door opened and
closed, and a chubby middle-aged man with thinning hair
and the sleazy smirk of a back-road car salesman made his
way out from behind the gears and settled in behind the
pulpit.

The crowd broke into measured applause. They weren't
clapping in sync, but they all applauded with the same cadence: three short claps, pause, one more clap, long pause.
Repeat. They stopped simultaneously at some unseen cue
and took their seats. All except Marco, who was still clutching my arm like a clingy father on his daughter's wedding
day. We stood in the center of the aisle, waiting, while the
balding man shuffled some papers.

"How you doing tonight, darlin'?" he asked me.

"A bit kidnapped, sir," I answered.

He laughed. Three short bursts, pause, one more, long
pause. Repeat.

"Well, we'll try to make this as quick as can be. Don't want to cause you any more inconvenience." He shot me a look that I guessed was supposed to be paternal but came off perverse and malevolent.

Someone in the line of girls to my left let out a soft whimper. One of the Empty Ones leapt from her front-row pew and wrapped her hands around the offender's neck. A series of snaps, like knuckles cracking. She dragged the dead girl away by the hair, and casually tossed her into a bin against the far wall. It was over in seconds. The woman took her seat, and nodded for the balding man to continue.

"Is she ready?" he asked. There were no cues to direct the question. He had lapsed into the non-state of the Empty Ones.

Marco answered: "Yes. She struggled, was beaten, and came willingly. There is still fight in her, but it is habitual."

"I take it we have incentive."

"She's here," another flat, female voice answered.

A young, dark-skinned woman with an impeccable pompadour emerged from behind the gears. A second later, she dragged another girl into view. I almost didn't recognize her. She was so skinny, pale, and lifeless. I didn't understand. It had only been a few days. She looked like a photo from a refugee camp.

"Jackie!" I cried, and tried to shake loose from Marco.

His fingers clamped down onto my arm so viciously that I went limp from the pain. My skin turned bright purple where it bulged out between his fingers. It looked like it was about to explode.

"Now, you're sure she's ready?" the balding man asked, feigning human impatience.

"The fight is reflex," Marco answered. "We are ready for the birth."

"Well, hell, then—let's get this hootenanny started!" The balding man slapped the podium and shot that sleazy smile at the gathered audience.

Three claps. Pause. One clap. Long pause. Repeat.

The car salesman wrapped his stubby little sausage fingers around the handle of the polished silver lever and gave it a pull. The gears turned, slowly at first, but quickly picked up speed. The jewels on them blurred together as the revolutions increased. The gears became a series of shining, interlocking circles.

I thought the first one was an accident. I thought she just fell.

But then they fed the second girl into the whirling gears. And the third. They made a sound like a lawnmower hitting a rock, then a fine mist of aerosolized blood filled the air. Two of the girls screamed, and the Empty Ones were on them in a blink: snapping their necks, dragging them to the side, and tossing them into the bin like you'd heft a particularly disagreeable garbage bag. But those were the only cries. The other girls had lost something inside. They stepped up to the gears, if not willingly, then with a conspicuous lack of resistance. I was looking around. Looking for somebody to stop it, to protest, or at least show some amount of surprise.

It was a stupid impulse.

And I saw her there. The pompadoured woman had led Jackie to the very end of one of the lines and just let her go. The girl at the front of Jackie's queue bent at the waist, reached out slowly, and put her hand into the space where two spinning gears met. It took her instantly, jerking her into the machine and pulverizing her into a bloody fog. When it was over, Jackie dutifully stepped forward one place in line.

"Stop. God damn it! Stop!" I pulled at Marco, trying to get his attention.

His face contorted and he beamed his *Homeroom* smile down at me.

"What's up, *chica?*"

"Please, I don't understand what's happening but—"

"Ha-ha." He snapped his fingers and shot me with a pretend pistol. "You failed high school biology or something? It was tough, right? I had to get that dweeb Skeet to do my homework for me, but Principal Belmoore found out and—"

"Th-that was on your show," I said.

All expression drained from his face.

"This is necessary. It is to prepare."

"Prepare for what?"

"For the birth. The division. The moment when the nucleus divides from one into two. You are here for a great purpose. The greatest purpose: With your help, a Tool of the Mechanic will be forged today."

"I don't understand. I don't understand what this is, but please—I will do whatever you want if you just let Jackie go. Don't let her walk into that thing. Please. Anything. Please."

"That attitude is good. That is where you should be. Your friend is the incentive. She is here to ensure you stay in alignment. If all goes well, perhaps we will not need her to lubricate the gears."

He flashed me the J. C. Sable grin.

"I mean, we're not monsters," he finished, laughing.

The machine picked up speed. The noise increased in pitch, like the machine was shifting gears. Then it shifted again. And again. *Wait—that's not—*

Daisy smashed through the old wooden doors of the chapel like a battering ram. Shrapnel exploded outward as her roaring engine revved even higher, spinning the rear wheel more freely now that she was off the ground. Time froze, and I saw Carey in a snapshot. His face was a mesh of blood and bruises. Two of his front teeth were broken. He looked to be missing a piece of an ear. And he was sporting the widest, most earnest grin I have ever seen. He looked like he'd just learned to fly. He knew what this moment was. He was a white knight. An action hero, here to rescue the damsel.

And then the snapshot was over.

Daisy's front wheel caught the edge of the closest pew, knocked the front end sideways, and sent Carey skipping down the aisle toward us. He landed on his ass and managed to shoot me a quick thumbs-up, right before the tumbling motorcycle caught him in the back of the head and knocked him unconscious.

My savior.

The Empty Ones barely glanced at him. As soon as it became apparent Carey wouldn't be getting up again, they turned their attention back to the machine. In the line opposite Jackie, a white girl with long dreadlocks put a foot into the gears—and was gone. In Jackie's line, a stunning young brunette with high cheekbones and electric green eyes opted to go facefirst. Jackie was only two spots back now.

Then one.

Then next.

NINETEEN

Do you have any idea how heavy a manhole cover is?

Me and Wash sure as hell didn't.

"One," I said, after we'd looped our fingers through the holes.

"Two," I said, as we set our feet.

"Three," I said, and we simultaneously threw our backs out.

The cover didn't budge.

After I finished flipping off the smug, impassive slab of iron, I limped over to where we had dumped the bike. I swung Daisy's kickstand down, put her in neutral, stood at the front end, and got a running start toward the side of a building. It took two shots for the stand to break off, leaving me with about ten inches of solid steel terminating in a jagged wad of metal.

"Here," I tossed it to Wash.

"What should I do with this?" he asked, looking around for something to hit.

"Pry the cover up, dimwit."

"Why me?"

"Because you got that retard strength."

He didn't move.

I rolled my eyes and took the metal bar back from him. I wedged it in between the street and the cover and pried until my eyes lost focus. I fell backward and the cover came with me. Wash slid it the rest of the way aside and stared into the black. I joined him.

There's no black like a sewer at night. Not the woods. Not even underwater. You can strain your eyes all you want, no details will pick themselves out of that darkness.

"I pry, you fly," I said to Wash, motioning down into the pool of black so thick you could scoop it up in your hand.

Wash nodded once, curtly, and leapt feetfirst into the hole.

"Jesus fuck!" I screamed after him.

There was a distant thump and some quiet moaning.

"There's a goddamned ladder, Wash!"

More moaning.

I swung my legs over the ledge and scrambled down the ladder. When the last cold rung slipped out of my fingers, I swatted around until I felt something Wash-shaped.

"You all right?" I asked him.

"I believe that I have taken most of the fall on my butt and elbows," Wash answered.

"Can you walk?"

"I think so, yes."

"Let's go, then," I said, and waited for the sound of Wash moving.

Nothing.

"Where are we going?"

"To . . . to the club, man. Come on."

"Yes, I know. But which way is that?"

"It's . . ."

Shit.

The air inside the sewer was stifling. I could feel the dark pressing in all around me, like a tangled sleeping bag. I tried to think how I'd been oriented when I came down, but I couldn't remember. If you pressed me, I probably couldn't have told you which way was down. I knew which way was up: The opening above us shone like the sun, though I knew the street we had just left had been mostly unlit. From one end of the tunnel, I heard a dull and distant rumble. It sounded like garbage trucks perpetually crashing into each other from about two blocks over.

"Hear that?"

"Yes. What is it?"

"I think it's the music from the club. Let's head that way. Here, put your hand on my shoulder."

I reached out in the general direction of Wash's voice and ended up with my palm flat over his face. He replaced it with his hand, and I put it on the shoulder of my jacket, right over the little metal spikes. I took a half step forward, holding Daisy's mangled kickstand in front of me like a torch.

It took us about six years to go ten feet.

"God damn it!" I lashed out with the metal bar and contacted nothing. "We're never gonna get there in time. If fucking Gus hadn't taken my lighter, we could—"

"Do you want a cigarette, right now?" Wash asked, confused.

"No, dipshit. For light."

"Oh," he said, and his hand dropped away from my shoulder. There was a metallic *clack,* and then a fucking meteor flared into life.

"Jesus," I said, shielding my eyes from the blinding flame. "Are you kidding me? Tell me that you're kidding me, Wash."

"I am not kidding you. What would I be kidding you about?"

"You had your lighter all this time, and you didn't think to use it?"

"You did not think to ask for it."

"How was I supposed to know you even had it?"

"You bought it for me last week."

Point, Wash.

"Give."

When my eyes finally adjusted, I had to admit that the cosmic flare I'd seen a second ago was actually a pretty meager flame. It illuminated an area maybe five feet around and wavered perilously from the slightest draft. Still, it may as well have been a lightning strike for all the difference it made. At least now we wouldn't stroll obliviously over a sharp drop or into some gator's mouth.

"You think those stories about the alligators in the sewer are true?" I asked jokingly.

"Absolutely," Wash answered, without a moment's hesitation.

We stopped talking after that.

We followed the rumbling for what felt like miles, watching for an opening into the club, or at least a branching path that might lead to . . . something. But we didn't find anything. Just a long, straight shot of concrete tube, stinking of mold and shit, pitch-black and forever.

Wash's Zippo got too hot to hold about ten minutes ago. I had it wrapped up in my jacket sleeve now, held aloft in front of me like a magic wand to ward off the dark. It couldn't have much fuel left.

"There's no way the club is this far," I finally said, breaking the silence.

No answer.

"Right, Wash?"

Silence.

Wash was gone. Wash was gone . . . and there was still a hand on my shoulder.

I spun about, brandishing the kickstand. I nearly bashed Wash's wide eyes right out of his head. He screamed. I screamed. It was not a dignified moment.

"What the hell, man?"

"What? What did I do?"

"Why didn't you answer me?"

"I did. I nodded."

I briefly considered bludgeoning him and leaving his body here to feed the mutant goldfish. But with a saintly effort, I managed to repress the anger and shove it into the little cubbyhole in my mind where I keep all the things I hate.

I repeated the question: "So you think we passed the club, too?"

"Yes," Wash answered, looking up at the sloping concrete ceiling. "Plus, there's no way it's this deep."

"Deep?"

"Of course. We have been walking downhill for some time now."

"What? How can you tell?"

"The water." Wash pointed at the thin stream of brownish gray trickling into the darkness. "It flows downhill."

"No, that's only . . . Fuck me. You're right. Why the hell didn't you say anyth—"

Flicker. Waver. Black.

The Zippo had run out of fuel.

We both lapsed into hopeless silence.

"I guess we go back," Wash finally said. He sounded dismal.

"I guess so," I agreed, "but at least it should go quick. We know there were no branching paths. No crap in the way to trip over. We can jog it. We'll just go 'til we hit the light from the open manhole. Maybe try the door again. Maybe just light the fucking building on fire and see if we can smoke the bastards out."

"Or we could just bar the doors and burn them."

"What the hell kind of talk is that? Jezza is in there."

"Jezza is dead. You heard him scream and you heard him stop. You saw what they were doing when we left hi—Ow! What was that?"

"That was a fucking kickstand to the knee, asshole. You don't say that. We lost your girl, and that sucks, and I'm sorry. But Matt and Safety Pins got away, and we'll get Thing 1 and Jezza back, too. We don't lose any more tonight. So you don't say he's dead until we see it with our eyes, you understand? You fucking understand, Wash?"

Silence.

"I can't see you nodding." I sighed.

"Yes, I understand," he said. "I am sorry."

"Let's get started," I said.

I reached out and gently pushed against Wash's chest. He turned and began to run. There was no sound but our shoes smacking around in the little stream of sewage.

Splish splash. Splish splash. Splish sp—

We had only made it a hundred feet or so when I grabbed Wash's shirt and pulled him to a stop.

"W—" he started, but I pinched the skin on his back and he fell silent.

We listened to the dark rumble.

Some sort of pumping station?

I kept my hand on Wash's shirt, waiting for . . . what, exactly?

I'm going fucking crazy down here.

I nudged Wash forward again. More splashing. The rhythm was hypnotic. You could pick up forms there, like a song. Our footfalls were even and repetitive: *Splish splash splish splash splish splash splash—*

I tugged on Wash's shirt again, and we both came to a sudden, synchronized stop.

Somewhere in the dark behind us, there was one single, solitary, mistimed *splash.*

It has been walking with us, hiding its footfalls with ours.

Splash.

It took an unconcealed step now. It realized the game was up.

Splish. Splash.

A girl's laugh, low and sweet and sincere.

Splish splash splish—

I raised Daisy's kickstand up in front of me, like that would do fuck-all. I tried to drop low, but there was nowhere to take cover.

Splash splish splash splish sp—

It was running toward us. Picking up speed. I couldn't place the distance with those echoes, but it was close. Louder and louder, faster and faster. I struck out with the bar. Nothing. I did it again, and sliced through more empty air.

Splash. Silence.

That last one sounded like it had come from right in front of me. It was out there somewhere. Waiting just beyond the reach of my pathetic little weapon.

I held my breath. I practically pulled a muscle in my eyelid trying to see something—anything—in that darkness.

"You were almost there." A female voice, thick and coy. Close. So close it was practically on top of us.

I lunged forward and brought the kickstand down hard, on nothing.

Laughter.

"You were almost at the party," the voice sounded in the darkness. *Slightly farther away?* "You can't stop now."

Splashing again. Rapid but fading. It was moving away from us, quickly and unerringly.

"Come see your friends," the voice said, giggling. It was far and faint. Almost inaudible beneath the rumbling. "Come see what we've done to them."

We waited in frozen silence, straining for any hint of movement. It couldn't have been more than a minute. It seemed like hours. I felt more than heard Wash stir behind me.

"You do not have to go, but I am going," he said.

I smiled at him, then remembered he couldn't see it.

"Like I'm gonna let you make me look like a pussy."

"It did not sound like she hit anything or fell down anywhere," Wash prompted. "It might be safe to run."

Yeah, fuck it. Why not?

I broke into a dead sprint. My feet flew, landing flat and sliding in the muck. Only my absurd momentum kept me upright. I laughed a little, if only at the stupidity of it. We were barreling down a dark sewer after an unseen assailant—two blind, aimless missiles firing forward into the void.

I had no idea how long we'd been sprinting through the pitch black tunnel, but my legs had gone numb five minutes ago.

I jumped and scraped my head on the low ceiling. I skipped for, like, maybe a quarter mile, just for some variety. I let out a whoop that echoed forever. I tried out a baseball slide—dropping onto one thigh and coasting for a good ten feet over the slippery mucus that had accumulated across every inch of the sewer floor.

It worked surprisingly well.

You know, sliding may be the single most underrated method of travel—

I bit a very small part of my tongue clean off.

I had forgotten to account for Wash, sprinting along behind me. He clipped the back of my head with his knee and went down in a heap somewhere ahead of me. We took turns swearing at each other and catching our breath for a bit.

"Fuck your mother raw, Wash. Watch where you're going," I said, spitting a few mouthfuls of blood in his general direction.

"Die in an avalanche of shit, please," he replied. "I do not understand why you were on the ground."

"I was sliding, dumbass."

"Oh," he said, then after a long pause: "Did it work?"

"Hell, yes. It's all slick, man! Like a giant waterslide."

"Oh," Wash repeated, then again: "Oh."

"The fuck are you doing, Wash?"

"Oh," he said. "My voice. It sounds odd."

"Maybe it's all the cocks in your mouth distorting the timb—Shit. You're right. Hoo!"

The noise traveled a matter of feet, then disappeared completely. Like something was out there eating the words. I had gotten so used to a tight echo after every sound that the absence of it unnerved me. It took me a minute to catch the meaning: We were no longer in the sewer. We were in someplace more open. Something that felt vast, now that I thought to pay attention to it. I wondered how long ago we'd left the relative safety of the tunnel. How long had we been running through this gargantuan unseen space, full of God-knows-what terrible obstacles? We could have fallen into anything—yawning pits, sharp rocks, vicious mole-men, masturbating hobos—but more worryingly, where the hell were we supposed to go? The tunnel was simple. I understood the tunnel.

She went thataway. Go get 'er.

Now what?

"It sounds like it is everywhere," Wash noted.

He was right. The rumbling wasn't louder, exactly, but it was more *present*. It ground at your ears from every direction equally, like tumbling around inside a giant cement mixer. I swiveled my head around, trying to hear if it was louder from any one particular direction. Something had to be causing it: a processing plant or water pump or some shit. Didn't matter. Whatever it was, it was running, which meant it would probably have some kind of passage or walkway workers used to get to it—maybe even an exit to the surface. No way in hell were we leaving without Thing 1 and Jezza, but maybe it would be smart to grab a rope, a pen and paper, some food, some water, some rollerskates, a flame-thrower, perhaps a couple of small howitzers, and above all, some goddamned motherfucking flash—

Lights!

They were almost invisible. Tiny pinpricks hovering in the distance. I thought they were more misfires, at first—you know how if your eyeballs go without light long enough, they start supplying their own? Those little shimmering pops and dazzles that float around your vision like jellyfish caught in the currents? I'd been seeing that crap for miles. But these lights only danced when I moved my head. They were fixed. They were real.

"Wash," I said, "look."

"Where?"

"Over there," I pointed, and immediately felt dumb. "To my left? Your . . . right? I don't know where you are. Just swing your head around a bunch until you find something to look at."

"Ah, yes. Lights."

I felt around in the dark until my hand landed on Wash's thigh.

This was getting downright erotic.

I helped him up and we stepped cautiously toward the specks. Having gotten some perspective, I could see now that they weren't small, just far away. A half mile off, at least. That couldn't be right. No way a space this big should exist underground.

After an eternity of careful shuffling (something about the wide-open space made sprinting blindly seem like a much worse idea), we reached the lights, though we couldn't see what was making them.

They are . . . below us?

We eased onto our bellies and pushed our heads over the lip of a dirt embankment. A hundred feet away and ten feet down, we saw the source of the lights: six waxy yellow bulbs hanging from a half dozen ancient, corroded streetlamps. They looked like something out of a period drama, all wrought-iron and decorative metal swirls. They were evenly spaced along the length of a low, raised platform. A busted awning covered in graffiti and weathered posters creaked above it. Below it, a narrow path ran along one side, with two parallel steel strips embedded in the dirt.

A train station?

If so, it was ancient. Like something you'd expect to find just outside a small country town at the turn of the century. I could even see a ticket window set in the side of a crumbling building in the shadows behind the lamps.

"Ah," Wash said. "I know what this is."

"Yeah. It's how the fucking mole-men commute. What the hell, Wash?"

"Some of the old subway lines were built over existing railways. Where they were not built over, they were built around. This station is abandoned, but do you see the tracks, farther out?" Wash pointed to a second set of rails, just at the edge of the light. "They are newer. They must use this place to store cars."

But Wash was wrong about it being abandoned: There must have been fifty punk kids milling about down there. I tried to see if I recognized anybody in the crowd, and came back with an impression like rubbing an old eraser over wet paper. Unnoticeables. They were all looking toward a mammoth set of gears—thousands upon thousands of them, grinding away pointlessly. The source of the rumbling. The gears looked ancient, maybe older than the streetlamps, and covered entirely in rust. All except for the teeth. Those were clean, bare metal. They saw regular use.

From the crowd next to the machine, faces started popping out at me. They weren't all Unnoticeables: There was a line of normal kids down there, too, stripped naked, beaten to a pulp, and muttering with dazed shock. They were standing single file, looking straight ahead at nothing. Beside the queue, his hand resting atop a giant copper lever, a man like a stick of dried meat smiled his hapless, dope-fiend smile.

Gus.

I heroically suppressed the urge to get up some major velocity and drop-kick his fucking lopsided smirk into the sun. Instead, I made myself scan the line again more carefully. I was looking for a skinny, pale kid with a ridiculous coif of overstyled blond hair, probably swearing at his captor in a fake Cockney accent. I was looking for a pretty blue-haired girl, probably spitting in somebody's eye for looking at her funny.

I didn't find them. I tried not to think about what that meant.

What I wasn't looking for—what I had secretly given up hope on, what I was so certain I wouldn't find that it didn't even occur to me to search—was the wide-faced, perpetually sneering son of a bitch at the back.

Randall!

He looked like shit. Like he hadn't eaten or slept since the pizza parlor. I almost yelled his name. I almost called him a motherfucker and ran up to punch him in the arm.

But he moved then, taking a small step forward and advancing one place in the line. I looked back to the head of it to see where they were going, just in time to see a chubby bearded dude bend at the waist and calmly insert his face into a whirling mesh of gears. He didn't even scream when they ground him into hamburger meat.

TWENTY

Eighteen wet concrete steps, and it wasn't raining. Could be somebody just washed something nasty away. Could be somebody hadn't washed something nasty away yet.

Three flights. Six landings.

Eighteen divided by six is three, multiplied by the number of rooms per floor—twenty-three—is sixty-nine; six minus nine is negative three, times the number of floors—two—is negative six, and it's always six, any way you cut it.

I saw it. I saw it coming when I counted out the bills that punk kid gave me and handed them over to the night clerk at the check-in desk. I gave him seventeen even. I said, "Keep the change, my good man," and he smiled all sad and said, "Looks like you need it more," and he slid one bill back to me, and I ended up giving him sixteen dollars, no matter how hard I tried not to. I went down to the corner store and I bought myself a candy bar and a bottle of cheap wine with a cat on the label. I looked at the prices for a good ten minutes to make sure, so that when I slid my cash over the counter I knew what I was getting back. Fifty-eight cents.

Ha-ha, you know what he said to me? You know what that little Korean fella said to me? He looked me straight in the eye and he said: "All outta pennies, man."

And he slid me sixty fucking cents.

I guess he expected me to be surprised, but I'm on to them by now. I know the game. So I just smiled and I gave him a big wink and I said, "Well, don't that just beat all," and I took my cat wine and my chocolate bar and I went back to my room.

At the Motel 6.

If you can't beat 'em . . . and all that.

But then something kinda funny happened. I locked that cheap plywood door behind me, I turned on the lamp with the chintzy tassels and fringe all across the bottom, I cranked the AC to full, and I lay down on the bed with its detergent smell and its busted springs, and the numbers . . . they just sorta stopped.

I could feel them there at the edge of my mind, nudging up against my thoughts like a dog pawing at the door. But they weren't getting in. I saw that somebody left the dial on the TV tuned to channel 6, and it almost bothered me. But then I flipped that son of a bitch on anyway, and *Scooby-Doo* was playing. I fucking love *Scooby-Doo*. That Velma girl—she has it going on. That tight sweater, short skirt, and knee socks? You can't tell me she got dressed in the dark. Some folks, they got it out for Daphne. But you know to look at her—she's one of those girls that talks it up all day, but when it comes down to lights-out she just lies there and acts like she's doing you a favor. Velma? You know she takes off those glasses and she gets *to work*.

I took a big ol' swig of rotten wine and killed the aftertaste with a tiny bite of chocolate, and damn it all if I didn't feel good for the first time in—

Christ, I don't even know how long it's been since my thoughts went this clear. Six months, maybe?

Ha, there you go again. You keep scratching at the door, six, you're sleeping outside tonight.

Shaggy was making himself a big sandwich, and my belly growled a little bit, but I shut that sucker down with a fat pull of wine and another bite of chocolate and I laughed some.

"Sammy," I told myself, "you got to take the good moments when they come to you."

There was a flash, and the room dimmed a little. I thought a bulb went out at first, but then I saw that wasn't it. It looked more like a new bulb had just turned on, making the rest of the lights seem less bright.

A new bulb that hovered about two feet above the burnt-orange carpeting, halfway between me and the bathroom.

"Like, it's a g-g-g-g—" Shaggy stammered.

The orb of light grew. Not brighter but more substantial, I guess. There was a sound like wind chimes—like wind chimes made up of static and screaming—that paused whenever I blinked. The carpet went gray. The TV went black and white. The color just bled right out of the world, wherever the light touched it. Something moved inside the light. It was too bright to see any real shapes, but I understood what it was.

I wasn't new to this game. I remembered Lisbon. And Mandalay. And Alicante. And São Paulo. I remembered no matter how hard I tried to forget. No matter how *important* it was to forget.

The fucking angels finally found me.

Couldn't have happened when I was huddled up on some stoop in an ice storm. Couldn't have happened when I was lunging at rats down in the subway tunnels, trying to catch dinner. No, it had to happen on my one good day. It had to happen right in the middle of Scooby-Doo.

It was a good episode too—no bullshit celebrity guests to muck up the plot.

Something vaguely like a hand formed from a refracting pattern of light. It reached out and opened a drawer from the end-table and withdrew the old navy revolver.

"Ha." I laughed, and clapped for the angel. "After all I went through to get that dang gun. That's great. That's downright poetic."

And then I realized it wasn't just the gun: Everything was significant.

The candy bar in my hand was a Snickers. My favorite as a kid. One of the few indulgences we ever got back in the bad old days. The wine wasn't anything I'd ever seen before, but it was cheap and red and burned going down, and that was as familiar as an old dog.

On the television, Fred was chasing down a werewolf, and I thought of Abby and her unibrow and what we used to call her. I came up with that nickname.

God damn. God damn it. I thought I'd see it coming when it came. I thought I'd have a chance to brace myself before it got this far. But no, I hadn't been paying close enough attention, and now they had it. They'd finally figured it out.

My solution.

The angel raised its radiant hand and slowly, gently pulled the trigger. I know you won't believe it, but I swear to God I felt the very instant that pockmarked old bullet brushed up against the lens of my eyeball. That's the second my humanity started swirling away like water down a drain.

TWENTY-ONE

"Markho," Carey spat through broken teeth, "kumm closhuhr, yuhr lippsh canch reash my dickh fruhm zhere."

"Shh! Shut up." I waved my hand in Carey's general direction, but I couldn't take my eyes off of Jackie.

She was unbalanced and unfocused. A few inches from her outstretched fingertips, a blurry weave of gears gnashed, waiting to seize the slightest part of her and pull her in.

She didn't move. She was frozen. Waiting.

Nobody was moving. *Everybody* was waiting.

Marco turned to me with an expectant smile.

"What?" I screamed, after it became obvious that I was supposed to do something. "I already said I'll do whatever you want! Just tell me, for God's sake!"

"Finish the ritual," the car salesman said.

It was picked up all over and tossed back at me in low murmurs from every direction, each equally toneless and firm.

"I don't know what that is," I pleaded. And I hated myself for it.

I am begging them? I am begging them to let me help?

A fist-sized lump of fury kicked over in my guts, but I held it down.

"You're the hero, lil' darlin'." The car salesman spread his arms wide and gestured at the motionless crowd. "This is your audience. Now you get to do your thing. Learn your lesson. Save the day. We're just here to watch."

"So I—what? I just get to take my friends and go?" I edged toward Jackie, afraid that moving too quickly might break whatever magical spell I'd apparently cast.

"No." Marco tried on a disapproving frown, but he clearly hadn't practiced the expression. He looked like some kind of deep-sea eel, only emerging to snap at the bothersome cameras.

"What's a victory without sacrifice? The audience needs to feel it," the balding guy said.

"You can take one of them," Marco supplied. "It is the decision that is important."

Marco pointed briefly to Jackie, then to Carey, and then appeared to forget about his own arm. It hung there immobile, stalled somewhere between the gesture and its normal place at his side.

I almost had to think about it.

That's not even true. I'm sorry. I'm so sorry. I don't want to admit it. I don't want to admit how quickly I made up my mind. But I had known Carey for what, a week? He was old and strange and probably crazy, and definitely smelly.

I'd known Jackie since I was twelve.

She gave me her brand-new sweater to wrap around my waist when I peed myself in gym class.

She told Bobby Mariano that I liked him, even when I begged her not to, and he asked me to the Valentine's Day dance.

She stole my car keys when I talked about giving up on this movie stuff and moving back to Barstow.

Our fucking cycles were in sync.

It was Jackie. The decision was Jackie, and I made it in a heartbeat.

I caught Carey's eye for just a moment, right before I turned away from him. He smiled at me. He flipped me off.

I tried not to run the dozen steps to Jackie's side, but I didn't try very hard. I grabbed her arm, and the second I touched her I watched life flare up again behind her glassy eyes.

"K?" she said uncertainly and took in her surroundings. "Why am I naked in a church? Oh, shit, did I get roofied again? These fucking Hollywood douche bags, I swear to Chri—"

"Jackie, quiet. I'll explain in a second. We just have to get out of—"

I turned toward the door and found that the church had dissolved in a ball of nuclear fire. A blur of light hovered there, the pure white shade of absence. Something acute shifted inside of it. I instinctually closed my eyes against the flare. When I opened them again, it sang to me in a voice like waves crashing against rocks.

"He has been abandoned!" Marco cried from somewhere behind the blinding light, and for the first time since I'd met him, I believed that the emotion in his voice—the unhinged, fanatical zeal I heard there—was genuine.

"He is ours! He is ours!"

The gathered crowd of Empty Ones—what little I could see of them through the light—leapt to their feet and began to flail with psychotic abandon. They screamed nonsense. They swung their arms and snapped their heads back and forth. All pretense of humanity had been dropped: Their

limbs bent at impossible angles, cracking and twisting grotesquely. The flesh on their necks split open as their spines
bent and burst through the skin. They lashed out and danced
and struck each other, bit each other, seized on and dug into
one another's flesh with their fingertips.

I watched a middle-aged woman wearing an impeccable
set of pearls tear at her breast until it came off. She flapped
it in the air like a patriot waving a flag. A blank-eyed child
reached into his mouth, tore out his tongue, and flung it at
the fat man holding his hand. They both gripped each other's
shoulders and spun about merrily, laughing. The balding
car-salesman guy was on the floor. He had his legs bent backward, broken at the knees. His torso moved in loose orbits
around his waist while his eyes rolled in his head. Both of
Marco's arms were dislocated. He was doing a mad sort of
jig, the loose limbs flopping side to side like empty sleeves.
He was endlessly repeating that joyous refrain:

"He is ours! He is ours!"

And so slowly you couldn't quite see it—more like it was
shrinking than moving—I watched as the angel approached
the spot where Carey was lying immobile, just trying not
to bleed.

It . . . it wasn't about me?

I was surprised to find that the tightly wound ball of anger I'd tamped down when Marco made me beg had been
growing tendrils and spreading throughout my belly. Wrapping around my guts. Taking hold.

*What was that crap? All the gibberish about the rituals and the
hero, and I was—what, incidental? Here to help some otherworldly
math nerd turn Carey into a sociopathic blob of light? No. Fuck
that. Fuck this.*

Jackie's eyes lost focus. She had been booted out into the

middle of this chaos from whatever haze the Empty Ones had inflicted on her, and it was too much. She had gone somewhere else for a lovely vacation rather than deal with the bloody monstrosities dancing all around her. I wrenched her hand and ducked forward, right under the singing ball of light. She moved perfunctorily, her body just waiting for direction. When we came up on the other side of the angel, I ran toward Carey. I expected . . . something. For the angel to adjust or attack or grow arms and give us all noogies. Anything, really. But it didn't seem to notice us, or care what we did. Not until I'd dodged past Marco's whipping limbs, reached down, and grabbed Carey by the collar of his patchwork leather jacket.

The second I touched him, the light behind us blinked out of existence. Then on again. And off. It flickered rapidly. I turned around and found the angel vanishing and reappearing at random points around the church. It was back at the gears now, then up in the rafters, over by the pulpit, and out among the pews. It wasn't so much an object as a blank spot where somebody had come down and erased part of the universe, so I don't want to anthropomorphize it or anything— but I swear, it seemed almost . . . frantic.

It wasn't until I started physically dragging both Carey and Jackie toward the door that I realized how strong my grip had become. My pinky—the sixth finger on my left hand— it didn't hurt. Every day of my life, the thing ached at the slightest movement, and here it was curled firmly into the black, brittle leather of Carey's jacket, and I felt no pain at all.

That had only happened twice before. Once on the night of the fire, when I lost my sister, and then again that day at my apartment with the Peeping Tom. The day that started all of this. I flashed back to the alleyway and that pervert hobo. How the angel had moved when I lost my sandal, how it popped into existence directly over the spot where I'd dropped my knife. Like it hadn't been aware of those things . . . until I stopped touching them.

It couldn't see me.

Marco and the Empty Ones were too far gone to notice anything was amiss. An old woman with perfectly braided hair was chewing straight through the thigh of a man I swore played the butler in an eighties sitcom about a rich family adopting inner-city children. A tan fellow with an intense widow's peak was holding two severed hands in his own, drumming them enthusiastically against the carpet. They didn't spare us a single glance as I dragged Carey's limp form with one hand and used the other to guide Jackie's remote-control body toward the exit. The angel blinked faster and faster—spot to spot to spot—and then stopped. It pulsed slightly. If I had to guess, I'd say it was thinking.

Then one of the girls, one of the few left alive from the second line, screamed.

Her body sucked up into itself, her guts expelled onto the floor by the force of her own collapsing torso. There was a deep *pop,* the floor shuddered, and she was gone. Next to where she'd been standing, a scene played in the air. The images were faint and transparent, like those from an old movie projector shining on a bedsheet. It was a dog chasing an old truck through the parking lot of a supermarket, over and over again.

A sound like bagpipes dropping. Another girl yelped, and her chest became a vortex that absorbed the rest of her body.

A third girl sniffed the air, panicked at what she found there, covered her ears, and began vomiting up a thick black sludge. It ran out of her mouth with unnatural purpose, slowly coating her face, her neck, her arms. She collapsed in a dark, sticky pile that shimmered like grease. It seemed to move of its own volition.

Clearly, it was time to duck out of this party.

I turned to reach for the doorknob. I had the cold brass in my hand and was squeezing the lever when I realized my mistake.

I had let go of Jackie's hand.

I panicked and snatched at her shoulder, but it was too late. She was watching something in the air in front of her. A ghostly rectangle of moving images. A television playing underwater. It showed a close-up of a little girl with two precocious, lopsided pigtails sticking out from either side of her head; one was tied with a ribbon, the other held in place by a cheap plastic clip with a little nub in the shape of a cartoon cat. She smiled.

There was no mistaking Jackie's goofy grin.

The girl twirled, and her pigtails spread out like a dancer's skirt. She laughed and hopped and spun so fast that she didn't even see the curb. It caught her foot and she was down. She barely had a chance to cry before an older woman in overalls rushed up to help her. Then I smelled burning plastic laced with dead flowers.

Jackie screamed, and a stale white light flared up behind her eyes.

"Jackie! Jackie, no." The inside of her skull was lit up like an airport. "Don't let it do this to you. Stay here. Stay with me."

She opened her mouth to scream again, and a stream of

faded color dribbled out across her lips, ran down her bare chest, and dissipated somewhere around her navel.

Carey tried to pull me toward the door.

"Emp . . . empchee won," he slurred around a mouthful of blood. Then tried again: "Emp. Tee. One. Run. RUN!"

TWENTY-TWO

I started to stand, but a hand on my shoulder held me back.
I looked around to find the offending party and punch him
in the fucking mug—and found Wash staring up at me.

"We need a plan," he said.

Another one of those hypnotized punk kids stepped willingly into the gears. A high-pitched whine and a deep stut-
tering growl, like stuffing a watermelon down a garbage
disposal, and he got pulped into a fine slop. Randall stepped
forward one place in line.

"I *have* a plan," I whispered. "I'm gonna go down there
and kick some ass."

A girl up next: She sat down at the edge of the rumbling
machine, carefully adjusted her posture like she was posing
for a picture, then reclined into the gears. The ragged metal
caught her hair, ripped part of her scalp off, and continued
yanking all the way down her torso. One of the Unnoticeables dutifully stepped forward and kicked the rest of her
skinned, twitching body into the maw. Two more, and then
it was Randall's turn.

"I think that is a bad plan," Wash said, after a very long moment's consideration.

"It's the only one I've ever had," I said, shaking Wash's hand off my arm and starting for the ledge, "and it hasn't let me down yet."

"I have a better idea," he answered, already standing and jogging off into the dark. "Stall for time."

It should say something about my mental state at this point, when motherfucking Wash—who carefully unfolds his burritos because he thinks the tortilla is a wrapper—tells me he has a plan and I listen.

Luckily, I found a way for our strategies to sync up. I decided to "stall for time" by bellowing a monumental, lung-splitting war whoop, then sprinting down the loose dirt embankment into a crowd full of monsters and hammer-punching the first one I came to.

Like I said: "Go down there and kick some ass" has always treated me kindly, and I don't switch horses midstream.

The first Unnoticeable crumpled like tinfoil at the blow I sent to his kidneys. He started to make a sound like *bloof* and then stopped because he was too busy choking on half of my fist. The blurry-faced man next to him turned to see what was going on and got my forehead in his nose for an answer. I planted a faded black Chuck Taylor in the groin of another Unnoticeable who, I saw too late, didn't have balls. When they were all grouped together like this, it was hard to tell even something as basic as gender. She still staggered a little bit from a firm kick in the ol' ladies garden, but obviously she didn't go down quite like I expected. I leaned forward and caught her with part of an elbow, as I struck for the one still reeling from my headbutt. They both collapsed in an indistinct heap.

I felt hands grab me from behind, so I bent over sharply and sent whoever it was flying over my back. I threw a wild punch in that direction, just in case he had backup, and connected with somebody's tit. She yelped and jumped away, immediately vanishing back into the bland mass of faceless people.

"I am a whirlwind of genital pain," I declared, laughing. But then my right eyeball flashed and I was on the ground.

A booted foot caught me in the gut. Another in the spine, then the side of the head, and I stopped counting kicks.

No idea how long I was out. It always feels like hours, but it's never more than a few seconds. When I came to, I found myself staring down at a bunch of feet and some gravel. Several pairs of strong hands were locked around my arms, carrying me. My legs were free, but I couldn't make them work right just yet. I sent them helpful commands like "kick" and "run," and they flopped about like lukewarm Jell-O in response.

A set of worn stairs passed by, then some old broken cobblestones. A hand twisted itself into my hair, and then I was looking up into Gus's distant eyes.

"You are very nearly as stupid as your friends," he said, his voice like wet cigarettes.

"I take offense to that," I tried to quip, but my mouth was thick and some asshole had put it on sideways. My reply came out sounding like a geriatric coughing into a bowl of soggy oatmeal.

Gus blinked and cocked his head.

"I take," I tried again, slowly steering my tongue around my mouth this time, "offense to that. I'm *way* dumber than those prissy bastards."

Gus laughed, all throat and no lungs. "You're right about that, my man! I mean, you walked into this? Into *all this*?"

"Into what?" I said carefully, trying not to let the drooling blood slur my words. "Your little poser posse playing with Tinkertoys?"

Gus's expression withdrew and his face went slack. He stepped toward me and slapped me in the mouth. Pain and probably some teeth went ricocheting around my skull.

"Do not joke about the gears," he said flatly. "They are the turning of the universe."

Gus took a step back, threw his ropy arms wide, and spun about, motioning at everything.

"Besides, you're so fuckin' dim, you probably didn't even see them, did you? Check it out, my man! *Really* check it out!"

I looked around at the half-erased faces of the gathered Unnoticeables and tried to think up a more eloquent way to call them all pussies. Then I saw what Gus was talking about. The darkness around the platform, just outside the reach of the faded yellow streetlamps—it was practically glimmering. Something out there was bouncing back the light. Something liquid, and large, and flowing like cold molasses.

Tar men. Thousands of them, lurking silently in the shadows. I could practically hear them slithering around now, though I knew it was impossible over the deafening rumble of the gears.

Fucking hell. Are the gears always that loud?

The ground had picked up a new kind of shudder, too. Something deeper and more immediate than the persistent *thrum* of the machine.

"It is funny," Gus said, "we did not think it was you, toward the end. So many doubted. It was all backward. You made the decision so early and so easily. You barely knew the pathetic old bum when you abandoned him in that alley outside of your apartment, and you were so very, very bad at the chase. But we should have known that the order of things does not matter. We should have had faith. Because now, here we are. It is all happening. We are . . . proud of you."

"You having a fucking stroke? Listen, save your babbling Manson crap for the groupies and just leave me and my friends out of it. For fuck's sake, haven't you got enough blood?"

"No," Gus answered immediately. "The needs of the gears are persistent. Without constant lubrication, they will seize. They will not process fuel. Without energy to turn them, the stars will no longer burn in the void. Without the un-ending warmth of the machine, without the rotation of the gears, the cold and the still will take everything. You do not understand it. You will not accept it. But we fight against en-tropy. We fight for motion. We fight for the machine. We are bits in that glorious engine, all of us. Even you. Even your friends. There may not be a final goal for us. We do not get the luxury of an end point. There is only maintenance, and our toil is infinite. But the work is good. The gears must turn. No, Carey. There is never enough blood."

That other rumbling again. Louder and closer. Some of the others were starting to catch on to it, too. The Unno-ticeable holding my arms started swiveling his head around, trying to find the source.

"I guess I was wrong before," I said, "about being dumber than my friends."

"What does that mean? Why say that now?"

"Because it sounds like my good pal Wash is about to do

the dumbest thing I have ever seen," I answered, smiling a bloody-toothed grin. "He's about to hit you with a fucking train."

It sounded like a giant cat trying to pass a steaming load of jagged scrap metal. Little puffs of dust kicked up from the corroded tiles. A single enormous flickering light grew swiftly larger, and the stink of burning oil swept across the platform like a tsunami. I pulled my arms together, throwing the Unnoticeables holding me off-balance just long enough to lift both of my legs, plant them on Gus's scrawny belly, and shove that junkie motherfucker right into the front of Wash's subway car as it jumped the rails and plowed past us. Gus disappeared in a corona of blood and flecks of tanned flesh. The train carried right on into the unsuspecting crowd like a bowling ball hurled into a set of bloody pins. They splattered like slugs beneath a car tire. It was horrible. It was nauseating. It was fucking *beautiful*.

And then the car caught something at the wrong angle. The whole train screeched, jumped sideways, and caught air. It lurched to one side, balanced there, then rocked back the other way. For a second, it looked like it might save itself, then it hit something large, wet, and black, flipped over onto its side, and ground to a stop in a hail of sparks. A dozen tar men went up like bottle rockets.

The Unnoticeables flew into a panic. They chattered and clucked like nervous hens, running to and away from the wreckage, wailing Gus's name. One fell to her knees, tore her top open, and beat at her own breasts. I only watched them jiggle for a second before getting to work.

I sent a telegram to my stubborn, ineffective legs. The message came through muddy, and there must have been a few typos, but the general gist was understood. I took my weight

on my own feet and off the Unnoticeables that had been supporting me. They hardly seemed to care. The smudge beside me grasped at my jacket a little when I twisted away from
him, but a quick jab in the old blurry area and he let go. I
stumbled over toward the gears and lost my footing in a
sticky pile of red stuff that I really wish I hadn't looked down
at. Randall was swaying gently in place when I found him.
He rocked back and forth on his heels, bopping to some un-
heard music. He looked like he'd had cigarettes put out on
his arms. There were thin cuts running up his side in ornate
patterns—a series of initials, I saw—and both of his eyes were
swollen almost entirely shut. I reached out for him, afraid
I'd shatter the poor bastard if I grabbed him too hard, and
closed my hand gently around his wrist.

At my touch, something clicked inside his head. He shook
his head, winced at the pain that simple gesture brought, and
for the first time actually seemed to see me.

"What, did you go queer on me?" Randall said. He was
confused and a little shell-shocked, but still clearly a total
asshole.

He's going to be okay.

Voices shouted in the distance, back toward the toppled
engine. I couldn't hear what they were saying.

"—is ours," one of them might have cried.

"Abandoned!" another might have hollered.

They sounded . . . happy?

"Wash is in there," I told Randall, and nodded toward the
unrecognizable mess of steel.

"What happened?"

"He drove a train right up Gus's ass."

"Who's Gus?"

"A guy that deserved a firm train up the ass."

"Good for Wash, then. Let's go get him."

I thought about telling Randall to run—that he was in no shape to fight—but we've had that conversation before, and it never went well. Admittedly the conversation usually took place when we were both drunk and arguing with some skinheads, and admittedly it was usually Randall telling *me* to run, and admittedly it usually ended with me taking a belligerent swing at him for daring to suggest such cowardice. But I knew he wouldn't listen, anyway. I threw his arm over my shoulder, and we hobbled toward the wreckage together.

I tried my best to ignore the shimmering liquid lurching through the darkness all around the smoking heap. I tried to disregard the glints of brass I caught here and there. I tried not to think about what we were walking into or what they were going to do to us. And then I saw what the Unnoticeables were dragging up through a gaping hole near the front of the overturned train, and I actually did forget all about the tar men.

It was limp and pale, knit through with deep splashes of crimson. It had a mottled brown three-foot-long chunk of steel through its chest.

It was Wash.

He was dead.

I clenched my fists. I ground my teeth together so hard I tasted the rough chalk of enamel on my tongue. I thought pure murder. I vividly pictured strangling every one of these motherfuckers so hard their eyeballs would burst in their heads. I wanted to watch their tongues loll out and to crack their fucking skulls like eggs against the ground. I wanted to burn this whole goddamned place down, with us inside of it, just so we wouldn't have to miss a second of their fucking flesh searing.

But that's not what I did.

What I did was look at Randall and see that he was barely standing. I looked over at the platform and the handful of half-naked punk kids still milling about in a daze there. I noticed a skinny girl with short blond hair, and I pictured what she'd look like with a blue wig. I turned away from my good friend's body—I walked away from the bastards that just killed him—and I tried to save the ones that were still alive.

When I get drunk enough to tell this story, and when the people around me are drunk enough to believe it, they all tell me I did the right thing. They all tell me I was heroic to leave revenge behind and focus on helping. "Noble," they call me. But every single miserable, hungover, dehydrated morning, I relive that decision for just a second—right after I piss out the last night's whiskey and right before I crack open the breakfast beer—and sometimes, I regret it.

Randall and I made the platform easily. What few Unnoticeables were still standing were too busy flailing and gibbering back by the train to stop us.

"He is ours!" I heard a familiar, raspy voice proclaim. I tried not to think about its owner.

I helped Randall up the steps and leaned him against a chipped concrete pillar. Thing 1 wobbled in place, mired in the same absent haze as the other punks. She looked so normal without the wig. So . . . *boring*. When I touched her arm, she instantly whirled on me and scratched half my face off. I swore and spat and called her a crazy bitch, at which point she realized it was me and stuck her tongue between my busted lips.

It hurt like a bastard. I coughed a not-insignificant amount of blood into her mouth.

It was easily the best kiss I've ever had.

When we finally broke apart, she smiled at me.

"I didn't know it was a wig," was the only stupid-ass thing I could think to say, still muddled by hormones and blood loss.

"What, you thought I was a natural *blue,* idiot?"

Randall laughed and snapped us out of it.

I went around and shook each of the three remaining punk kids. At my touch, one broke into an immediate sprint. She disappeared into the darkness before any of us could get a word out. One started crying, folded into a little ball, and refused to move. We tried to drag him and he nearly clawed our eyes out. Maybe there's something else we could've done, but we didn't. I hope he got out of there okay. The last kid thought we were friends of his college buddies, pulling some elaborate prank. He refused to believe what was happening. Randall spat in his eye and I punched him in the crotch. Twice. The reality of the situation dawned on him quickly.

I pointed up the embankment, and we all started our slow, pained crawl out of that dank hellhole with its gibberish-spouting freaks. We got maybe ten feet before the world lit up like Times Square. It was a lightning strike that didn't fade. A flash so white it stole the color from everything else. I turned and looked right into the face of a tiny star. Which was, oddly, hovering in place about three feet behind me. Something twisted deep inside the light. I don't know that "thing" is even the right word. It was more like an idea— just the very loose concept of sharp edges and absence.

From no direction at all, I could hear stone waves crashing on a glass beach.

From the whiteout area behind the star, I heard Gus's distinct jackass guffaw. It grew and grew into a manic pitch. All the false, detached cool of the dopehead was gone. In its place was utter and complete ecstasy. An unrestrained glee you'd only normally hear from a little girl waking up to find a pony beneath the Christmas tree.

We had been through too much, too quickly. There's only so much fear you can experience in such rapid succession before it all gives way to numbness. I had used up all my terror in those early days with the tar men. I had been wary of the Unnoticeables. I had been sickened by Gus and the business with the gears. But if you had asked me yesterday, I would have told you I'd forgotten how to be really afraid.

There was something turning in the white void of that star that made me remember.

I turned to Randall, to tell the dumb son of a bitch to run until his feet ground away against the earth, but he was looking at something with such intensity that it made me stop. A confused, thin little smile bounced around his face, trying to pin itself down.

"That's weird," he said in a strangled voice. "I taste beer and chocolate milk."

His pupils caught on fire.

Brilliant light poured out from somewhere deep inside his brain. He made a sound like icicles breaking in a storm, and hacked up a thin liquid the color of everything. It shimmered, prismatic, when it first dribbled out between his lips, but as it ran down his chin, the fluid thickened and turned black. When it clotted on his chest and started running back up his neck, I could see it was still shimmering, just a little bit, like oil on water. I tried to wipe it off him with my jacket sleeve, and it came back partially melted.

I turned to Thing 1 for help, but she was gone. Already running up the embankment. Told you she was a smart girl.

I looked around for something to do. Something to hit. Something to hit something with.

There was nothing.

I watched as the light spread behind Randall's eyes, hollowing him out.

I did the only thing I could think of. I called the malevolent star's mother a cheap whore, and I dive-tackled the son of a bitch.

TWENTY-THREE

I was holding on pretty good there for a little while. I thought I might make it: I'd put up nonsense barriers around all of my emotional core concepts, just like Yusuf had taught me—but then something shifted in the attack patterns. The angel punched through my psyche like a meteor, leaving a frozen trail of little pieces that used to be me. I perceived the attack sequentially, at first, when I was still holding the bastard off. Then the angel flared through, and all sense of chronological order vanished.

I could see what happened ten minutes ago about to happen any moment. I watched the events unfold exactly 1,296 inches beneath the moldy floorboards of my shitty motel room as they happened, had happened, would happen, and did. I saw the dark arena in the subway tunnels from the angel's point of view: a series of infuriatingly cluttered equations, constantly shifting and evolving in unproductive directions. It reached out and gently rearranged some bits, and a small chunk of the world that used to be a boy named Randall started to simplify. It projected the most probable event flow resulting from that action and was pleased when everything went according to its nature—when the candidate named Carey offered himself bodily unto the angel. The interface was . . . less than seamless. He had been prepped sloppily by the algorithm—this one had proved difficult—but he had been taken through experiences similar enough to my own. He had been through the chase, he had made the decision, he had abandoned the old candidate to save his friends, and he had voluntarily touched the angel. Giving it his code. Code that was now close enough to mine to provide the last missing piece for the most important problem of the day.

My life.

That stupid kid jumped headfirst into the angel, just like it wanted, and it gathered up his neural patterns, now carefully conditioned to be compatible with my own, and used them to shatter the last stubborn fortress of my humanity. I couldn't really blame him.

After all, I'd done the same thing, exactly thirty-six years ago.

Well, not quite: I had skillfully maneuvered a speedboat in a thrilling chase through the Puerto de Alicante. And in that palace in Alicante, I had swung down into my angel on a rope, just like Errol Flynn. It was far classier than an unbalanced motorcycle ride and some clumsy dive-tackle. But the sentiment was the same. As soon as I had touched the lukewarm light, I felt part of myself shunt away, never to return. And though the Empty Ones let me leave with Isra, we never saw her dad again. They turned poor Yusuf into an angel, though he'd fought against it his entire life. But I had made my decision and sealed his fate. And now a different one was being made for me. Just like, thirty-six years from now, some other fool with similar core concepts—a violent sort of loyalty, a longing for purpose, a knee-jerk disdain for authority—would do the same to Carey. Abandon him. Let him become one of these monsters. It was the cycle. It had repeated and would repeat forever, until the universe was a smoothly idling engine of sterile perfection.

In another part of my brain, the more superficial elements that comprise my self—the cadence of my speech, a key set of memories, my emotional responses to various stimuli—are being solved, simplified, and erased. I am being transformed bit by bit into one of these calculating aberrations. But I knew that was going to happen, and I was prepared. Yusuf taught me how to split my mind apart a long time ago. It wouldn't last. I was stalling, not winning. It was clear I would not be the one to break the cycle after all. Even with the training. Even with the preparation. The second that stupid fucking kid hit that light, I was done, and now it was just a matter of time.

But man, you have to put up the effort. That's part of being human: That arrogant little part of you that says you're special, that you can beat it, that when the time comes, it won't happen to you—*you and you alone are immune!* We all have that delusion. It's one of the core concepts of humanity, as a species. And it's hardly ever correct. But at least I'd spent twenty years preparing to be wrong. Two decades stitching one very simple, fundamental idea into my being— and then systematically erasing every part that even remembered why.

God, it took so many lives to get that idea. My darling Isra, the Gator, that cunt Tomas—all hollowed out or disappeared entirely, just to get me into the Citadel for thirty bloody sec-

onds. But I got in, and I got out: I walked through that inferno and came out the other side with a beautiful killer of
a concept seared into my head. I came out with the number
six.

It has to be simple, you see. Anything too complex can be
restructured and dismissed. You can't count on an idea retain-
ing the same value, or even existing at all, after an angel fin-
ishes with you. And if you have too much psychic buildup
around a concept—memories, explanations, tangents—the
angels will burn all of that away and the idea will still be
there but hold no importance. So I made it into something
they couldn't understand.

I made it into madness.

I spent twenty years repeating the number six to myself.
Twenty years finding it in everything I saw. Counting my
steps by sixes and shuffling on the seventh. Every sixth
breaths, I inhaled twice. Six beats of the heart, and I blinked.
I found multipliers of six everywhere I looked: I broke down
addresses, transcribed new alphabets and, most important,
I drank myself into oblivion. I ruined every brain cell that
remembered why I was doing it. I drowned every single neu-
ron that knew the significance of the six. I burned the number into my soul even as I erased it from my brain. Even now,
looking back at all I've given up for it, I could not tell you
what the number six is supposed to mean, or how in God's
name encoding an affinity for it into the angel I will become
will help anybody.

I just know that the angels can clear up madness most
times, if it's just a simple matter of tracking it back to the
source. But true insanity? Irrationality and obsession that
come from nowhere, with no explanation? That would have

to be left behind, as a sort of spiritual remainder. Junk characters in an otherwise perfect equation.

It wouldn't bother the inhuman light I was about to become. Not much, anyway. Most angels had some garbage floating around in them. Little quirks that gave them a bit of personality. The one that got Yusuf thirty-six years ago, it liked the sea. No idea why, but the ocean held some kind of importance to the man or woman it once was, and so it kept popping up in coastal towns. That's how we tracked it. How we found the Citadel. How we came to know about the six.

And this one? This twinkling ball of asshole sorting out my insides like a stock boy, filing away and destroying my most important memories just so it could reproduce and turn me into a glorified lightbulb? This one, when all was said and done, would have one tiny quirk. A little thing it couldn't quite explain.

It would like the number six.

It would seek it out. Favor it. Maybe even tend toward candidates somehow associated with that number, when it came time to reproduce again. A harmless little foible that, with a little luck, would someday kill the bastard dead. With a lot of luck, it might kill them all.

I felt my love for bicycles go. I could never explain that. I just liked them.

Then it was the taste of cheap wine.

Shit. That was getting close. That was *really* important to me.

I should say something meaningful. That's what one does, typically, when they're about to vanish from the world forever. But I have no memories to draw from anymore. No experiential basis with which to impart wisdom. I have only information.

Information is everything.

Information is purity.

TWENTY-FOUR

The fluid dribbling from Jackie's chin started off the color of a rainbow reflected in murky water, but somewhere around her chest, it ceased its natural downward flow and reversed. It clouded up. Thickened. Grew cancerous. It looked sort of like those pictures they showed you of smoker's lungs back in health class, but alive. It raced up Jackie's neck and poured back over her jaw, her cheeks, her hair. It didn't seem to be hurting her physically, but good God, with all that screaming, how could you tell?

It wasn't the sound of pure animal agony. I mean yes, it was absolutely that—Jackie was screeching like a trapped rat—but it wasn't *just* that. She was trying to communicate something: She barked out unrelated words, numbers, ratios, little snatches of music.

She started hollering out the start of a funny anecdote I recognized. It was one of her favorites. She was always such a good storyteller.

"So there I was at the prom in a full-on old-fashioned diving costume—we're talking metal helmet and—"

Then she went back to reeling off digits. I think I recognized my phone number in there.

If the sound didn't make it clear, the light pouring out of her would have been enough of an explanation. It fired up small, at first, like a sparkler behind her pupils. But now it was all through her. I could see her veins illuminated through the skin.

The whole church smelled like burning plastic.

Jackie was being hollowed out from the inside.

And nobody cared.

The Empty Ones hopped around idiotically, hooting like drunken monkeys and tearing their own flesh from their bodies. I looked to Carey for help, but he couldn't have given a shit if you paid him for it. Here we were, watching my best (if I'm being honest, my only) friend burning up like a meteor in the atmosphere, and all he could do was yank on my arm and scream for me to run.

Ha-ha. Where would I run to?

What's the point, without Jackie? She's why I was in L.A. in the first place. She was so sure we'd make it. That we both had something special and amazing that we couldn't capitalize on anywhere else. What was I going to do, if I left her here? Go back to my shitty overpriced apartment and count roaches? Turn up to work so I could sling drinks and absorb the auditory poison of a thousand vapid L.A. douche bags?

I looked around for Marco. For the blank-eyed bastard that started all of this. It was hard to recognize him with half of his own face yanked off. But he was there: standing in front of those bloody turning gears, whirling and raving. They weren't words. Not that I understood, anyway.

Nonsense. All around me. Nonsense.

Carey saw that I wasn't moving and that he wasn't in good

enough shape to make me. He looked sad. He released my hand.

Right now, I couldn't remember why I wasn't supposed to let him do that.

"Sammy," he yelled to the angel, "Sammy, is that you?"

I laughed.

The living inferno that was killing my friend was named fucking *Sammy*? That's something you'd name a hamster.

The angel directed some of its focus toward Carey.

"Come on, Sammy. That has to be you. I'd recognize that rotten wino-breath anywhere, you ugly son of a bitch."

The angel processed. It wavered, and then a brief snippet of clashing guitars faded in from nowhere. A moment of silence. Then a scent like a thunderstorm in the desert. It was trying to figure something out.

It was trying to figure out Carey.

"Knock that off, dumbass," Carey snapped. His broken teeth gave the last word a whimsical little whistle. I laughed again. *It was all so goddamned funny.*

"You know, I've been around too long to fall for that bush-league shit. Please, Sammy. I didn't know you well when you were still around, but we were always all right, you and me. I'm sorry that I only got a sense of who you were—who you really were—after you were gone. That was my fault. But I know what you were trying to do that night. I guess it didn't work, but you can still stop it here! I don't know what happens when you turn. If there's some little piece of you left in there or what—but you seemed like kind of a stubborn dick back in the day, so I'm going to bet that there is. If that's true, then you gotta stop it, Sammy. Don't let this fucker win."

The angel flickered. It withdrew a bit. It dimmed a little. Carey smiled. It was a sad, gentle expression that I didn't think his crumpled paper bag of a face was capable of. And then the image of a half-burned T-shirt with the Spanish flag on the front flashed in the air in front of him. Carey's face curled up and he tried to spit something out. Then he screamed. His voice echoed. It was the only sound that did.

I looked to Jackie.

I couldn't see her anymore. Just slick, black ooze in the shape of a woman. Blinding white voids where her eyes and mouth should be.

I looked back to Carey. He was clutching his head in both hands. Bent double in pain. He saw me looking and grinned feebly, trying to reassure me.

I took a step toward the angel.

"Oh, son of a bitch." Carey lunged for me, but he fell short, wracked with sudden spasms.

I took another step.

"Don't be a fuckin' moron!" he shouted from somewhere behind me.

But it was too late. I was already flying.

I don't know what I was expecting. That I'd go sailing straight through the light, unimpeded? That I'd, like, bounce away from its force field or something? No idea. I just know that I sure as hell didn't expect an angel to feel like crème brûlée.

Maybe surface ice on a frozen lake is a better analogy: There was a thin, fragile shell that gave way the second I touched it. Then the light inside, dimmer but somehow bigger, with a texture like air in a library.

From the outside, the angel looked like a blank spot in the universe—impossible and deep and *wrong*—but not very big. The thing only had a diameter of a few feet, depending on how closely your eyes could stand to look at it. But when I cracked through the shell and into that vacant space, I didn't fall or impact or puncture the other side. I just drifted right on through into nothing.

I'm not explaining this right. I didn't have any literal sense of my body. I wasn't moving, but there was motion and sensation and . . . Look, I jump through windows and serve sandwiches for a living. I'm not a poet, and I've certainly never had to explain being removed from existence before, so cut me some goddamned slack, okay?

I figured I knew what was actually going on. Back in the real world, I was being solved. Purified or whatever. I was dead, dying, or just vanishing, and all this was the result of a few random brain cells firing, trying to make sense of visual information when they were no longer attached to eyeballs.

I was kind of okay with it. Maybe it would help Carey. Maybe it would help Jackie. Or maybe I just wouldn't have to deal with this crap anymore and I could get some rest.

God, I was going to miss my bed.

I felt a strange release of pressure all around me. An emotional atmospheric change. Have you ever been in the room at a party at the exact moment when two people decide to hook up? It's like you can feel their sense of impending accomplishment. Their restrained glee.

It was like that, but magnified and cruel and everywhere.

The angel was . . . *happy*. It was so satisfied that I was here. I was supposed to do this, I realized. This was exactly what it wanted all along. This was where it needed me to be.

I felt a pull on my brain stem. Not a physical pull, and not my physical brain stem, but that's how I think of the core of my being. Where I store whatever crude central impulses that make me who I am. And somebody had just put both of their greasy hands in there and taken out a heaping scoop of Kaitlyn.

It was a strange, violating sensation. Painful in an abstract, nostalgic way. Like hearing about a childhood friend that you haven't thought of in decades suddenly dying in a car crash.

I wanted to give it up. I wanted to be ready to let it all go because this was all just too goddamned much.

But I couldn't. I was just too mad about the whole thing. The angel wasn't just happy, it was *fucking smug*. There was no relief to the sense of satisfaction, because there was never any doubt. The angel always knew that I would do this. It wasn't like getting the big promotion; it was like telling your snotty kid brother "I told you so" after you warned him not to touch the hot pan.

I tightened my fists, though strictly speaking I don't suppose I had hands anymore. But I could feel my phantom extra finger there. It didn't hurt. In fact, it felt good. Stronger than ever.

I pictured swinging that fist into some self-satisfied ball of light's stupid face. Again and again and again and . . . something broke.

A little shard of light shook, dislodged, and fell away. I could see a two-inch snatch of varnished wood out there, beyond the whiteness. I gritted my teeth and mentally swung again. The void around me shook, or shimmered, or I don't know—it felt the impact somehow. Another shard fell. Bigger this time. I could see a weathered old hand, clutching at some thin brown and gray hair.

I gathered myself up, took a few metaphorical strides, and I sent a leaping soul-uppercut right to that radiant bastard's angelic balls.

More shards fell and the gaps widened. But, more important, I could see there was something in here with me now, floating around in the void like it had been dislodged from its anchor point. It was small. Made up of bits of broken glass and faded cloth. It sat just below me, rotating listlessly among the splintered light. It was a tiny little sculpture of the number six. It was crude and so simple, but there was genuine care put into it. You could tell just to look at it. Macaroni pictures on the fridge. An ashtray from camp.

I reached out with my immaterial hand and thought about touching it.

Warmth ran through my absent body. It settled in the empty space behind my eyes. It wanted to reassure me. It wanted to thank me. But it didn't have the words. So much of it was gone. It was just a little piece. Just the smallest remnant of a human being. A man named Sammy.

And he was so happy that it had all worked.

Then he was gone.

I took another look around the fractured null space. There were dull brown veins of corruption tracing their way through the pristine light. The atmosphere was different. Now it was like standing next to a coworker while he got chewed out by his boss.

The angel had done something very stupid, and it knew it was going to pay for it.

I thought of myself growing larger. I tapped into that smoldering little ball of fury in my gut that I can never seem to fully get rid of. I felt it cool and harden into iron. It gave me weight. I pushed out with my intangible hands and the white void strained. I pushed harder and it buckled. I reared back, curled the fingers of my left hand into a shaking fist, and I punched the bastard right in its heart. The light shattered into a million pieces, disappearing as they fell. Flecks of glass buried in the sand.

I laughed.

It all went black, and I finally got to rest.

TWENTY-FIVE

I dreamed that I was floating on an impassive black sea. Its surface was glassy, unbroken and unending. Something in the water was sapping my strength, so I couldn't paddle or even turn my head. The moon was high above me, bright and cold. No clouds up there, just a flat, deep blackness. There was no border between the sea and the skies. They flowed into each other, a seamless sheet of stillness.

It was peaceful, in a way, but it also filled me with unease. I couldn't quite place why. Something about the depth of field in that sky was wrong. It took me a bit to figure it out.

The stars.

They were going out.

There was something swimming in the murk beneath me. I was sure of it now. I couldn't see it, and the waters didn't so much as ripple to betray its presence, but I knew it was there. You know the feeling: You're sitting in your living room, killing time—watching TV, playing on the Internet, just generally wasting the few unclaimed hours left in your life—when you suddenly drop the book or mute the television.

A few seconds later, there's a knock at the door. You must have heard something, felt a vibration that gave away the visitor, but if you think about it, you can't place exactly what that something was. You weren't aware, and then suddenly you were.

So it was with this thing beneath me. I could feel it moving down there, like a planet through empty space: far away, unimaginably vast, and unspeakably uninterested in me. Then something changed. The entity shifted direction. It noticed me. It had a long way to go, but it was coming my way, and when it got here it would swallow me and barely notice.

I tried to move my arms. My legs. There was a weight on my chest. I recognized the feeling.

Sleep paralysis.

My eyes shot open, but it took a dozen panicked breaths and a careful effort to get my hands and feet to respond. I was in my own bed. I could see that much, though my room was dark. A sliver of light split clean through the gap between my closed door and the frame. There were voices out there. Hushed but happy. Giggling. I could hear music but couldn't make out what it was.

I focused on my fingers. I tried moving them, and though I broke out in a thin sweat from the strain, I eventually got two of them to twitch. With a shattering effort, I closed my right hand into a weak fist. I did the same with my left, and was so relieved when it moved that I almost didn't notice the ache in my useless extra finger was gone.

I tried to sit up slowly, but the head rush still exploded behind my eyes, tunneling my vision to a few bloody pinpoints. It passed. There wasn't room to stand—my bed takes up the entire room—so I shuffled on my butt toward the door.

I twisted the knob, the chipped white paint coming off on my palm, and eased it open.

The voices paused.

My legs felt like half-inflated balloons. I moved like I was on wet stilts. I leaned heavily on the wall until I eventually made it to the living room. When my eyes adjusted to the light, I saw Carey frozen in place, obviously in the middle of telling a story of some kind.

At least I hope that was the reason he was miming a two-handed death grip on a giant imaginary cock, paused in mid–pelvic thrust against my recliner.

"K!" Jackie fired up out of the sofa like her ass was made of gunpowder. She flew across the room and locked her arms around me.

I laughed and tried to return the hug, but my arms were still weak. They rested uselessly on her back.

"Carey said you'd be okay, but Christ—you slept for, like, three days."

Carey released his phantom phallus and gave me a knowing smile.

"I'm fine," I meant to say, but instead I made a sound like a sick frog.

"I know three things," Carey said happily: "You're going to sound like Clint Eastwood for at least a week, you're not going to poop for four days, and you can't remember the tune to 'Amazing Grace.'"

"What?" I wiped the crust out of one eye and laughed at him. "What's that supposed to mean? Of course I remember 'Amazing Gr—.' Holy crap."

"I am the magic man. I take payment in cheap beer and cheaper women."

"No, seriously. How did you know that? I honestly can't—it'll come to me, won't it?"

"Nope." Carey shook his head. "It's totally gone. You'll have to relearn it. No idea why that is. The angels take different things when they do that nasty soul-scoop business. You'll be finding blank spots for years. But for some reason the melody for 'Amazing Grace' is always gone."

"What the hell are you talking about? This happened to you?"

"Sort of. A long time ago."

"And you didn't think to fucking warn me?"

"Excuse me? I told you to never—*ever*—touch one of the cocksuckers. I told you to run the second you see one and you—"

"So, hey," Jackie piped in, "not to interrupt the angry Alzheimer's convention here, but now you're going to explain literally anything that happened back in that whack-job church, yeah?"

"I, uh . . . I'm still a little muddy myself," I admitted.

"Don't look my way." Carey threw up his hands. "I explained what I could to your merciless cockteasing friend here, but Christ, Kaitlyn, you blew one of the bastards up! This is uncharted fucking territory."

I shuffled into the kitchen and poured some nasty L.A. tap water into a coffee mug with a faded picture of Steve Urkel on it. DID I DO THAT? it tried to say, in barely legible purple Comic Sans.

I went to down it, but my throat was too weak. I coughed, sputtered, and slumped on the edge of the couch.

"It was trying to turn you into another angel, wasn't it?" I finally got enough breath to ask.

"Yeah," Carey said.

"Because you went through something like I just did, when you were younger?"

"A little bit. The details were different, but yeah. Same shit."

"So someday one of those angel things is going to come for me, like it came for you?"

"Maybe." Carey picked up a half-filled bottle of dark brown liquid from the table. He sloshed some into his mug—Frosty the Snowman, if you must know.

"But it won't be this one," he continued, "when you nose-dived into the bastard's guts. It looked like it ate something that didn't agree with it, then it exploded from the inside out. Disappeared up its own bright and shiny asshole. Sounded like an orchestra caught in a tornado."

"We were deaf for half a day," Jackie supplied.

"We figured we'd pass the downtime getting hammered and screwing," Carey said, and he moved to slap Jackie's ass, but she jumped away.

"Like hell," she chided. "You look like somebody stepped on a dried apple, dude. I'm not above flirting a little, but I'd rather suck off a shotgun."

"We'll see about that when we get to the bottom of this bottle." Carey laughed.

"Marco," I said quietly.

The jokes died out.

"He got away," Carey finally said. "Hell, 'got away'! Like we were in any shape to go after him. Your friend's lucky she still knows English after what the angel did to her. If you'd been a few minutes later, you'd be changing her diapers. Or watching her do the psychopath dance with Marco. It was all we could do to walk out of there under our own power."

"So it was all for nothing." I nearly spat on the floor, before remembering that it was mine and I'd have to clean it.

"No way!" Jackie leaned forward and took my hands. "God, you should have seen it."

"That was some *Raiders of the Lost Ark* shit," Carey agreed. "The Empty Ones standing too close when you took the angel out just melted like government cheese. Well, better than government cheese, actually . . ."

"Most of the faceless dudes just shut off. Somebody flipped a switch and they went full vegetable," Jackie said. "It was awesome."

"And I don't mean to overstate this, but I'm pretty sure you killed that son of a bitch. As in, for good. And I'm also pretty sure that's never been done before. Ever. In the history of everything."

"K," Jackie said, laughing, "I think you're, like, the chosen one."

Carey tipped his mug back, drained it, then thumped it solidly on the table.

"A drink for the messiah," he said, and moved to pour whiskey into my empty cup.

I put my hand over it. He looked at me sideways.

"Jesus, Carey," I said, "I feel like microwaved death. I'm pretty sure I'd take one sip of that rotgut and throw up my nervous system."

"Suit yourself," Carey said, refilling his own mug instead. "But if there's a problem bottom-shelf bourbon can't fix, darlin', I don't think it can be solved."

TWENTY-SIX

I dreamed I was floating on a sea of breasts. Just coasting from one boob to another, completely free and unhinged from society. It was majestic.

Then I opened my eyes and tried to come to terms with being in my own shithole apartment again, living my shithole life surrounded by my shithole friends.

The broken, sagging cot that hilariously failed to pass for my bed almost fell apart when I shifted my weight on it. I had barely gotten my eyes open when something limply whacked up against my face. Not quite hard enough to hurt. I looked up into Randall's lopsided smile. He had a partially crushed can of Schlitz in one hand and a drooping slice of pizza in the other.

He had pizza-slapped me. The bastard.

"Wake up, my precious little sleepyhead," he said.

I tried to swing for his balls, but the second I moved my arm, I found I couldn't support my own weight without it, and slumped backward into the wall. My head *thunk*ed painfully. The world wiggled a bit, then settled down once it decided I was nauseous enough. I took a few breaths and tried to ignore the sound of somebody peeing in the bathroom behind me.

The toilet flushed and the bathroom door opened, clipping the frame of my bed. It moved my head a fraction of an inch.

I very nearly threw up on myself.

Matt the Black Unicorn was wiping his hands on his shorts. He froze when he saw me sitting upright on the faded green army cot.

"Holy shit! Carey's awake," he yelled into the other room, and I learned to hate him a little just then.

There was a minor commotion. Somebody was coming this way, but I couldn't focus on that right now, because Randall was waving a moist and flaccid slice of old pizza under my nose.

"You hungry?" he asked.

I swatted it away.

Safety Pins poked her head around the corner. She smiled broadly at me. You didn't see that much from her—she was usually too concerned with looking unattainable. Which, Jesus, she still did, in that low-cut beige tank top and those skintight jeans.

Wow, am I horny already?

"Are you okay? Do you need anything?" she asked, kneeling down in front of me. I could see right down her top.

"If . . ." I tried to speak, but my throat was packed with wet sand and cat litter. "If you could . . . bounce around a little. I think that would really help."

Safety Pins rolled her eyes and stood. She refrained from

slapping me, thank God, but when she pushed off of my knees, even that little jostle was like being rolled in ground glass and deep-fried in shit.

"What the fuck happened?" I asked.

Randall drained his beer and tossed the can aside. It clattered off the wall and fell into one of the many, many piles of empties.

"I'm not really sure," he said. "I blacked out for most of it. I can remember a piece here and there, but most of it is gone. Mouthless dudes. Gears. Blood. Screaming. Then you and Thing 1 hauling me away. Then light and burning."

"She get out?"

"Jenny?" Matt said. "Yeah, man, she's here. She's doing a beer run. Be back any second."

"She said you tackled a fuckin' fireball." Randall laughed. "Too bad I missed that. You'll have to do it again sometime so I can see it."

"What about Gus? I'm assuming he had a massive coronary after witnessing my heroism, right?"

"No dice. I was conscious for the after-party," Randall said, kneeling down and rummaging beneath my cot for something. He came up with another can of warm Schlitz. My emergency stash.

The son of a bitch.

"When I came to, you were lying in the dirt while the faceless kids all clapped and cheered. The ball of light was gone, whatever it was. Gus gave some big speech. Mostly gibberish. Stuff about engines and numbers. Then he went a little gay on you."

"Wh-what?"

Is that why I feel like such crap? Did I get molested by a monstrous Iggy Pop impersonator in my sleep?

"Ha!" Randall gestured at me with the hand holding the beer, and some of it sloshed onto my leg. I thought about lapping it up, but I doubted I could move that far right now. "You should see your face. Not like that. He came over while you were out and rearranged you. Put your feet together, crossed your arms over your chest. He kissed you on the forehead and thanked you."

"What the very fuck?"

"I don't know, man," Matt said. "I mean, we saw some weird shit a few nights ago. That black thing, the faceless kids—but the stuff Randall's been telling us is a whole new kind of strange. I mean, evil balls of light? Are you guys sure you didn't just huff a bunch of glue in the sewer?"

"My grandma saw one once, way before any of this happened," Safety Pins said, "those balls of light. She thought it was an angel. It spoke to her in my dead grandpa's voice."

"Shut the fuck up," Randall said. "Your crazy grandma is full of shit. Whatever that thing was, it sure as hell wasn't an angel."

"They just, what, let us walk out of there?" I asked.

"They didn't give a hot god damn what happened to us," Randall said. "They just packed up and filed out after Gus got all romantic on you. They walked off down the tracks. They sang the whole way. Like the Seven Dwarfs."

"Whugho?" I got some spit down the wrong pipe and nearly choked on it. When I recovered, I tried again: "Where did they go?"

"No idea." Randall shook his head. "We've been asking around, but nobody's seen any of the faceless kids for a few days. Gus's club is all boarded up. But I think I know where we might be able to find him. . . ."

Matt jumped a little. I got the feeling he'd already drilled

Randall about the rest, but apparently this was news to him.

Randall pulled a crumpled sheet of paper from his back pocket. He handed it over. I unwadded it and smoothed it out on my leg. It was part of a magazine column—an editorial about the importance of domestic beer at local punk shows—with a lined box off to one side. Inside the box was a list of dates and places. Most I didn't recognize. One I did: "The Roxy—28/12—The Talentless."

It was a show date. At a venue in London.

"Are you kidding me?" I tore the page in half. "Gus's fucking band is going on tour?"

"Guess they got signed a few weeks back." Randall smiled bitterly.

I thought for a minute.

"He's not getting away with this," I said.

"No way in hell," Randall agreed.

"What?" Safety Pins spat. "Do you hear yourselves? They're gone! They left! They're somebody else's problem now. Fuck London! We barely got out of this alive. Some of us didn't. . . ."

"She's right." Matt nodded. "Melissa—uh, Safety Pins— her and me are getting out of here, anyway. She's got an uncle out in L.A. that has a guesthouse we can crash at. I bet we can sneak you guys in there for a while."

Safety Pins looked at him unhappily, but she didn't say no. Sweet girl.

"Thanks," I said, and weakly snatched at Randall's beer. The monster pulled it away. "But no thanks."

"Besides," Randall added, "those London posers have been going around saying they invented punk. Somebody's gotta go over there and set 'em straight."

I laughed and it was a terrible mistake. I was so busy coughing, I didn't hear the door open.

When my vision came back, I saw Thing 1 standing there. She had gone back to the blue wig. My jacket hung over her shoulders, huge, filthy, and limp. A case of beer rested on one cocked hip, and a brown paper bag nestled up against her breasts. She smiled at me. It was the sexiest thing I had ever seen in my life, and the girl wasn't half bad, either.

Thing 1 set the beer down on the floor and reached into the bag.

"I don't know if you're feeling up to it," she said, "but I bought this for you. It's like a 'thanks for not letting me get crushed by a weird cult' present."

She pulled out a bottle of Wild Turkey.

I was shaking. A strong wind would disperse me like a pile of leaves. Every movement sent shock waves of nausea through me, and my throat felt like I'd tried to swallow a belt sander.

This was the perfect time for alcohol.

I grabbed the bottle, twisted the cork out, and took two deep swallows.

"God damn," I said, "if there's a problem top-shelf bourbon can't fix, I just don't think it can be solved."

Randall looked at me with plain jealousy and sneered down at his own tepid beer. Thing 1 eased gently onto the cot beside me, like she knew that the slightest jostle felt like a punch to the gut.

Safety Pins got up and went into the living room. I heard her rummage around in there, then the slide and shuck of a record being pulled from the stack and out of its cover. A few clacks, some muffled pops, and distorted guitars spilled out like drunks leaving a bar after last call. I took another swig of whiskey and offered the bottle to Randall. He smiled and yanked it out of my hands. For a while there, it was just booze and friends and music.

It was pretty all right.